THE SPINNER OF DREAMS

FINAL ART TK

THE SPINNER OF DREAMS

K. A. REYNOLDS

HARPER

An Imprint of HarperCollinsPublishers

Also by K. A. Reynolds

The Land of Yesterday

Dedication

[TK]

FATE WHISPERS TO THE DREAMER,
"YOU CANNOT WITHSTAND THE STORM."
AND THE DREAMER WHISPERS BACK,
"I AM THE STORM."

Once upon a time, before the War of Fates, the Mazelands had been ruled by powerful elves, twin brothers who controlled the fates and dreams of every being in all worlds: one ruled the left side of the Mazelands, the realm of fate; the other ruled the right, the realm of dreams. They kept order, gave purpose, bestowed hardships and hope, and especially loved the humans living in the world below. For centuries, all was well. Until they died in the great Faerie War, and the fates and dreams of every new creature born died with them.

Every day, above and below the sky, children were born

without purpose, without dreams, without any destiny at all. It was as if they were alive but asleep. Parents were afraid. Citizens of the Mazelands had waited centuries for the new twins of legend born with marked hands to restore fate and dreams to all worlds.

It had been foretold. And now that day had finally come.

Queen Saba and King Noll ruled the realm above the earth's sky known as the Mazelands. Though they were said to be barren, they had given birth to two children—twins. They could not have been more proud of their newborn daughters, each marked with strange black-hearted birthmarks on their palms. The girls were neither elf nor faerie, yet old magic ran in their blood. The marks on their hands had sealed their fates. They were to follow in the footsteps of the ancient rulers. They were to become enchantresses.

The Mazelands had been waiting.

The day after the twin daughters were born, Mogul, the wisest sage in the land and the grandest forest troll in existence, paid the new parents a visit in the castle. Mogul had skin as tough as bark, beady eyes, and a bulbous nose enormous enough to cast shade. He'd arrived in earth-colored robes draped to his hairy algae-coated feet and tied at his great waist with rope. Mogul's beard of moss, twigs, bird nests, and flittering, fluttering birds ran so long it trailed him like a train. The wise troll ducked through the nursery door, hunched over the twins' cradle, and drenched the girls in shadow from the encumbrance of his precipitous nose.

"With the birth of your twin daughters, a new age of order, balance, love, and necessity has dawned, dearest Saba and Noll." Mogul's eyes crinkled as he brushed the crying babes' cheeks. They both stopped fussing immediately and cooed at the troll. "Behold, the Enchantresses of Being are born."

"Enchantresses of . . . ?" The king, dark-skinned and handsome in white-feathered robes, bubbled over with wide-eyed joy. "Truly? These are *the* enchantresses—from the old stories?"

"Indeed they are," replied Mogul in his deep, resonant voice. "The daughters for which the Mazelands have been waiting these many long years: the Spinners of Fate and Dreams."

The giant gazed lovingly upon the twin girls. With gravity, he splayed the right hand of the babe with dark skin and black hair. Marked on her palm was a solid black heart like those on playing cards.

Mogul declared, "This child shall be loved by all and rule the lands beyond the Mazelands, the realm of dreams known to all as Dreamland. Her name shall be *Reverie*."

He observed the other child with skin as pale as her hair, crying once more. Marked on this child's left palm was a crumbling black heart.

"And this child shall be loathed by those who love her sister. She shall be known as Kismet and rule the Mazelands, including the abandoned labyrinth, and govern the realm of fate."

The parents gasped at the marks, unbelieving. Saba twisted her large silver heart-shaped locket. She wished to protest—to cry out and fight this declaration—but held her tongue. Nobody, not even the queen, disagreed with the enchanter, Mogul. Noll tapped the silver dagger at his side four times, as he did when anxious thoughts came, yet he remained silent.

"From this moment on," Mogul continued, "the lives of all living beings shall bend to their will. The sisters shall work in direct opposition to each other, and though they may try, they shall never be friends." He stroked his beard and regarded Saba and Noll. "The old magic of the twin elven kings runs through your daughters' veins. And like them, Kismet and Reverie will not be able to enter a mortal's home, forcibly take a mortal's life, or trick them into the Mazelands or Dreamland against their will. It is important you hold them to this. For if either Spinner ever tries, they will instantly crumble to dust. This is the law, and so ever shall it be."

Their parents hated that one of their precious girls, who they loved with their entirety, should be loathed. It pained them to hear that their twin daughters would never be close. But they accepted the terms and rejoiced nonetheless in their daughters' exalted births.

Perhaps, Noll and Saba hoped, time might change Kismet's fate.

The wise representative of the Mazelands slapped his massive hand on the king's back and spoke with the timbre of middle earth tearing in two. "They may not both be loved by their people, but they will have you to watch over them." A shadow passed over the forest troll's granite-gray eyes, darkening them to the shade of wet stone. "Having the love of one's people isn't everything, old friends. Often it's the hard necessities that make us who we are and give us the tools we need to find our way to our greatest dreams. Your darling Kismet can give that gift to all."

After Mogul dragged his heft and his scent of damp soil from their bedchamber, the king and queen cuddled their daughters dearly. They whispered words of love to each, not knowing that over the next eleven years, Kismet, currently holding her father's finger and smiling up at him, would grow into a jealous and angry girl. That she would lock herself in the tallest tower of her ruby palace, unable to understand why her people detested her yet pledged their lives to her sister, Reverie. They didn't know she would brood over why her parents and Mogul would do nothing to break her curse.

They didn't know their brokenhearted daughter would become a monster.

Chapter 1

THE BEGINNING OF *THE END*

The day Annalise Meriwether was born, charred black hearts rained down from the sky. The crisp, crumbly things descended through a crack in the heavens like burnt leaves from a dying world. They blew west on the tail of foul winds, blotting out the sun. Neighbors watched the dark storm propel to the Meriwethers' front door as the babe released her first cry. Strange wolves howled. The land blackened and died. A legion of white crows gathered on the Meriwethers' roof and stayed. Frightened towns-folk bolted locks and shut windows—but that would not be enough to deliver them from their ill fate.

A plague of darkness and ruin descended, and everyone knew who to blame.

"What's wrong with her?" the girl's parents asked the doctor. Their gazes fixed on their baby's left hand—twice the size of her right. When the grim doctor splayed the child's clenched fist to reveal a birthmark resembling a shattered black heart—the mark of the Fate Spinner herself—a wisp of black smoke rose from its center and danced away like a thing with wings.

The doctor scowled at the infant and answered, "Everything."

From that day forward, the folks of Carriwitchet blamed their bad fortune on the marked girl. Every storm, drought, sickness, and death, natural or otherwise, was considered Annalise's fault. The townsfolk faulted her for breaking their sky and stealing their sunlight, which never did return to their town. They loathed her for their dead crops, increasing poverty, and unsellable lands—even for her odd, blackberry-colored hair and plum eyes ("the color of dark magic, they are!"). They were certain that the girl cursed by the Fate Spinner had doomed them all. And no matter how kind the girl was, or how much she loved or tried or gave, the world spat Annalise Meriwether out.

At least it did—until the Fate Spinner, watching Annalise from above, made a terrible mistake.

Chapter 2

Foolish Girl, You Know
Nothing Ever Works Out for You

The big day had finally arrived.

Annalise sat at her desk in her bedroom at the peak of her small crooked house—shaped like a scrunched witch's hat—trying hard not to panic. Given that the sun had not shone over her town of Carriwitchet since her birth, Annalise brushed her long blackberry hair by candlelight in comforting rounds of four. She gazed at the dark morning sky out her diamond-shaped window, past the bars of the giant iron cage surrounding her home (built by her dad to keep the vicious townsfolk and night wolves at bay). And, beyond the fence circling her mom's garden of deadly nightshades, Annalise watched the petrified forest, more anxious than ever.

After last night, how could she be anything else?

Brush-brush-brush-brush.

One-two-three-four.

Countless white crows blinked at her from the craggy trees, as they had since her birth, eleven years past. Night wolves howled from the vast dead field past the garden, hunting anything that moved. Annalise brushed her hair harder and counted louder inside her head, trying to drown her worry. Her insides flipped and flopped anyway. Her head still whirred like a worry-thought-making machine. Annalise clenched her big fist tighter around her hairbrush, trying to ignore the pain slicing into her marked palm.

What horrible thing might happen today, if her dark mark decided to act up?

Who would she hurt next?

Stomach sour, the sharp pain in her hand getting worse, Annalise set down her hairbrush. She straightened her severely cut bangs, separated a chunk of hair above her right ear, and placed a braid near the crown of her head. As always, she tied her four black silk ribbons at the top of her braid—one for each of her deceased grandparents, dead because of her curse. Finally, while inhaling four cavernous breaths, Annalise cleared the worry-thought cobwebs from her mind and focused on the unbelievable, impossible possibility of today:

In a few hours, one of her most desperate dreams might come true.

For years, Annalise had asked her parents for a cat. Yet despite her mom working at an animal shelter, her answer was always the same: "You know your dad has fur allergies. He gets all sneezy and snotty—and just so *wet*. As it is, I need to change all my clothes after work before I can even walk through the door." Her mom, a tiny, stylish woman with wild, sometimes green, other times blue, but right now brown chin-length hair, shook her head with a sad sigh. "I'm sorry, sweetheart. A cat just isn't in the cards."

Her father, the goofball that he was, would raise his dark eyebrows and chime in after her with something like, "How about a snake, or a turtle—or an iguana?"

But snakes, turtles, and iguanas, as nice as they were, didn't purr or meow or have whiskers and fluffy little dagger-like feet, and the thought of cuddling them didn't feel quite the same. So always, Annalise would smile sadly and reply, "No, thank you." The discussion over, she'd slink away, cursing her left hand as it flared with pain, thinking what a cruel mistress the Fate Spinner could be.

But yesterday, as if by some divine miracle, a hypoallergenic Siberian cat—one that wouldn't make her dad puff up into a six-foot-four stuffed pastry that sneezed gooey

11

filling—arrived at her mom's shelter. She'd come home so excited with the good news, the three of them danced around the kitchen laughing with joy. Overwhelmed with happiness that one of her dreams might be realized, Annalise had forgotten to contain her big hand, which proved a horrible mistake.

Because sometimes, when she got too excited, panicked, or afraid—and sometimes for no reason at all—if her cursed hand wasn't clenched into a fist and hidden in the dark—and occasionally even when it was—the shattered black heart on her palm would smolder. And then it would burn.

Like last night. Sparks and fiery ash burst from the black mark and blew into the air as they'd danced. The curtains caught fire. The cheerful happiness stopped. Annalise's spiral of panic had begun. Despite her mom and dad shouting, "It's okay! It isn't your fault!" with forced smiles while battling the rising flames.

Annalise had run and hid in her bedroom anyway, pinching her big, cursed hand for doing this to her again. Upstairs, she'd crouched in the corner, squeezed in the grips of a full-blown panic attack. Heart pounding like a million hooves on the plain of her chest, her throat closed. Her soul writhed. The air in her lungs turned to stone as she gasped for a breath—any breath—and her mind buzzed with ever darkening thoughts. And all Annalise could do was stroke her hair and count things to four until she could breathe again. And when she'd caught her breath, she hugged her shaking legs to her chest and cried. With each four she counted, she wished that she was uncursed and had a normal left hand. Wished that the Fate Spinner had left her and her family alone.

Later, when Mom and Dad came upstairs to say good night, again they'd told Annalise not to worry, that everything was fine. "We love you," they'd said. "And don't worry. Come morning, your new cat will love you, too."

Annalise had nodded, wanting to please them because they were so good. But what if her hand did something bad to the cat? What would they think of her then? Would they loathe her like the rest of the town?

Would they wish to get rid of her, too?

Now the day of the dream cat had arrived. Annalise should have been excited, thrilled even, yet a terrible dread soaked her through and whispered in the hollows of her mind: *This dream will be snatched away like each of your dreams before.*

"Annalise," her mom called. "Breakfast!"

One-two-three-four.

Balancing on noodley legs, Annalise changed out of her black fox pajamas with the hole in the knee and put on her nicest outfit. Her mom had scrimped and saved for this outfit

13

at every chance she could: leggings inscribed with famously tragic poetry—in dark plum, to match her eyes; a knee-length black skirt; a button-down black top with a white collar that stood tall at her neck; fake leather black boots worn to maximum comfortability; and a hooded dark plum cloak.

This last item was essential to Annalise's ensemble. The cloak, which once belonged to her mom, was well-worn and big enough to hide her cursed hand; Annalise rarely went anywhere without it. Last and most important, she gathered what little courage she could find and tucked it into her pocket. Then, while clenching her big fist in a knot beneath her cloak, Annalise hurried toward her fate.

The scent of coffee and dried-apple biscuits drizzled with butter called to her from the kitchen. On her way through the dim living room, their ancient black-and-white television, the cord held to the wall by a patchwork of tape, flicked on as she passed. Her cursed mark had that effect on electronic devices, which Annalise disliked immensely, especially when it came to the TV. They only got one channel: the local Carriwitchet news, much of which revolved around her.

"Good morning, good people of Carriwitchet," said newsperson Penny Fabius. A squat woman with short red hair—not a nice natural red, orange, or auburn, but extreme fire-truck red—a sharp chin, and cold blue eyes. "Today the skies will be dark and broken, the weather chill and reeking of death." The newscaster held up the familiar talisman draped around her neck and sneered at the TV screen, as if speaking directly to Annalise. "No thanks to the accursed child marked by the Fate Spinner—the devil-spawn, Annalise Meriwether, who blighted our town—say true, say evil, say curse!"

Annalise's eyes pinched and her chest heaved. Static crackled across the screen when her dark mark spiked in pain—she clenched her big hand tighter. "Please," she begged her shattered black-hearted mark. "Not today."

For now, her cursed hand listened.

"Our man on the scene, Richard Inglehart," Penny Fabius continued, "reports that the accursed parents have not left their home since yesterday, and the Accursed One, not for the last forty-four days, thank the Fate Spinner for that." Penny spat on the ground and glared proudly at the screen. "Stay tuned to channel seven, the Eye on the Sky, for hourly sightings, locations to avoid, and updated Meriwether reports. And," she finished with a grin, "may a better fate be yours."

The burden of all she was, and the harm she'd caused simply by being born, settled like a thundercloud over Annalise's heart. Many times, she'd pleaded with her parents to leave

Carriwitchet—move somewhere no one would know their name. But always, their response stayed the same: "We'll not flee because we've been bullied into thinking we don't belong here," her mom would say first. "One day, maybe you'll understand."

"We were not born to run from oppression," her dad would add with pride. "But to stand bravely inside it and *defy* it. This is our home, Annalise, and we refuse to go."

"Yes, that," her mom would continue, her face worn and a bit ashamed. "But we also have very little money. Your grandparents left us this place, thank goodness. And I know you'd like to move. But I'm afraid even if we wanted to go, we couldn't afford another home." Then she'd smile and say, "At least we always have each other."

And as happy as Annalise was to be anywhere with her parents, standing in the hallway staring at the television screen flickering with an old image of Annalise's face labeled *Enemy Number One*, all Annalise wanted was to flee the town that hated her and never return.

Annalise forced herself to keep moving toward breakfast but paused at the kitchen door, just out of sight. Her mom and dad sat at the decrepit table (its legs held on by rope and clamps), sipping hot beverages—Mom, watery tea; Dad, coffee from yesterday's grounds. The shadowy sky hung lower than usual outside the cracked kitchen windows. Low fog crowded the field. Dead branches scratched the window glass like charred claws. Annalise avoided the curtains—old yellow ones from the attic, replaced in the night. She tried to ignore the scorch marks on the sagging wood ceiling but failed miserably. Now the burns were all she could see. Crisp, heart-shaped black leaves, the only kind that survived after Annalise's birth, bustled past the house carrying on with their pretty deaths, as if letting go was the easiest thing to do.

For Annalise, letting go was the hardest thing ever.

The memory of flames from the night before. The worry her parents would change their minds about letting her get a cat. The secret thought that maybe her parents hated her, that maybe they wished she'd never been born. The creeping fear that the Fate Spinner would one day take her mom and dad away from her, like she did her grandparents. Worries whirled about inside Annalise as she hovered outside the kitchen.

Four breaths, in and out. Four more strokes of her hair. Four times Annalise threw her worries away; four times they returned with force. Until she finally forced her feet forward and stepped into the kitchen light.

"Morning, shweetheart," Mom slurred. She peered over her notebook, pen clenched in her teeth as usual. Her mom,

17

Mattie, had a friendly, heart-shaped face, smiling brown eyes, and skin like blended autumn leaves, a shade darker than Annalise's own. She smiled at her as if nothing had happened the night before. As if children spat burning ash and black flames from their hands regularly. As if Annalise was the rarest and most lovely star of them all.

"You look nice," her dad said happily. Harry Meriwether, the handsomest man in Carriwitchet, was tall; had longish, straightish dark hair; chiseled cheekbones; a short black beard; and a kindness that radiated from him like sunlight. He regarded Annalise over his black glasses and chipped coffee mug that read: Poetry Is Life. "You ready for the big day?"

Annalise slid out her wobbly chair and sat across from them. She wanted to tell her parents how sorry she was for being cursed and setting fire to things again. Except only strangled air escaped her throat.

She stroked her hair and clenched her cursed fist tighter instead.

"Annalise?" Her mother's forehead lines deepened. "Are you okay?"

Nodding quickly, heat singeing the backs of her eyes, Annalise inhaled and exhaled, as always, exactly four times. The number four reminded her of a square—four sides, four

18

walls to break to escape her fear. Sometimes it worked; other times, not so much. Annalise watched the lemony fabric of the new curtains lift and fall, fall and lift on repeat, until she'd calmed enough to ask the question she'd dreaded to ask.

"Are we still going to the animal shelter today?"

Her mom peered over the crest of her notebook, pity crossing her face. Knowing how much Annalise disliked pity, her mom traded it quickly for a spark of excitement. "Yes, of course. As soon as I finish this chapter."

Fresh hope lit in Annalise. Although, in the time it took her mom to finish writing her chapter, the sky could shatter completely and the earth could crumble to dust (some of her sentences took days to complete). But Annalise kept her lips zipped, not wanting to ruin the chance of her first dream coming true. "Do you mean it?"

"I wouldn't say it if it wasn't true." As if she'd heard Annalise's thoughts, her mom snapped her notebook shut and stood. "You know what? I can finish this later. Let's get in the car and go. Right now."

Annalise broke into the world's fattest grin and hugged her mom as fast as a spring wind. "Thank you!" she cried excitedly. "You won't regret this!"

"I know we won't," her mom replied, and kissed Annalise's cheek.

Her dad nodded in agreement. "We never have regrets when it comes to you."

Everything seemed so wonderfully, exceptionally perfect—

Except for the panic stalking her life's peripheries like a panther, growling from the shadows of her cruel-hearted mind, *Foolish girl, you know nothing ever works out for you.*

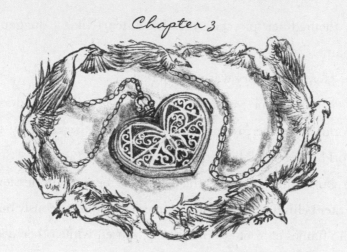

Chapter 3

THE WHITE CAT

Before Annalise was born, her dad dreamed of being the best boat builder in the world. He'd spent years learning his craft. He'd carved sacred creatures into helms, burned designs into planks, and brought his dreams to life. Each design was a gift to behold. He'd sold boats around the world and eventually became a great success. That is, until his daughter's birth, when his boats—and reputation—crashed and burned. Sailors died. Families were torn apart. And Harry Meriwether had earned a new name: *the Devil's Boatman.* Forced to give up his dream, he carved only models of longboats these days—their house was full of them. Each pierced Annalise's heart like a dagger of shame.

Her mom's story was no different.

Mattie spent years writing books, building fantastic worlds from the ground up. But each was rejected by the world. "Give up," literary gatekeepers would tell her. "Stick to gardening and leave the dream of being a professional writer behind." Some of her manuscripts spontaneously burst into flames en route to publishing houses, while others were lost. It didn't matter that her mom woke at 2:00 a.m. each morning to write before work, or if she was good and gifted and determined. No matter how wonderful her books were, fate's answer remained the same: No.

Annalise blamed herself for her parents' failures. So much so, she felt she needed to be extra good in return for their love. They'd already given up so much because of her. So when her big hand did wicked things, Annalise grew especially anxious.

And it grew more wicked each day.

The time to go to the animal shelter had arrived. Though she didn't feel she deserved it considering the trouble she caused, a secret flicker of hope in the dungeon of her heart refused to die: that maybe, even after everything, she was worthy of one very slight, cat-shaped dream. Her mom unlocked the cluster of locks barring their front door. And together, they stepped into the dark.

The Meriwether house sat at the far edge of town, bordered by a charred field and the petrified forest, dead as the sun over Carriwitchet. Their funny, hat-shaped home hung onto its togetherness by a thread. Shutters drooped. Black shingles flaked off like dragon scales. The circular wraparound porch—the brim of the witch's hat—was a study in *How to Sink into the Ground*. Each of the three floors slid off in different directions. Moonglow drenched their garden of poisonous nightshades, which Annalise's mom sold by mail order to apothecaries outside Carriwitchet under an assumed name.

The bars of their cage glinted in the dark light. Icy night winds greeted them with the scents of mildew and death. Annalise's blackberry hair whipped back in a gust as they stood between the door of their house and the one to the outer cage. She called this *the space between worlds*. She smiled as her dad popped the enormous padlock. Hands clasped, her parents' heads high, they led Annalise to their ancient car.

Somewhere channel seven's man on the scene, Richard Inglehart, would be reporting her cursed family *on the move*. They had hidden cameras posted in the trees—ones her parents never could find. Annalise held her mother's hand tighter, listening for the night wolves. She couldn't see them but knew they were watching, too.

Inside her cloak, her big hand burned. Annalise imagined reporters waiting for her cursed hand to do something bad. She forced this thought away and kept moving toward the car.

On the other side of town, a train whistle blew.

Annalise stopped in her tracks and hugged herself tight.

"Hey," her dad said, softening his watchful eyes. "It's okay. The train isn't coming for you." Her mind seized regardless. One after the next, worry-thoughts wrapped her lungs in cold cloth.

Your existence is a curse.

The train came for your grandparents and killed them, thanks to you.

You're the plague of your parents, this town, and every soul you meet!

Mom: "Annalise?"

You should be ashamed.

Dad: "Annalise."

Ashamed.

Ashamed.

Ashamed.

Ashamed!

Annalise took four breaths deep into her lungs and tried

wishing the worry-thoughts away. *You have the right to be happy,* she told herself. *Mom and Dad love you and you know this is true. It's okay, Annalise, it's okay.*

Your dreams might still come true.

"Annalise," her mom said quickly, opening the car door, face blooming with hope. "Come, sweetheart. Your new cat awaits."

"Okay," she answered. Forcing a smile, Annalise got in their rusted tank of a car and quietly shut the door.

And they drove, white crows cawed and swirled overhead, following as always. Sometimes Annalise thought the crows were protecting her. Other times, they felt like curious strangers—as if Annalise was an animal on a stage, and they'd come to watch her dance. Night wolves howled from the petrified wood, an eerily lonesome song that covered her bones with frost. She'd often dreamed of running a sanctuary for hunted and mistreated animals like the night wolves. Those attacked for their nature, for being themselves.

Behind their cries came another haunting call of a train. The moment felt frozen. Like a photo in a book captioned: *Just a few minutes before it happened . . .*

But the drive out of town was always fraught with danger. Their old car, with its dents from thrown rocks and scorch marks from tossed torches, rattled from a mile away. All of

Carriwitchet heard them coming. Townsfolk peered out their ramshackle doors when they passed—to jeer, spit, hold up amulets of protection—a shattered black heart with an eye in the center—to ward off the Fate Spinner's curse. "Don't look at them, Annalise," her dad said, gazing at her from the rearview mirror. Annalise nodded and cast her gaze aside. Away from the dilapidated black houses lining the road—on her birthday, every house in town turned black. Same as the trees in the petrified wood, and the farmlands beneath the cracked sky.

For hundreds of years prior to Annalise's birth, Carriwitchet was blessed. Some said it was the Spinner of Dreams who'd given their town prosperity, luck, security, and life. Not until Annalise was born wearing the mark of Fate did the Fate Spinner turn her dark eye onto them.

"Fate hates us," the townspeople gossiped. "We've loved her sister too much."

"She sent the girl as a punishment!"

"We must prove our loyalty to the Fate Spinner!" they cried.

"If she has cursed this girl, we must show the Fate Spinner we detest the girl, too. Mayhap then Kismet will return our sun and set our world to rights. . . ."

Annalise squeezed her eyes shut. She couldn't see the

angry faces of the townsfolk holding their amulets out against her, but they were there. Each stone they threw at their car made her spirit jump out of her skin.

She counted her breaths, but it didn't help—nothing really did.

"Sweetie, take my hand." Her mom reached into the backseat. Annalise opened her eyes. She clasped on to her mom like a life raft in a stormy sea as the townsfolk cried, "FREAK!" and "DEVIL!" and "CURSE!" and "Leave and never return!"

A strangled cry escaped Annalise as tears slipped down her cheeks. But still she was smiling at her mom, because her mom was smiling so lovingly at her.

The car swerved as her father stepped on the gas. "You know you're none of those things, right?" Harry Meriwether asked, skirting the rocks flying into the road.

Annalise raised her big purple eyes onto his in the mirror. "Yes," she answered softly, but only for him. Her heart knew no such thing.

Annalise took four deep breaths and tried to push her pain away. Sometimes deep breathing worked. Other times all it did was keep her alive.

Classical music played in the background—dark and dramatic, as they liked. The farther away from Carriwitchet they drove, the brighter the world became. No more venomous looks, the black stain of Carriwitchet left behind them. Here, the heavens opened blue as a gem and the whole world sang.

Annalise pressed her nose to the window. She wanted to pluck the colors like flowers and hold on to them forever. They'd been driving for what felt like hours when finally, after cresting the lovely, rolling green hills, they arrived at the animal shelter one hour before it opened.

A few employee cars dotted the lot. Since her mom was the shelter's resident Cat Lady, she came and went as she pleased. A glorious ray of sunlight drenched them in muslin gold. The warmth flowed through Annalise like magic, leaving the darkness from earlier behind. Annalise made sure her big hand was hidden as they paused on their way to the door to bask in the sun, faces up and smiling. Even though the shelter owners knew the truth about her family—and liked them regardless—Annalise didn't trust her big hand to behave.

Two dogs ran to the chain-link fence, barking and wagging their tails. *Hello, hello,* they seemed to say, *are you here to take us home?* Annalise beamed. The dogs were beautifully unafraid of her. In Annalise's perfect world, every animal would be surrounded by warmth and love and whatever else their pretty hearts desired. She made a silent wish that both dogs would find perfect forever homes soon.

Mother's coworkers let them though the double set of doors. Annalise greeted the nice-looking man and woman kindly, all the while stroking her hair and wondering if they'd like her if her big hand did something wicked. She wanted to think they would, but her experiences made her doubt.

The first room they entered was the cat room. It smelled wonderful—like fur, second chances, and hope. Annalise followed behind her dad. He'd put on a special mask and taken several outrageously giant pills beforehand to lessen his allergies. "Hope I don't puff up like a balloon," he joked, and joined her mom at the counter.

Annalise tightened her cursed fist under her cloak, furrowed her brow, and begged her dark mark in a whisper, "Please don't do anything bad."

Her left hand pinched ominously in reply.

Annalise walked softly down the first aisle of kittens and cats, stopping at each cage to say hello. As she approached the end of the aisle, a shock of joy struck to her toes. On the floor in the last cage on the right sat the large fluffy Siberian, no-sneezes-for-Harry cat. He had long white fur, and, much to her amazement, large plum-colored eyes like hers. Annalise had never seen a cat, or another person for that matter, with eyes the same shade as her own. He was beautiful and strange and looked especially good at keeping secrets—those too private to even share with her parents.

Annalise had always felt having a human friend would be quite different from having an animal friend and felt certain that one needed both. But as she turned to tell her mom and dad she'd found their cat, she saw that they were speaking in hushed tones with a shelter employee Annalise had never seen before.

The woman eyed Annalise suspiciously.

A chill of winter rippled Annalise's scalp. Heart revving, ears buzzing, Annalise counted—*one-two-three-four*. Regardless, the usual worries came. Maybe the woman hated her family? Maybe she knew of Annalise's big hand and wanted her to leave?

Trying to make herself smaller, Annalise crouched before the cat enclosure and gulped breath after breath over the lump in her throat. A moment later, the woman laughed at something her dad had said.

Annalise nearly melted with relief.

Thank you, Dad—thank you!

Annalise wiped the panicked sweat from her brow and smiled nervously at the white cat. Immediately, the black heart on her big hand flared in pain and fought for freedom from under her cloak. It jerked this way and that trying to seize the cat. The other cats in the shelter howled, growled, and spat.

Please, Annalise begged her big hand. *Please leave us alone.*

Her big hand shook and burned and then stilled.

Embarrassed, worried, yet enchantedly hopeful, Annalise exhaled a sigh of relief and read the tag on the cat's cage: *New arrival: Hypoallergenic Siberian male. Two to three years old. Dislikes other cats. Detests dogs. Nervous around people.*

The long-haired white Siberian sat up in his blanketed box and gazed intensely at Annalise. The more he blinked his hypnotic plum eyes, the quieter the other cats became, until their cries eventually ceased, and the room grew silent as a stone.

Curious.

Annalise cleared her throat. "Hi," she said softly. "I see your sign says you're a nervous type." Annalise contemplated sticking the fingers of her good-natured hand through the bars to let the cat sniff her but didn't want to frighten him—getting bitten wasn't part of her plan. Annalise told him the truth instead. "If I had a sign, it would say I was nervous around people as well." Shoulders slumped, she stroked her hair and sighed. "Actually, I'm nervous around a lot of things. Even myself."

The cat narrowed his eyes, appraising her as if trying

to decide something. His puffy white tail flicked, yet he remained inside his box.

Annalise observed him closer. Something was wrong with him. The skin beneath his fur was covered in wounds. He had several gashes on his upper body in various stages of healing, and some missing fur. Annalise glared and gritted her teeth.

He'd been abused. Not much angered Annalise, but people who hurt animals were at the top of her list.

"Did someone hurt you?" she asked, not expecting an answer, though she swore she saw him nod. "How terrible." Annalise dropped her eyes and squeezed her cursed hand tight. "Sometimes, people hurt me, too." The cat craned his head closer toward the bars, ears flicking, shifting on his paws. This time, she was sure he nodded back.

Next, to Annalise's delight, he began to purr.

He purred—because of her! Even though the tag said he was nervous around people and *she* was a people, he didn't seem anxious around Annalise at all.

The cat stepped out of his oversize shoebox. Annalise glanced down and gasped: his left front paw was bigger than his right, like her big hand.

"Mercy," Annalise exclaimed. "You have a big hand, too?" A 'double paw' her mom had called others like this before. A surge of gratefulness flowed through her. Annalise loved the unusual white cat even more with the peculiarities they shared.

Maybe my dream of having a friend will work out after all.

"Ah, I see you've found Mister No Name." Mom grinned down at her. Annalise had been so engrossed, she hadn't heard her parents approach. "Look at him, Harry. He didn't seem to like anyone else, but he looks absolutely in love with Annalise."

Annalise, sitting cross-legged on the floor, spun around hopefully, heart fluttering. "May I let him out?"

"Of course," her mom replied. "Just be careful. He must have suffered terribly—it seems he was chained for some time." Her mom narrowed her face like a dagger. "I hope whoever did this to him pays in a most satisfactory way."

Annalise nodded hard in agreement but hesitated.

Her dad's reddened eyes tipped into smiles over his mask. "Go on. Open it." He waved Annalise on. "He likes you. It'll be okay."

Annalise had a moment of panic as she reached for the cage door. Animals had responded unfavorably around her marked hand in the past—scratching, lunging, biting—a raccoon once chased her for fourteen blocks!

"Annalise," her dad mumbled through his mask. "No

matter what happens, we're here for you."

Big hand tucked in the shadows under her cloak, Anna-lise took four quick breaths and unlocked the cage.

The door creaked open. Annalise made no sudden moves. "Try not to be scared," she said. "I won't let anyone hurt you ever again."

The large white Siberian didn't hesitate. He climbed out of his enclosure, plopped into Annalise's lap, and rubbed his head against her hidden hand.

An electric shock zinged through her dark mark. Anna-lise gasped. The cat snuggled closer, and she cuddled it back.

Could I finally have found a real friend?

"Well, well!" Dad cheered, with no small amount of emo-tion. "He's smitten. I think we've found our cat."

This close to one of her dreams, Annalise finally allowed herself to relax. "You're perfect." She stroked his fur with her nice hand. "I can't wait to tell you all my secrets." The cat nuzzled close to her ear. "Mostly," Annalise told him, "I can't wait to take you home."

"Likewise," she swore she heard the cat say.

Annalise froze, eyes huge. "Excuse me?" she whispered. "Did you just say what I think you—"

The bell to the entrance dinged. Two volunteers swooped in from outside, one holding the door for the next, looking

34

at each other and laughing. A chilled wind gusted inward. Autumn leaves skittered across the floor. Papers *whoosh*ed off the front counter, scattering free. The world wound down to slow motion.

And stopped.

When Annalise's cursed mark shot with one of the worst pains of her life, she doubled over and nearly screamed. Black smoke bled through her cloak. And in one fast jerk, her big hand fought its way free from hiding.

No!

The cat's muscles tensed. His gaze flicked to her smoking big hand and then to the open doors. The other employees were at work in the next room. The volunteers still hadn't noticed her. Annalise's parents regarded their daughter with dawning fear.

"Harry," her mom said gently, crouching to reach for the cat.

"Mattie," her dad replied, stooping alongside her.

The cat glanced briefly at Annalise, an apology in his eyes, before bolting for the open doors. He ran so fast, he blurred. Mattie and Harry raced into the parking lot to catch him, but it was too late. Annalise's new friend was gone.

Instantly, her big hand erased of hurt, smoke, and flame. As if her cursed hand had done it on purpose. Like it had scared her new friend away to hurt her. And now that the cat was gone, her big hand was happy.

Annalise clenched her fists at her ears, chin trembling, heart pounding with loss, the inescapable pain of being so close to a dream and having it snatched away.

The Fate Spinner had stolen her happiness once more.

Annalise turned away from the cage and hugged her knees to her chest, cursing her big hand and her fate for stealing what felt like her last chance at having a friend. Annalise wasn't an angry girl. She loathed feeling full of fire and darkness, ready to explode. Annalise was a girl of love and care and dreams, not of hatred.

But oh, how Annalise hated her big hand and the Fate Spinner both!

She was tired of someone else controlling what happened or didn't happen in her life. All she'd wanted was a friend to share secrets and laugh with. Someone who knew her thoughts and likes, her oddities and the dark depths of her anxieties. Someone who liked her anyway, and knew, without a doubt, the evil things she did were not who she really was, not in her true heart. Someone who saw that underneath her curse she was kind and gentle, a friend who knew how to be good. How was she supposed to keep dreaming when every dream she'd ever had died before it was born?

Seconds before her parents rushed into the shelter, a new determinedness sprouted through the tired foundation in Annalise's spirit. A resolve to never let anything like losing the white cat happen to her again. Perhaps it was time to say goodbye to her many smaller dreams, like having friends and even a cat. Time to dream bigger than she'd ever allowed herself to dream before.

Just then, a strange wind blew in through the doors. And as Annalise stroked her witchy purple hair, a zap of not-entirely-unpleasant energy coursed through her marked palm, electrifying her senses, as a new dream sprang up within her.

Annalise raised her chin, focused her gaze on the door, and whispered her new dream, "I wish to rule my own destiny and rid myself of this curse."

Once and for all.

Chapter 4

GHOSTS OF CURSES PAST

Once upon a time, Annalise had lived with her parents and grandparents—both sets—all of whom treasured her despite her curse. She'd been a happy baby. Annalise had cooed and burped and farted while laughing, as all good babies should. She'd sucked her toes and drooled and sighed with contentment when her family tucked her into her crib and sang her to sleep. Annalise grew fat and happy, fed on love and joy, sheltered from the madness of a town gripped by fear. Not realizing the townspeople loathed her. Or that they'd tried to burn down her home—twice. If it wasn't for the white crows attacking the townsfolk and driving them away, her family might not have survived.

Until Annalise got older, she hadn't known she was cursed.

Once, at twelve months old, Annalise and her mom were walking defiantly through town. Unforgiving townsfolk huffed and scowled and crossed the street to avoid them, white crows trailing their steps. Occasionally, a few crows would caw and dive-bomb someone—Richard Inglehart, reporter for channel seven news, for example. Despite the townsfolk's cruelty, baby Annalise had giggled in her mother's arms.

At least she had until she and her mom were almost to the car—and a rare black crow landed on Annalise's head. Her happiness soured to fear. And for the first time, a plume of fire erupted from baby Annalise's mark.

Mattie jumped. Townsfolk scattered. White crows attacked—caw-caw-caw-caw. Annalise screamed—her small body contorted in pain. The news crew arrived in seconds, ready to spew propaganda and hate across televisions far and wide. "Breaking news: the Meriwether child is a demon!" Richard Inglehart shouted into the camera as Mattie and Annalise rushed to their car. "Here's your proof for you— she's set the whole town to burn!"

Mattie batted her hair, which had caught fire. She tried to extinguish her child's left hand, but the damage was done. The awning beside them caught next. Flames spread, and they escaped just in time.

At three years old, Annalise's grandfather, Jovie Meriwether, who bore a wart on his nose and a twinkle in his eye, drove her a few towns over to the bookstore. Annalise had wandered to the back, which, she discovered, was the most magical part of the shop. She'd found a quiet spot in a red velvet chair, a book alive with art, and a window filled with sunlight. Lost in the beauty of it, she'd met a friend.

"Wanna play?" the black-haired girl asked, extending her hand. Annalise beamed like a firework. Grandpa Jovie's wrinkled face lit with delight. When Annalise unknowingly clasped the girl's hand inside her cursed palm, the girl screamed and fell. "It burns, Mommy—she burnted me!" A red welt in the shape of a shattered red heart imprinted on the girl's palm. The girl cried and ran into her mother's arms.

"You should keep that . . . *monster* locked up!" the girl's mother told Annalise's grandfather before storming off in a huff.

From then on, when Annalise's family took her to town, they covered their tender-eyed girl's ears from harsh words and threats and reassured her that she was loved. "You are our darling girl," they'd say. "And we shall always love you." And, despite everything, for a long while, Annalise regarded the townsfolk with kindness when they passed her by.

But all good things must come to an end.

Not long after Annalise turned four, her grandparents got on a train and never returned. Newspapers said the train crashed in a freak derailment and burned. Even then, Annalise knew the truth: the fault was hers. Soon, the townsfolk's whispers grew too loud to ignore.

"It's the girl that killed them."

"Annalise Meriwether is a demon."

"Fate's number one enemy."

"That girl's wicked heart will kill us all!"

Haunted day and night by those who would do them harm, Annalise's father built the giant cage around their home to lock strangers out and safety in. As the years passed, Annalise's smiles weren't so easy, and she feared the unknown waiting beyond her front door.

Annalise had asked her parents about her curse once, when she was seven, after lighting a mean boy's hair on fire. "What's wrong with me, Daddy?" Annalise had asked, curled in his lap. "How did I curse Carriwitchet on my birthday?"

He tapped Annalise's nose. "Do you know what I remember about that day?"

"Uh-uh," Annalise replied, stroking her hair.

"The joy on your mom's face when she looked at you. How flocks of white crows and a snow of black hearts arrived with you. How the air crackled like static, and everything

41

felt more alive." His soft voice hitched. "I remember staring into your bright eyes and thinking how magical you must be to transform a town from ordinary to extraordinary just by being born." Annalise burrowed closer to her dad and the *lub-dub* of his heart. "And you know what I thought? *How amazing.* If the girl can do that without even trying, when she grows up, imagine all the magical things she'll do."

Her dad was being kind, as always. Still, Annalise frowned. "But what if the magicalness inside me is bad? What if *I'm* bad, like the townspeople say?"

Her mom walked up and swept strands of hair from Annalise's forehead. "You? Bad? Never. The only people behaving badly are the ones attacking you for being different. Your *magicalness* is a gift. One I hope you might learn to love."

Annalise clenched her big hand tighter. How could she love something that caused so much pain?

Annalise asked one more question, her gaze fixed to the floor. "Why did the Fate Spinner curse me?"

Annalise's parents were quiet a long time. Finally, Mattie took Annalise's face in her hands, peered deeply into her eyes, and said, "I think you were so powerful, the Fate Spinner knew she could never tame you. I think that scared her then. And I think it frightens her still."

They never spoke of the Fate Spinner again. But every day

since, Annalise's anxiety and panic had worsened. Her fear of the outside had ballooned into a beast too big to control. A slithering monster that whispered through the petrified, black-hearted trees:

"One day, the Fate Spinner will take your parents. And then, you accursed little thing, she will come after you."

Annalise tried very hard not to hate anyone or anything.

However, two things came close: spiders, and her tormentor, the Fate Spinner.

Chapter 5

A CURIOUSLY HIDDEN BOOK

With the sweet white Siberian cat of Annalise's dreams gone, and her parents outside chasing after him, Annalise found herself alone. She pressed her forehead to the cat's empty cage and recited her new dream four times:

I wish to rule my own destiny and rid myself of this curse.

As her parents pushed through the shelter's doors, Annalise spied something curious in the Siberian's shoebox at the back of his cage.

A small, book-shaped object, nestled in a nest of the cat's shed white fur, peeked at her like a secret. Something meant only for her.

Annalise wiped her snotty nose and damp eyes and

glanced at her parents behind the front desk. Her mom gestured to Annalise as if to say, "Be right there" and spoke quietly to the other employees ("I'm sorry." "I'll work extra hours. Please don't tell anyone what you saw." "Yes. She'll be all right."). Her dad approached Annalise, scratching his allergy-reddened ears like a dog. As discreetly as possible, Annalise slid her nice hand inside the cage and reached for the tattered old book.

A jumping spider leaped onto the cover.

"Mercy!" Annalise withdrew her hand at once. Spiders were the one creature she'd had a hard time warming up to, especially the jumpers. "Please move," she asked politely. The spider hissed and scuttled away.

Pulse throbbing, Annalise reached again for the worn binding, longing to bring it to her nose. Books were like rare paper flowers one should always stop to inhale. Her dad, almost to her place on the floor, suddenly turned to ask her mom a question. Annalise made a quick grab for the book. The instant her fingers wrapped the binding, a charge of electricity surged through her, toes to scalp, freezing Annalise in place.

Then, in the depths of her mind, a vision appeared . . .

Annalise saw herself at four years old, right before her grandparents passed away, sitting at the top of their home's spiral staircase. The house, dark and moon-drenched. Annalise wore pajamas, ready for bed, a book of unicorns and dragons in her lap. Annalise's grandparents circled the table in the kitchen, talking quietly over night-cabbage soup and tea, when an unwelcome knock banged at the door. This was before her dad had built the iron cage. Before they felt all-the-way safe. Annalise craned her neck to peer through the slats of the railing as her dad swung open the door.

A brisk wind rushed inside. Crisp black-hearted leaves tumbled past her parents' feet. Tiny flashes of lightning zapped and zinged in the doorway between her parents and the someone outside. A severe-looking young woman, with skin as white as the moon and hair the same, stood on the threshold. She wore a long fitted black dress with a stiff collar rising at the back of her head. Buttons, small and hard as her black eyes, ran from her throat to her knees. Ruffles of lace twisted at her throat. Her lips, as well as her eyes, were painted in thick black kohl. The woman seemed familiar, as if Annalise had seen her before, but she couldn't place where or when.

White crows cawed in a mad scramble around the woman, diving in to attack. But when the woman swung her walking stick at them, the crows screamed and flew away.

"Pleased to make your acquaintance," the woman said, bowing, in a voice as soothing as chamomile tea. The shiny veneer of her staff resembled a dark mirror of many closed eyes. The longer Annalise stared at the staff through the banister, the hotter the black mark on

*her big hand became. When the woman flicked her gaze up at Anna-
lise, her dark eyes widened, and Annalise's cursed hand stabbed with
pain.*

*"Can we help you?" her dad asked coldly, wrapping an arm around
her mom. The grandparents quieted in the kitchen.*

*After a long silence, the stranger ripped her gaze from Annalise,
more flustered than she was seconds ago, and said, "Yes. I've . . . come
for the girl."*

*Annalise whimpered and crawled backwards toward the wall.
Her big hand, hot as lava, trembled. Annalise held it against her chest
and sang it a soft song in her sweet child's voice, "Go to sweep, go to
sweep . . ."*

*Her dad glared. "We don't know who you are, but if the town put
you up to this, you've wasted your time. This is our home, and Annalise
has as much right to live in Carriwitchet as anyone else!"*

*"I'm afraid you don't understand," the strange woman said as if
each word caused her pain. "I have a very good reason for being here. You
see, a mistake was made the day of your daughter's birth. Somehow, she
defied the laws of fate—the laws that govern your world." She flicked
her soulless black gaze onto Annalise. "She stole something from me, and
I've waited long enough to take it back."*

*The woman moved to step over the threshold. Electricity zapped in
the doorway, pushing her back, crumbling part of her dress sleeve to dust.
When the woman raised her hand in surprise, Annalise caught a glimpse*

47

of her marked left palm. At the shattered-looking black heart, identical to Annalise's own.

"Who are you?" Harry asked the stranger.

"I know who she is," Mattie replied with breathless awe, staring at the woman's marked hand. "This is the Fate Spinner. The enchantress who ravaged our town and cursed Annalise."

The Fate Spinner grinned her display of perfect white teeth. "If you want your child to live, give her to me. I promise she'll live a long, useful life. But if you let me leave without her, life for you will . . . not be so kind." Annalise's grandparents entered the room and stood behind Mattie and Harry. The pale woman leaned in as close as possible without getting zapped by the membrane of electric current between them. She said something Annalise couldn't quite hear. Every word was muffled except these: "Mazelands . . . Labyrinth . . . Dreamer!"

Annalise's mom grabbed the door, readying to shut it in her face. "If you really are the Fate Spinner, you're not allowed to touch us or enter our home. Try, and you'll crumble to dust. We know the laws, too, Kismet, and since you're most certainly not invited into our home, leave and never return."

"Hear me, and hear me well," the Fate Spinner shrieked for all Carriwitchet to hear. "The next time we meet—and we will meet again—it will be on my terms. And none of you shall survive." White crows screaming behind her, she banged her staff on the porch. Sparks

and smoke plumed in a wash of black. The stranger bowed before her
parents, then grinned at Annalise as her mom slammed the door.

"Hey there," Annalise's dad said, jolting her from the vision.

Annalise jumped. Her heart galloped too fast, her breath lost in the stampede. Her back still to her dad, Annalise re-hid her big hand and slid the strange book behind her.

He adjusted his glasses and knelt at his daughter's side. "Sweetheart, are you okay?"

Was she? Annalise didn't know. What had just happened? That couldn't have been a real memory. Could it? And if so, why did it come to her now, when she touched the odd little book?

"Annalise?" Her dad repeated, "Are you okay?"

Finally, Annalise swung around to face him, wondering if she'd imagined the whole thing. "I'm, um . . . just sad, I guess?" And alarmed, worried, confused, and heartbroken about losing her feline friend. "I really just wanted that nice cat to like me."

"Yeah, I know." Her dad sat on the floor beside her. "And I'm sure he did, too. I think, in the end, his fear got the best of him."

"I'm so sorry, Annalise." Her mom knelt before Annalise,

her dark eyes glinting with love. "After enduring so much abuse, maybe the poor thing just needed freedom."

"And you," her dad added, "were the one to give it to him. I'm sure he'll think of you fondly for that."

Annalise closed her eyes and sighed deeply from her scared, worried heart. Inside her dark mind, she recalled the Fate Spinner's face.

Annalise hugged her parents fast and hard. "I love you," she said quietly. "No matter what, I will love you forever."

"And we love you back," they said together, and helped Annalise to her feet.

Annalise slipped the strange book into her cloak pocket before anyone saw.

"Now," her dad said, "let's go home so I can take off this ridiculous mask. What do you say?"

"Yes," her mom agreed, and wrapped her arm around Annalise. "And hey, no matter what, we always have each other, right?"

Annalise smiled and nodded at her parents. "Right."

What would she do without them?

The Meriwethers drove home in silence. Annalise sat in the backseat inside a clean ray of sunlight, safely out of her parents' sight. She slid the black book, its cover the texture of batwings, into her lap. No shock of electricity or vision came.

It seemed like an ordinary book. There was a title on the cover in gold she hadn't noticed before: *The Book of Remembering.*

There were very few pages inside. They all appeared blank until suddenly, charcoal sketches began to appear— drawings of ferocious monsters and people battling them inside a large skull-shaped maze. Pristine crystalline palaces and strangely colored beasts flew in stranger-colored skies. Golden butterflies fluttered around a king and a queen in rich robes. Beneath them, words bloomed onto the page. And Annalise read the story writing itself before her eyes:

The Twin Enchantresses: the Fate Spinner and the Spinner of Dreams

Once upon a time, in the Mazelands on the flip side of the sky, there lived a set of very different twin girls: Kismet, the Fate Spinner, and Reverie, the Spinner of Dreams.

Kismet, born first, had hair like silk spun from moon-light and frost-pale skin. Her eyes, as large and dark as the polished night sky; her clothes, always black; her hair, severe and fantastic. She carried a powerful staff of enchanted mirrored eyes said to see into her subjects' souls. Kismet held charge over all events that occurred in each person's life. She bestowed hardships, luck—both kinds—along with love, pain, mercy, death, good health, disease, and curses.

The Fate Spinner decided each person's fate.

Reverie had dark brown skin and black hair, both of which glittered with mica-like stars. Her eyes were gold and warm; her clothes, bright and wild and ever-changing to suit her mood. Her crown bore horns and crows. Reverie held charge over people's dreams. Not those found in sleep, but rather one's most heartfelt desires: the wishes they longed for with their entire being.

The Spinner of Dreams granted the power of dreams.

The gifts of the twin enchantresses came with four unbreakable laws:

1. If either perished, the surviving Spinner would inherit the other's gifts and lands.
2. The Fate Spinner (All That Must Be), cannot possess the ability to see or change her sister's fate.
3. The Spinner of Dreams (All That One May Become), cannot possess the ability to see or change her sister's dreams.
4. If any mortal challenges Kismet's assigned fate, said mortal maintains the right to enter the Mazelands, conquer the Labyrinth of Fate and Dreams, and earn a dream of their choosing. However, at no time are they to touch,

hurt, aid, or influence anyone by any means, magical or otherwise, once inside the labyrinth.

If either Spinner disobeyed any of the above four laws, the other Spinner would immediately take their crown.

Many traveled far to challenge the Fate Spinner, but most were never seen again. Still, if one had a devastating fate and a dream worth fighting for, if one wished to find the Mazelands and the enchanted labyrinth, one only needed to follow the arc of moonlight on the night they were ready to go, and it would lead to an extraordinarily dressed cat with an exceptionally large paw. Follow the dream cat, the right hand of the Spinner of Dreams herself, and it will show you the way to the labyrinth, where one's most desperate dreams might come true.

If you be such a dreamer, a word of caution. If you survive the journey to the Labyrinth of Fate and Dreams, know that anything you see within the labyrinth's walls might be real—or it might be an illusion borne of the maze that bears a mind of its own.

Eyes wide, Annalise shut the book. Heart fluttering like a dove with glass wings at what she'd read, she felt the car bump and rattle in sync with her thoughts. She knew about the Mazelands and the Spinners, of course. And she'd heard murmurs of a labyrinth before, but she'd never heard of a cat guide with an exceptionally large paw.

Like the one from the shelter.

Mercy.

The book seemed to hum in her hands. Annalise took another peek inside.

The pages had changed. Now an elaborate sketch of a white cat in a top hat and monocle stared back at her with deep purple eyes. Could the cat from the shelter be the same as the one in the book? Had he come to show her the way to the Mazelands, to help her find the Fate Spinner and break her curse?

Had she missed her chance?

Sketched in charcoal on the next page was the Fate Spinner, the same woman from her vision, the enchantress who ruled her destiny and marked her with a curse.

Alongside the drawing of the Fate Spinner was another of her twin sister, the Spinner of Dreams. She wore a crown of crows and horns, and a dress of white crow feathers. Her lips and eyes were gold. Color and light moved through her dark skin like sunlight through a prism, alive with creation, empathy, and love. Annalise skimmed Reverie's face with a finger from her kind hand. At her touch, ripples of memory returned, of every happiness, wish, and beautifulness

Annalise had ever experienced.

Annalise smiled from the back seat. Until an electric bolt of fire pierced her blackened mark and she cried out in surprise.

"What's wrong?" her mom asked while elbowing her dad to keep his eyes on the road. Annalise hid the book behind her, tears in her eyes from the piercing hot pain.

"Annalise, answer your mother." Dad's eyes bored into her through the rearview mirror.

Tapping her small hand against her thigh—four times, repeat—she answered, "It's just my mark. I'll be okay. Don't worry." Annalise forced a reassuring smile while trying to count her hurt and fear and anxious thoughts away.

"Try not to worry, sweetheart," her dad said, taking a curve. "We'll be home soon."

Dad turned up the music. He'd just passed the wooden sign for Carriwitchet—topped with four white crows—when a rivulet of smoke seeped through her plum cloak from her cursed hand. Annalise clamped her fist tight, gritted her teeth, and recited her new dream under her breath, "I wish to rule my own destiny and rid myself of this curse."

The powerful words pushed everything else away and left only one truth behind. Tonight, even if her panic attacks came one after the next, she'd run away and not look back.

Annalise would leave the last people who loved her and begin a quest for her dreams. She'd follow the moonlight and find the cat in the top hat and monocle. She'd rule her own destiny and escape the Fate Spinner's curse.

Then Annalise would be free.

She removed *The Book of Remembering* out from behind her back, held it close, and imagined the Fate Spinner's face.

I am coming to find you, Annalise thought. Shadows veiled her face as she stared out at her broken town. *And then I will show you just what a dreamer can do.*

Chapter 6

GOODBYE

Later that evening, after Annalise had opened and closed *The Book of Remembering* until the pages cleared, she, Mattie, and Harry played a rousing game of Castles, Angels, and Fiends—sort of like chess, but with wizards, ghosts, and monsters. Her father won—again. Miraculously, Annalise's devilish hand behaved itself the whole time. They enjoyed a supper of her favorite foods: mashed potatoes, sweet-and-sour noodles, and appleslaw. They even had a rare treat: chocolate brownies with whipped cream and bright red winterberries, purchased several towns away. The night wolves stayed clear of the Meriwethers' field, despite the full moon. The crows were suspiciously quiet, asleep on the bars of their home, nary a flutter in sight. They enjoyed a perfect last night together as a family. But soon, Annalise would have to say goodbye.

Annalise stroked her braid with her nice hand as her parents tucked her into bed. She wanted to remember them this way forever. Her dad, smelling of cedarwood, donning his famous goofy grin and onyx-rimmed glasses. Her mom, kissing the crown of Annalise's head, perfumed in moonlight, black roses, and home.

Before closing the door, Annalise's mom paused. "Annalise?" The candle in the corner of her bedroom cast everything in a golden glow, including her mom's face. "If you could have any dream in the world come true, what would it be?"

Annalise's nerves zinged, and her hairs raised. She shifted onto her back and focused on the shadow-bars on the walls, not wanting her parents to see her in case she cried. "Anything?"

"Yes," her mom answered. "Anything."

A whirlpool of emotions swirled inside Annalise like a hundred mixed colors of paint. If they'd asked her what she wanted most a week ago, even more than an end to her curse, her answer would have been, "My grandparents, alive," every time. But after everything that had happened, only one answer remained.

"I'd want to rule my own destiny. I'd want to decide my fate for myself."

Something within her big hand *moved*. Like a monster was growing and writhing within her, gaining a life of its own.

"Now that is a fabulous dream," her mom replied. "I hope, more than anything, that it comes true."

"Ditto, kiddo," her father said warmly, straightening his glasses.

Together, they returned to Annalise's side. Her mom scooped her up and latched on. Her father stroked her strange purple hair. And Annalise held tight to her family, knowing, when she let go, she might be letting go for good.

Suddenly, all Annalise's pent-up heartache and woe, worry and pain, shook from her chest like a solid thing, a dragon birthed from a rip in the earth. "I'm so sorry! Sorry I'm such a burden"—she gulped—"such a broken and ugly, cursed thing."

"Annalise." Her dad's eyes twinkled sadly behind his glasses. When he continued, he was uncharacteristically stern. "Don't ever say such things about yourself. You are one of the only two stars in my sky, and don't you forget it."

Mom perched on the bed beneath the cracked window and midnight moon. "That's right. You were our greatest dream; did you know? It's true! Before you came along, we wished for a daughter just like you." Mom's smile jigged nervously around the edges. "So, whatever you think of the Fate Spinner, she let us have you. Your dad and I are grateful for that, and we wouldn't have it any other way."

Annalise sighed. How could she leave the last people who loved her?

But, if there was even a small chance that the Fate Spinner would take her mom and dad from her, hurt them as she'd done her grandparents, how could she not?

Annalise whispered the words that swam up from her heart, "I don't know what I'd do without you."

They kissed her and stepped into the hall. "Good thing you'll never have to find out," her dad said. "Good night, little love."

"Good night, sweetheart." Her mom waved her way out the door.

"Goodbye," Annalise said instead of good night, alone with her monsters once more.

Outside, the night music played: wind twisting the spines of dead leaves; crows, feathers, and wings making eerie harmonies; night wolves howling at the ghost moon. If Annalise listened closely she could hear all the fears of the dying world sing. It was an incredibly lonely sound.

In the room beneath hers, her parents snored. The clock

read 11:02 p.m. The numbers added up to four.

That was her cue from the universe: it was time.

Annalise needed to check the book's instructions to make sure she remembered them correctly. But given her experience with *The Book of Remembering*, she wasn't sure what she'd find. Carefully, sneakily even, Annalise pulled back the enchanted book's cover. Thankfully, the instructions were waiting for her:

. . . if one wished to find the Mazelands and the enchanted labyrinth, one only needed to follow the arc of moonlight on the night they were ready to go, and it would lead to an extraordinarily dressed cat with an exceptionally large paw. Follow the dream cat, the right hand of the Spinner of Dreams herself, and it will show you the way to the labyrinth, where one's most desperate dreams might come true.

If the white cat in question *was* the same cat she'd found in the shelter, he had escaped too fast to follow. Plus, the shelter was filled with sunlight, not moonlight.

Maybe it's a coincidence?

Maybe not.

Either way, Annalise decided to follow the moonlight across the field and see what happened. The thought of doing so made her insides shrivel and curl with worry.

But, she told herself, *if you want to be free, you're doing it anyway.*

Quietly, Annalise slipped from her bed. Her home's perfume—of static, warmth, and the unnameable scent of family—circling her head, she snuck about and packed a bag with essentials. Some of the water and snacks she kept in her closet for panic-attack emergencies. *The Book of Remembering.* The small wooden heart her dad gave her for her second birthday that read: *My Heart Is Yours.* She almost brought a change of clothes, but nothing more would fit. Finally, she donned her favorite plum cloak, which would remind Annalise of her mom.

How nice it would be, Annalise thought, *to be a normal child. Not having to worry about my fate or curse or leaving my loved ones behind.*

The part she'd been dreading had arrived. Annalise took a deep breath and exhaled in a whisper directed at the room below, "Please forgive me. I love you. Goodbye."

Anxiety slithered through her veins and grew and grew and grew until Annalise felt too choked to breathe. But she wouldn't let her anxiousness stop her. Stubbornly, perhaps even bravely, Annalise would do what she dreaded, for better or worse.

Before leaving, Annalise wrote her parents a note and left

it on her pillow.

Dear Mom and Dad,
You always tell me to follow my dreams,
and that you're always there for me. Try to
remember that when you read this and find
me gone. I'm tired of my curse ruining our
lives, and I'm finally ready to do something
about it. I hope you won't be angry with me.
Hopefully, I'll return with a dream come true.
How happy we'd be then!
I love you more than all the stars in the sky.
Always, your Annalise
XXOO

Annalise unlocked every lock on the front door, followed
by the giant padlock on the bars, and relocked them behind
her. White crows, perched on the bars of the cage, ruffled
their feathers and blinked at her in the dark. Annalise nodded to them, and she swore the largest bird, perched on the
bar to the right, nodded back.

Beyond the iron enclosure, Annalise crunched through
the dead grass and leaves, past the shadowshine berry trees
dotting their backyard. She used to help her mom in the

garden often. Something about digging in the earth with bare hands was soothing. Her mom used to sing faerie songs while they planted their nightshades, and Annalise's favorites always involved the strange fruit.

"One whiff of shadowshine berries will wake those poisoned with sleep. One bite of shadowshine berries will kill those fated to eat. And keeping thorns close, when you need them the most, protects fair dreamers from harm . . ."

Her mom said the shadowshine berry trees were a gift from the Spinner of Dreams herself.

A twig snapped close by.

Annalise flinched.

The cameras. Was Richard Inglehart watching her escape from the trees? Was her guilty face flicking on to every townsfolk's TV screen?

Annalise listened closely. But no more twigs snapped. No shoes rustled dead leaves. No voices crept into the night.

She spotted no night wolves in the field—not yet, anyway.

When her pathway cleared, Annalise stepped forward, bag clutched close to her chest, and left her old life behind.

Chapter 7

THE WHITE CAT RETURNS

In the backyard, the mid-October night arrived blustery and crisp. The field past the fence shone like a pale white diamond. Dew coated the dead lawn and fall decorations scattered about the yard. The white crows slept soundly in the dead poplar. The brisk wind cooled Annalise's flushed cheeks as she crunched through the dead grass, listening to her worry-thoughts whirl. Annalise had just paused in a shaft of moonlight beneath the poplar tree to gather her thoughts when a branch snapped above her. With a fright, Annalise slowly raised her eyes.

A white cat in a top hat and monocle smiled down at her.

Annalise gazed up into the tree in shock. Tail high, gaze

firm, deep plum eyes steady, the cat was immediately recognizable.

"Y-you're—" Annalise stuttered. "You're the cat from the shelter." Intelligence far beyond that of a regular cat gleamed back in his stare. "The cat that I thought liked me but ran away from me instead."

The white cat, which may or may not have been a guide to the Spinner of Dreams, nodded once.

"I see." The rejection stung. But still, the cat felt like a friend. Annalise noticed missing fur and a thin trickle of blood at the cat's neck. He had other fresh wounds as well. "Fate hasn't been kind to you, has it?" Her blackberry hair rose in a rogue breeze. The cat rubbed the half-healed wound at his neck, then shook his head so hard his monocle nearly popped out. "I'm sorry. Fate hasn't been kind to me, either."

The cat observed Annalise for a moment before showering her in a warm grin. "But your kindness saved me."

The gentlemanly feline leaped down from the limb and landed on a stump behind the tree. Annalise gasped with excitement and followed. "I knew you could speak!" she said. "I knew I hadn't imagined it!"

Moonglow tipped the cat's fur in a glaze of liquid mercury. He blinked up at her and replied in a wise, velvety voice, "Cats, like all animals, have always spoken. But only those touched by the magic of both fate and dreams can hear us." The cat's eyes twinkled beneath his hat's rim.

Annalise had to admit, she really did like this cat. There was something unusual about him—something dark and bright at once.

The cat lowered his head and tapped his top hat. A word appeared in a glitter of gold across the black ribbon at its base.

Muse

Annalise's eyes went wide. "Your name is Muse? That's a wonderful name!" Annalise glanced over her shoulder, making sure her parents hadn't come outside, and whispered, "You're a dream cat, aren't you—a guide into the Mazelands?"

Muse nodded sadly. "I am. And for the record, I would have liked to have left the shelter with you earlier. Please know I didn't run from you out of fear but to retrieve something I'd lost when they locked me up in that cage. Something I needed in order to help get you to the Mazelands."

Annalise shook her head and circled the cat on the stump, stroking her hair in rhythms of four. "I don't understand. Why would the Fate Spinner try to stop us?" In the vision Annalise had seen, it had seemed like she *wanted* Annalise to go to the Mazelands with her.

"Because you possess something the Fate Spinner would do anything to control." His voice deepened. "Something rare. Something that she doesn't want inside her labyrinth."

Annalise's breath came faster. "What could a powerful enchantress want from me?"

"I'm afraid I'm not at liberty to say." Muse faced the frosted night field. "All I can say is, on the night you were born, the Fate Spinner made a terrible mistake. And today, she made another."

The Fate Spinner made mistakes? Annalise knelt alongside the cat in the moonlight and stared into his plum eyes. "What mistake did she make?"

The cat turned toward Annalise and grinned with all his teeth. "She underestimated us. And it will be her undoing."

A small, hesitant smile played at Annalise's lips. Muse had given her new hope. Out of the corner of her eye, she thought she spotted a butterfly with golden wings flutter past. When she looked again, it was gone.

"Thank you, Muse," Annalise said, scanning the air for the butterfly. "For coming back here and sharing your knowledge with me."

Muse bowed. "Anything for those on the path to their dreams."

"If you don't mind me asking," Annalise asked quieter, not quite ready to leave the safety of her yard, "what was it you needed to find when you left the shelter?"

Muse patted his hat with one paw and tapped his monocle with the other. "These were gifts from the Spinner of Dreams, given to me long ago. When worn in your world, the Fate Spinner can't see me or anyone I'm with. But when the cat-catcher found me, my hat and eyeglass fell off. Since they're essential in getting you to the Mazelands, I needed them back." He swished his tail and focused his plum eyes on her. "I'm sorry about running from you earlier, but I'm glad you found what I left you in the cage."

Annalise brightened. "You're the one who left the book in the box?"

"I am," Muse answered with a bow. "That book is elven made, and twice as magical in the right paws. Pass it to me and see for yourself."

Muse stuck out his large left paw, waiting.

"Oh, hold on." Annalise dug into her bag, pulled out the tattered book, and placed it in his paw. Immediately, it shrank to the size of her cursed mark. "Mercy." When he handed it back the binding resumed its proper size. "That's brilliant."

Muse half laughed, half purred. "I thought you'd enjoy that. I smuggled it into the shelter hoping you'd find it." He glanced at her hidden big hand. "I wanted to make sure you knew what you were up against with the Fate Spinner. Also"—he may have blushed—"so you'd recognize me."

A flush of kindredness warmed her cheeks. "I definitely recognized you. The book showed me sketches and information about the Mazelands and Spinners and—" Annalise shied with ambiguous worry. Would Muse believe that she'd had a vision? What if she imagined it? Would he think her too strange to be her friend?

"And what, Annalise?" Muse asked, looking more curious now than ever.

One-two-three-four. "When I touched the cover, I remembered something odd—a memory from years ago. Of the Fate Spinner at my home."

The cat leaned in closer, tail tick-tocking like a metronome behind him. "*The Book of Remembering* gave you a memory. Interesting."

Dry grass rustled close by. The white crows swiveled their heads toward the field. Annalise searched for night wolves but saw nothing except tall, undulating grass.

Annalise stroked her blackberry hair, slipped the enchanted book into her pocket, and said softer still, "Do you know . . . I mean, could you tell me . . . did what I saw really happen, or was it a dream? Because sometimes, especially when I'm scared, my imagination sort of . . . runs away from me."

Muse appeared to weigh his next words carefully and

gave her a sideways glance. "I'm not surprised you saw something when you touched the book. *The Book of Remembering* is a diary of sorts, written by the Spinner of Dreams when she was about your age."

Annalise gasped. "Really?"

"Really." Muse gave her a wistful grin. "As children, Reverie and Kismet were never close, but they were the only playmates they had. They used to play hide-and-seek in the labyrinth, knowing none of the beasts could hurt them. Reverie was always forgetting things about the maze. She wrote in the diary to help her remember details in case she got lost. The pages are even enchanted to erase after each close." Muse straightened his monocle. "It can't tell you which way to go or how to win, since the labyrinth is always changing. But, if you stay true to your dreams, the book may help you recall certain memories, as well as give you clues and visions along the way."

Annalise's big hand tingled but didn't hurt. "If it belongs to the Spinner of Dreams, why did you give it to me?"

Muse gestured toward her pocketed book. "What belongs to the Spinner of Dreams always comes to those who need it and hides from those working against her. Keep it close and remember: no matter where you are on your journey toward your dreams, the magic you hold within yourself is greater

71

than any curse. You are a dreamer, Miss Meriwether," Muse said, leaping down off the stump. "Try not to forget it."

A blaze of fire cut through her marked palm, greater than any pain before. Annalise inhaled a fast breath through her teeth. Smoke slithered through her cloak in plumes, too thick to ignore. She dropped her bag to the ground and released her cursed hand into the moonlit air. "Not now," she ordered it. Panicked thoughts slithered over her brain like tentacles and squeezed. "Please," she whispered, "stop!"

The cat stared in alarmed wonder at her hand spewing black flames. He was about to speak when something sharp pierced the broken heart on Annalise's big hand. Something resembling . . . the tip of a horn.

Annalise raised her big hand and spoke directly to the monster beneath the shattered black heart: "I won't let you rule me any longer. Do you hear me?"

The ugly horn tip vanished at once.

Was she imagining it, or had her cursed hand . . . obeyed her?

The wind gusted sideways, carrying scuttling leaves toward the field.

Muse gave her a strange look—wonder, pride, hope?—and cleared his throat. "The journey to the Mazelands is dangerous. Are you ready to fight for your dreams?"

Annalise glanced over her shoulder, past the bars surrounding her home. The night-light shone steadily from the kitchen. Upstairs, her parents slept safe and sound inside their bed. They wanted to protect her with bars and locks and kind words, but with the Fate Spinner guiding her path, how could they ever keep her truly safe?

The only way to get the Fate Spinner to reverse her curse was to face her head-on inside the labyrinth. Maybe then, she and her family's sad tale would change for good.

Annalise nodded to herself and reburied her cursed hand. "Yes," she answered over the worry-thoughts pounding her brain and her rib-cracking, too-fast-beating heart. "I'm ready."

I wish to rule my own destiny and rid myself of this curse.

Muse straightened his monocle with a grin and purred, "Wonderful."

Her big hand ached but no longer stabbed or burned. She clenched it hard anyway. "Before we go, would you please promise me something?" Annalise asked.

"Anything."

"If you're going to abandon me again, this time, would you warn me first? Because," she said with a nervous blush, "I do rather like you."

Now, Annalise may have been mistaken, but she was

almost certain the fur at the dream cat's cheeks pinked when he replied, "And I, you, Miss Meriwether." Muse held out his big paw. "Friends?"

Friends? She'd never had a real honest-to-goodness friend before.

Excited beyond all imagining, Annalise shook Muse's big paw with a laugh. "Yes. Friends." A flutter of warmth surged through her palm where they touched.

Muse let go of her hand and winked.

Then lickety-split, he spun on his heels, sprang over the short picket fence, and bounded into the moonlit field. And, for better or for worse, with the lush perfume of dreams fading into the night, Annalise picked up her bag and followed the dream cat into the dark.

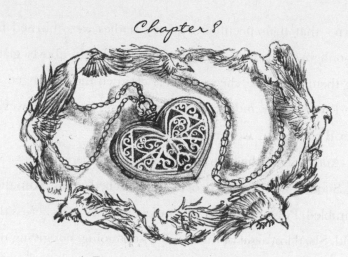

Chapter 8

A FIELD OF FIRE AND WOLVES

With nothing but his tail-tip to follow, Annalise sprinted after the cat.

Her bag of possessions bumped against her leg. Lengths of wild blackberry hair swirled out behind her. On the borders of the large grim field, night wolves howled a cry that said: *The Hunt Is On.*

Since Annalise's birth, half the population had either left or died because of the night wolves. The townsfolk used to hunt the foul creatures until the hunters were killed by their fangs instead. Many in Carriwitchet said the beasts fell through the crack in the sky the night Annalise was born—that their peculiar leathery bodies were burned by moonlight when they plunged from the world above, glazing them in a silver sheen. Others claimed they belonged to the Fate Spinner and were sent by her as spies. But, however they'd come, they were always out for blood.

And tonight, the blood they wanted was hers.

Sudden howls echoed over the parched grass. Annalise stumbled. Pulse pounding, she quickened her steps across the field. She'd lost sight of the cat, but kept going, not giving up. Not even when the blades of dead grass sliced into her as she ran.

"Muse?" Annalise called ahead.

No reply.

The wind died. Sweat slicked her skin. Annalise's breath rattled and chugged. She imagined the wolves closing in.

Stop, she told her anxious brain when it showed her exactly how the beasts would take her down. Annalise imagined them biting her ankles. Dragging her away. Ripping her to shreds. Running faster, she thought louder.

Stop! Blood hammering in her ears, the movie of her death playing out in her mind, Annalise sprinted faster than ever.

"Muse!" Suddenly, her dark mark burned as if seared with a red coal. She thought she saw eyes and the tips of black wolf tails through the grass. "Where are you?" Her eyes darted left and right but found no sign of the white cat.

Why would he leave her alone with the wolves?

White crows appeared overhead in a swarm—caw-caw-caw-CAW! Behind her, the crunch of claws on dead earth. Annalise ran faster. She shouted to all that would hear, "I will rule my own destiny and rid myself of this curse!" before tripping on a rogue rock. She stumbled and dropped her bag. A wolf snapped and growled at her back. Icy breath swirled around her and she huffed and puffed and scooped up her bag—and ran. "And after that," she sputtered, ignoring her worry-thoughts, *(You're going to fall. You'll never make it. Dreams are no match for Fate!)*, "I have another dream, too. One day, I want to run a sanctuary for mistreated animals. A sanctuary," she said louder over her shoulder as the wolves closed in, "for hunted animals like you!"

The thunder of paws faltered. From every direction, the throng of night wolves howled. Their cries sounded sad. The moment hung on, like a kite at the edge of the world. Still, Annalise kept sprinting through the tall grass. "And I would love you," she said, tears in her voice. "I wouldn't ever let anyone harm or hunt you again."

A breath-stealing pain shot through her marked hand.

Annalise dropped to her knees. If the night wolves got her, she'd be ribbons in seconds. Frozen in pain, Annalise removed her big hand from her cloak and stared at it in horror. Again, the tip of a black horn had broken through the center of her

77

dark mark. A ring of fire circled the horn's tip. Sparks flew from her cursed hand and caught on the wind. Afraid it would ignite the dry grass, Annalise clenched her marked palm, raised it over her head, and scrambled to her feet.

Too late.

Smoke plumed from the field. Red eyes peered at her through the grass, inches away, as the muzzles of night wolves taller than her parted the grass on all sides of Annalise. "Get back!" Panic readied her heart to explode. Shaking with adrenaline on noodley legs, she spun in a slow circle and extended her big hand like a weapon. "I don't want to hurt you—but I will."

The crows circling above cawed and watched but did not intervene.

"*We* don't want to hurt *you*," the largest wolf spoke, teeth bared, inches from Annalise's shoulder. "We just want to rid you of that *thing* growing behind your mark." A smaller wolf growled alongside her cursed hand. "Our mistress won't let us live in our true home or control our own lives until you give us that hand." They snapped. When Annalise jumped, they grinned. "Besides, we'd be doing you a favor. Do you not agree?"

"Yesss," the smaller wolf to her left hissed. "Let us relieve you of that ugly hand—we'll take your whole arm if you like." Those hidden in the tall grass laughed. "Nobody escapes their fate, you know," she snarled, "not even you. You may as well give us what we want. Then we promise to be on our way."

"Don't come any closer!" Annalise's braid whipped as she spun in a circle, big hand thrust forward, spitting black flames. "Turn back. And let, me, *go!*" A sudden beam of black fire shot from her hand. Sparks sprayed around her. The wolves nearest her jumped back—leathery skin on fire, yipping in pain. "I said I didn't want to hurt you!" She felt terrible. Was she terrible? "You should have listened!"

Grass kindled in a ring around her. The field went up in a *whoosh* of black flames.

"You can't win, little one," the largest wolf growled, fading backward into the field. "We will see you again!" The beasts sprinted to the petrified wood, crying and growling in rage. The crows cawed above her as the wildfire spread.

Still, Annalise found no sign of Muse.

Shaking all over, clenching her cursed hand into a ball, encircled by smoke and magic black flames, Annalise fell to her knees and cried. She was so bad—so, so bad. "What have I done?"

Behind her, Annalise's parents were asleep in their bed. If they were hurt from her fire, it would be because of her. She couldn't let the flames reach them.

Annalise sprang up. Using the adrenaline flying through her body, she stomped on the blaze. Choking, she batted down the fire she'd caused, one flame at a time—but it was spreading too fast.

Caw-caw-caw-caw! The flurry of white crows assembled overhead. Wings and feathers and eyes and beaks flashed inside the moon as they circled directly above Annalise. Then, everywhere, snow. Fat white snowflakes sifted down from the crows' wings to extinguish the black flames.

The crows were helping her. Sizzle and pop; crackle and hiss. They circled and snowed until the wildfire died and the field was coated in drifts of white, and steam rose from the field. Then, finally, the monstrous thing inside her hand retreated, along with the burning pain.

"Thank you!" she cried gratefully four times. The crows cawed and flew. Annalise raced on to the stone wall at the edge of the field after them, until the only fire anywhere was the dream in Annalise's heart, raging bright and clear.

Beyond the wall was the cemetery where her grandparents were buried. Annalise approached the barrier, shaking the snow from her cloak.

A fluffy streak of white fur donning a black hat caught her eye.

Sitting atop the stone fence, Muse the cat was waiting for her.

Chapter 9

The Train of Dreams and Wings

Annalise stood before the white cat in the top hat and monocle at the end of the newly burnt field. Giant dead trees lined the length of the stone wall. A flurry of white crows flapped the last flakes of snow from their wings and settled in the bare branches above. Snow landed in Annalise's hair and on the tip of her nose.

Her cursed palm pulsed as if it had gained a heartbeat of its own. Worries swirled through her mind like black dust, covering everything.

"I'm glad you made it," Muse said. "I was beginning to wonder." The cat paced the stone wall, then calmly paused to lick his larger paw—as if he hadn't just abandoned her to a pack of night wolves. Like cursed girls, burning fields, wolf attacks, and snowing crows were the most boring thing he'd ever seen.

Then he yawned, and that was it.

Annalise brushed the snow from her face, trying not to feel hurt. Trying not to feel anger. But she was hurt. She was angry. Her thoughts and emotions tangled and stretched inside her and then, she fell apart.

"Why did you leave me?" Annalise asked, clutching her bag to her chest. "I thought . . ." Her hands shook. She dropped her bag and inhaled noisily through her tightening throat. "You were supposed to be my guide—my *friend*. You weren't supposed to leave me."

Muse resumed pacing, purple eyes on Annalise. "Just because you didn't see me, didn't mean I wasn't with you." His mouth tipped up in apology. "I am sorry, but a part of my job is making sure you're ready to stand on your own. If you're going to finish the labyrinth, you'd better get used to figuring things out by yourself." He pointed at her hidden hand. "Maybe what's growing in there can help you with that."

An image of the black spire in her hand—*a horn tip; definitely a horn*—rushed back and pinned on the corkboard of her mind. The beast inside her grew stronger, more dangerous and hurtful every moment. And Annalise couldn't imagine it ever helping her.

"Why are we here?" she asked, pushing thoughts of the horn aside. The last place she wished to be was the graveyard that held her grandparents. Jovie and Thessaly, Frida and Hugo; all beloved, all hers, all gone.

"Because the end of one journey is always the start of the next," the cat replied, wrapping his paws with his snow-damp tail.

Annalise stared at her feet. "How can death be the beginning of anything but sadness?"

"Many of the most significant events in one's life begin with an ending." Muse leveled his hypnotic eyes, so like Annalise's own, onto her. "Endings are pathways to doorways that open onto hidden things—things one cannot see until they reach that end."

Muse popped out his monocle and held it up to the crack across the sky. The glass caught the slight reddish glow gleaming through from the other side. Muse twitched his whiskers, closed his other eye, and peered through the monocle curiously.

"What are you doing?" Annalise moved closer, trying to glimpse what he saw within the magical-looking glass.

"You'll see." The glass flashed once, then reddened to rose-colored smoke.

Everything quieted. The black leaves stilled. The world might have turned to ash for all the sound Annalise heard.

All was dark until, beyond the cemetery, lights on houses began to flash on.

Maybe the townsfolk saw the smoke? Maybe the cameras had found them? "What if we've been followed?" Annalise whispered to Muse. "What if they come and take me away?"

"We were not followed," Muse replied quietly. "When I'm wearing my hat and monocle, dreamers I am guiding cannot be seen. The Spinner of Dreams made them this way."

Annalise sighed. "Why should dreamers have to stay hidden, Muse?"

The cat's plum eyes flashed. "Dreams are very powerful things, Annalise. Know another's dream, know their heart. Know a dreamer's heart, and you know just how to control them." His tail twitched. "Dreams are one thing that must always be followed alone."

A sudden spotlight bright as a sun burst through the break in the sky. Annalise shielded her face with her bag. But the light grew, blighting her vision, turning the darkness to day. Annalise's hair and cloak blew back in a wind threatening to knock her down. The white crows caw-caw-caw-cawed. Raising their wings from the trees, they flew directly into the beam of white light until they vanished.

Muse returned his monocle over his eye as leaves whipped to and fro.

"What's happening?" Annalise shouted over the gale. "What is this light?"

The cat's voice boomed, "The secret to outrunning your fate!"

In the distance, a lonely whistle blew.

Annalise froze.

Panic lit.

Blood raged in her ears.

Annalise stumbled backward on rubbery legs. The light and whistle belonged to—

"A train," breathed Annalise.

Seven years ago, her grandparents died on a train. Usually, just the sound of one passing by triggered a panic attack.

Annalise's body shook in a pulse of terror from scalp to toes.

The train is coming for me.

"M-muse." She couldn't breathe. Couldn't move. Couldn't think. Annalise couldn't do anything but be afraid. "I don't—I don't know if I can do this."

The cat howled over a second whistle, one paw holding his hat, the other his monocle. "It's the only way to the Mazelands—the only way to become the master of your own fate! I am your guide. It's my job to point your way."

At her feet, shimmering white train tracks pushed out

of the earth in a ripple, twisted up into the sky, and wound through the crack into the next world. The train whistle blew louder. More white crows than she could ever imagine dived out of the light toward her and Muse in a flurry, heading straight for them.

"What are the crows doing?" They'd saved the field from fire and had protected Annalise and her parents for her whole life. Everyone in Carriwitchet thought the crows wicked and devilish, like her. But they were always there for her, and she didn't want them to get hurt. "They're in the way of the train!" Her pulse boom-boom-boom-*boomed*. "They have to move—before it hits them!"

The cat set his monocle over one eye and smiled at her gently. "You needn't worry about them." He paused. "The crows *are* the train."

Annalise spun toward him. "*What* did you say?"

He was enjoying this. "The crows are messengers of the Spinner of Dreams. Not unlike myself, they help deliver dreamers to the other side of your world. Keep your eyes on the break in the heavens and see for yourself."

A shape barreled toward them on the tracks between worlds—the shape of a train, made up of thousands of snow-white crows. The white-winged train doubled and tripled and quadrupled in size until it finally slowed and stopped on the tracks before them.

Gossamer smoke of infinite colors puffed from the smoke-stack. The scent of ozone, like the air after a warm rain, rolled from the train's feathers in waves. Each car had a large set of wings that folded as it came to a stop at their feet.

Feathers the length of Annalise's big hand made up the cars in place of metal and paint, as if the multitude of crows had joined to construct this giant magical beast. Each window was curved, tinted black glass, like the round eyes of birds. Annalise couldn't see anything inside the enchanted locomotive.

Suddenly, Annalise got the itch to run—to Mom and Dad and the safety of her caged home. But going back wouldn't help her break free from her curse.

So, as Annalise's heart chugged louder than even the train, she tried to hold tightly to her new dream:

I want to control my own destiny and rid myself of this curse.

The darkness within her mind laughed. *"You are a selfish child to want such a thing. You should never have left your parents behind."*

"Annalise?" Muse spoke softly, his voice drifting up from the ground. She hardly heard him over the war of words in her brain. Beads of sweat sprang up on her brow as the reality of running away from her parents hit her hard and fast. "Annalise," Muse said loud as thunder. "It's time."

Annalise glanced distractedly down at Muse. Her hair

blustered left and right, as fickle and scared as her thoughts: If she did not board this train she'd have no chance of escaping her fate, completing the labyrinth, or finding the Spinner of Dreams.

But what if she got on the train and died like her grandparents? What if she got lost in the maze and never saw her parents again?

Or . . . what if she beat the maze and won?

"Are you ready?" the cat in the mystical hat and monocle asked.

Annalise clenched her big fist and counted until her heart slowed. Then she nodded and answered, "Yes. I am."

But what if, what if, what if . . . ?

"No. Wait." Annalise shook her head. "What if I don't have everything I need? What if I get lost and hurt myself? What if I run out of food and water?"

Muse tipped his hat, purple eyes twinkling. "In the game of 'What if,' nobody ever wins. In times of trouble, I find following my instincts usually leads me right where I need to be. That said, before I forget . . ." Muse removed his hat, pulled out a small round *something* like a rainbow gumball, and replaced the hat between his ears. "Here." He passed her the bright candied something. "Eat this."

"What is it?" Annalise scowled at the rainbow orb. It was *moving*.

"It's a rare bit of magic, actually. A treat created by the Spinner of Dreams. Eating it keeps dreamers from starving inside the labyrinth, where nourishment can be hard to find. But, be warned, though you won't starve to death, this candy will not satiate your hunger—at times, it may make you hungrier still. Oh, and it might alert certain *things* that live in the maze to your presence once you're inside. The choice to eat it is, of course, up to you."

Annalise clenched her fist, wondering what to do. She wasn't very good at decisions. Whether choosing between chocolate or tangerine ice cream, or staying home versus running after one's dreams, each one felt like a life-and-death situation. Like her entire future rode on her choice.

Annalise suddenly realized how little food and water she had in her bag. She might be in the labyrinth for days, and she was already hungry.

On the other hand, the idea of *things* within the walls had her worried. . . .

But starving to death in a labyrinth had to be worse, right?

Annalise decided to worry about the somethings in the maze later and held out her nice hand. "I'll—I'll take it," Annalise said.

"Excellent," Muse replied, and dropped the gumballish orb into her palm.

Annalise curled her fingers around the candy and recalled

her other concern. "You don't happen to have a magically endless bottle of water, too, do you?"

Muse's whiskers bobbed up and down when he laughed. "Afraid not, but there should be refreshments on the train." He winked.

Annalise regarded the strange candy, took a deep breath, and plunked it into her mouth.

Her eyes burst wide as she chewed. The gumball tasted like every color of the rainbow, mingled with her favorite fruits and happiest memories. Annalise swallowed.

Feeling instantly full and a bit sad, she glanced far across the vast field of dead grass toward her house. She could just see the night-light shining from her kitchen window. *This is it. There's no going back.* Under her breath she whispered one last goodbye.

The train whistle blew.

Speakers clicked on, and a woman's voice blared: "ALL ABOARD! The Train of Dreams will now be departing for all points between Carriwitchet and Dreamland. Passengers, please have your tickets ready." *Click.*

Tickets? Annalise's pulse soared. *I don't have any—*

Suddenly, cats of every size, color, and shape appeared from thin air with the *pop-pop-pop!* of bubbles popping. Cats sporting suits and ribbon-heeled boots. Cats with and without glasses. Cats with briefcases, canes, and hats, walking on their hind legs, each with one double paw like Muse gathered before the many doors of the long train. Several pushed in front of Annalise attempting to board before her. The fancy felines gave terse nods to Muse yet avoided Annalise.

"Who are they?" Annalise asked.

"They are guides to Dreamland, like me." Suddenly, his image grew hologram thin.

"Mercy. What's happening to you? You're disappearing, like a ghost." Her plum eyes flashed with dread. Annalise knelt at his side. "You're not leaving again, are you?" Her lungs chugged faster. "You said you'd warn me if you were going to leave."

A few of the dream cats looked on.

Muse's body faded to little more than a silver shadow. "I'm not leaving you. I'm letting you take the lead." He held out his large paw. "Please, give me your hand and I'll show you."

She shook her head and stood. Cats grumbled and jumbled out of her way. "No—I can't find my way alone." Panic rose dark and horrible, a leviathan whipping inside her chest. "Please, don't go!"

She felt small and needy, but above all, scared.

"Take my hand, Annalise. Do you believe in your dreams? If so, you must trust me."

Annalise set down her bag and let her anger and endless

91

list of sad questions blow through her. *Why was everything always so hard for her? Why was she cursed? Why did she have such impossible dreams? Why was her mind, heart, body, and world, filled with so many cruel ghosts?*

In the end, her answer was always the same. "I do believe," Annalise said. She extended her small hand.

Muse regarded her kindly but firmly. "No. The other, if you please."

Every cat had gathered around them to watch. The eyes of the train were on them, too. After a moment's hesitation, Annalise removed her accursed hand from her cloak, and did what Muse asked. A bolt of static passed between their skin. This time, at their touch, Annalise smelled colored roses and sunlight, pine needles and fields of fresh crops. Annalise closed her eyes. On the backdrop of her mind, she saw towns-folk laughing and shopping and gardening, working in the sun in their fields. Parents and their children dancing happily as they laughed. She watched her mom writing outside in a warm breeze, and her dad building boats alongside her. The lands were green and the water clean, and the sun shone warm and whole. In this vision, Annalise was happy, free of pain and free from her curse.

This dream is mine.

Tears of happiness rolled down her cheeks. "Thank you,"

she told him. When Annalise let go of his big paw, the scents and vision faded away. "Thank you for reminding me."

"I am here," Muse said. "And don't forget about the book. Beat the labyrinth, find the Spinner of Dreams, and remember—I believe in you." He tipped his hat before shifting like smoke in wind and smudging out of sight.

Annalise buried her big hand in her cloak, grabbed her bag in her other, and counted *one-two-three-four*. And the cats blocking her path parted to let her through.

Four steps made of white feathers unfolded at her feet. The train door hissed open. Annalise's hair and skirt blew back in the sudden vacuum gust as a peculiar, misty light wafted down the steps. The besuited felines tapped her legs and waved their arms, gesturing for her to go through the door. "Oh," Annalise said nervously. "Forgive me. And thank you."

Without looking back, Annalise threaded her dream like warm silk through her brain: *I wish to rule my own destiny and rid myself of this curse.*

She repeated her dream, four times.

And *I can do this*, four more.

The spike in her cursed hand twisted as the train whistle blew.

Chapter 10

A Mysterious New Friend

I can't do this.

Standing before the open train door, every atom in Annalise's body seemed to spin ever faster. She counted stars, cats, worries—anything to stop her heart from banging too fast at her ribs—as her growing fear stole her breath.

I can't do this.

Panic squeezed.

I can't do this without Muse. I can't leave without Mom and Dad. I can't-can't-can't-can't.

Knuckles white, Annalise clutched her bag tighter and glanced far across the field toward home. The light in her bedroom was on.

94

Mon and Dad were reading her note!

The grip on Annalise's bag slipped. Her bag dropped. Her knees buckled. Annalise lost her balance and fell.

Several cat eyes watched her through the train windows. Were they laughing? Calling her names? The reality of leaving home crawled up her spine like a million baby spiders and nested in her heart.

Stop! she told herself with a shiver and pushed herself off the ground. *If I'm to have any chance against the Fate Spinner, I must believe in myself and my dreams.*

But how could she leave her mom and dad?

"The first step toward one's dreams is always to believe," Annalise's mom had always told her. "Sometimes the world feels like a dark hallway lined with locked doors. The key is imagining with your entire being that on the other side of one of those doors, there's a table set in a sunny meadow with a seat bearing your name. That there is a crowd gathered in celebration and they've only been waiting for you. And that, when you finally walk through that door, they will cheer and raise their cups and welcome you like an old friend. Keep this belief in your heart, and eventually, when you least expect it, you will find the right door, and it will open for you. Believe in your dreams, Annalise, and nothing, not even Fate, can stand in your way."

Hair rushing wild in a strong wind, Annalise faced

the train. She counted slowly to four as she walked up the white-feathered stairs. "I believe in myself and my dreams," she said at the top. And with a *whoosh*, the train doors whispered shut behind her.

The train of crows climbed the glowing tracks into the sky. Signs began flashing from the ceiling: *Please Take Your Seat.* Turbulence hit hard and fast. Annalise's nerves jumbled, and her feet stumbled. She grabbed the backs of two seats holding two cats who were less than impressed. "Sorry," Annalise mumbled, cheeks hot as a supernova, and kept moving.

Other night travelers murmured softly. Every cat on the packed train stared.

At her.

This was one of Annalise's strongest triggers for panic. Her first instinct was to run. Beg the conductor to take her home. She contemplated leaving her dreams behind but pressed on, counting light fixtures instead. Each lantern on the white-feather walls cast a warm apricot glow within the train car. Outside the round windows, the night rose like a bird and cocooned them in black.

Annalise spotted no empty seats.

To her left, a couple of cats watched her intently. One nodded to her. The other was reading a newspaper. She recognized them from the platform before boarding the train.

When Annalise passed, the cat with the paper hid the headlines. But not before she'd seen the front page of a paper called *The Daily Eye of Fate*. The caption read: *WANTED DEAD OR ALIVE*.

Below the headline was a sketch of her cat guide, Muse.

Wanted dead or alive?

Annalise leaned in closer to the cat who'd hidden the headline, momentarily pushing her anxiousness aside. "Ex-excuse me," she stuttered. "I couldn't help seeing your newspaper. Do you know my guide, Muse? Can you tell me what he did wrong?"

The cat in the heeled boots and top hat shifted awkwardly and crumpled the paper under the seat. "Ah yes, Muse." The one beside him, wearing a severe black dress and monocle, hissed. "Now, now, Despiteous, you can't stay angry at Muse forever, can you?" The perturbed cat growled and resumed reading her book: *When Love Goes Wrong: A Cat's Tale of Tears, Claws, and Woe*.

"Let's just say," the first cat continued, "Muse and the Fate Spinner don't see eye to eye. Haven't for, oh, about eleven years, if you get my meaning. They've been playing cat and mouse ever since."

Eleven years: the number of years since her birth.

The cat laughed at his own joke and glanced toward

Annalise's marked hand, squirming under her cloak. "She wants his hide, but she'll never catch him. He's a wily one, that Muse." He patted her small hand. "Once you leave our company, what with our magical hats and assorted whatnots, the Fate Spinner will be able to see you." He tapped the side of his nose and winked conspiratorially. "The white crows of the Spinner of Dreams can only protect and help you outside the maze—they're not permitted to do so inside the Fate Spinner's walls. So, eyes open, dear girl. Stay focused and forget about Muse. The Fate Spinner doesn't play nice."

Annalise grew even more confused. She couldn't help wondering why the white crows, which were governed by the Spinner of Dreams, wished to protect *her*?

The cat in the severe dress leaned over her seatmate and added, "My best advice to you, young miss, is to find a friend—someone who's got your back when the Fate Spinner pushes you down. Not like that good-for-nothing—"

"Despiteous . . ." The other cat smirked at her and she cooled her claws at once.

"Sorry about that. As I was saying." She nudged a chin at the cat at her side. "It helps knowing you're not alone."

Annalise inhaled through her nose and bravely lifted her chin. Muse was a friend, but he was gone. Friend or not, she wouldn't let the Fate Spinner stop her from going after her dreams.

"Thank you," Annalise said brightly. "Good luck to you both."

"And to you," they added together. "May the magic of dreams be yours."

Annalise continued in search of a seat. Finally, at the very end of the train car, a dark shape stole her eye. A small black fox lay curled in a ball on the last bench seat on the right. Its nose was hidden in a fluffy tail, and its copper eyes were fixed on her.

At first, the fox's gaze was curious. But the closer Annalise drew, the quicker that curiosity morphed into fear. Annalise didn't want to frighten it further, but the only empty seat on the train was next to the scared black fox.

Putting on her gentlest smile, Annalise stopped at the empty seat beside the terrified creature. She clutched her bag to her chest like a shield and said in a quick voice, "Hi."

The black fox scrambled atop the seat, trying desperately to shrink closer to the wall, or perhaps merge with it. The fox had only three legs: one of its front legs was missing. This endeared her to the fox even more.

"I'm sorry to bother you," Annalise went on. "But . . ." She peered hopelessly at the full seats and then back to the fox. "Would you mind terribly if I sat with you?" She lowered her eyes and said softer, "I could use a friend."

The three-legged fox trembled, eyes giant as copper pots.

Until, eventually, it nodded, just once.

"Wonderful!" Annalise smiled and slid in beside the fox, dropping her bag into her lap. Sometimes her anxiousness loosened her words, other times it tied them in knots. Currently, all the nerves and worry unraveled inside her and spilled off her tongue all at once. "Sorry, I'm a bit nervous. I'm sort of frightened of trains. I also recently lost the friend I came on this journey with."

The fox blinked at her through the fine hairs of its tail. It opened its muzzle as if to speak, when the dull pain in Annalise's big hand shifted into high gear. Annalise clenched her big hand tighter. The pain worsened as the horned thing within it pushed through.

Please, stop, she begged it, nearly bursting into tears. *For the love of dreams, STOP!*

The pain died immediately. The horn retreated.

Annalise relaxed a bit. Though the fox remained silent, its curious, wary gaze remained. "So," Annalise asked, tapping in fours on her bag. "Are you here with anyone?" The fox trembled harder and sank lower. Its fur shone in the light like polished onyx. "Um," Annalise stumbled as her mind went blank and mouth dry. "Uh," she said and stroked her braid. "Are you from Carriwitchet, too?"

Silence.

A cold shiver brushed her skin at the panic in its eyes. It feared her. It sensed her differentness—her dangerousness—her monster. The frightened fox pushed farther away. Then things got worse.

From the car behind them, the voice she'd heard on the speaker boomed, "Tickets please, have your tickets at the ready."

Ticket. Right. She didn't have a ticket.

The fox lifted something out from under its black tail—a long rectangular ticket—not taking its eyes off Annalise for a second. One half of the ticket was black with red writing; the other was white with gold. Curly script was emblazoned on them both:

Single Passenger Ticket: Nonstop to the Mazelands

"You're going to the Mazelands, too?" Annalise asked. It must also have a dream. Annalise wondered what it might be, and if the black fox had also left its loved ones behind. "I am as well. If they let me get there." Muse never mentioned how to get a ticket. The creases of her brow deepened.

Outside the windows, everything glowed in a mist of shimmering pink. They were halfway from earth to sky.

Breathing faster, Annalise returned her attention to the fox.

"May I ask where you got your ticket, um . . ." She didn't know how to address the fox and had forgotten to ask earlier. "I'm sorry, what's your name?"

The fox blinked. Slowly, it sat up and gave her a cautious, but warm, smile. "Hello. My name is Mister Edwards." He extended his shaking paw. "Pleased to make your acquaintance."

Mister Edwards. What a suitable name for a shy black fox. Annalise relaxed a bit at his gentle voice and took the fox's small paw into her own. "Pleased to meet you, Mister Edwards." They shook. A jolt of heat burst through her marked palm. A beat later, it was gone. Annalise's smile only faltered for a moment. She hoped the fox hadn't noticed. "My name is Annalise Meriwether." She blushed and took back her small hand. "And the pleasure is mine."

Mister Edwards stared at her for a moment, then lowered his gaze to his tail. "I'm . . . sorry, Miss Meriwether, if I seemed rude before. It's just," he whispered, "people haven't been very kind to me lately." When the fox raised his eyes to hers, within them she witnessed an ache of pain as raw as her own. She wanted to protect him—to wrap him up and keep him warm. "But you seem rather kind. So, in answer to your previous questions, I do live in Carriwitchet. And, as for my ticket, my dream cat gave it to me." He frowned. "You don't have a ticket? Didn't you follow a dream cat to the train of crows?"

Annalise scanned the train car. The dream cats acknowledged her briefly, then returned to their newspapers, conversations, and books. Annalise worried about Muse and hoped, wherever he was, that he was all right.

"Yes," Annalise answered. "I had a lovely guide called Muse." Her expression darkened. "He didn't give me a ticket, but I'm heading to the Mazelands as well."

The fox curled his fluffy black tail around the stump of his missing leg. "I'm sorry to hear you have no ticket," he offered, leaning in close. "But, as my guide said before she left me, *"Only from inside the struggle can we attempt to break free."*

Her dad had told her that exact thing once. So many things were a struggle for Annalise and her family. So much persecution, sorrow, and pain. Yet sitting here talking to the fox, Annalise already felt better knowing she wasn't alone.

"Do you know where I could get a ticket like yours?" Annalise asked. The bellow of the ticketier drew closer from the next car. The train lurched higher into the sky. "I *really* need to get to the Labyrinth of Fate and Dreams. Without a ticket, I'm afraid the ticket master might not let me go."

The fox's face fell. "Hmm." Mister Edwards's nose

twitched, and fingernails tapped before peering over the seats in front of them. "I'm not sure how to find one at this late date."

The cat with the newspaper a few seats up faced Annalise. "We all have different paths to our dreams. Some have tickets to ride. Others," he said grimly, "must fight for everything they've got. Sorry, miss, but we're not your guides. We're forbidden to help you any more than we have already."

That didn't sound good.

The door between cars hissed open behind them. Annalise didn't even have time to react before the owner of the stern voice was upon them.

Chapter 11

MISTER EDWARDS'S TERRIBLE TALE

"Tickets, please," the ticketier demanded. The mumblings inside the car ceased immediately. Annalise, too scared to face the ticketier, contemplated the window instead. Mister Edwards's gaze darted between Annalise and the ticketier, now standing directly beside them.

"Of—of course," Mister Edwards replied, stumbling on his words as he passed over his ticket with his shaking paw. His nervousness made Annalise nervouser.

While staring intently at the window, a sleek white wing brushed her cheek. Slowly, counting the whole way, Annalise faced the owner of the wing—and gasped.

The ticketier was a six-foot-tall white crow.

Its black-seed eyes round as balled glass, its stare sharp enough to cut leather, the crow stamped Mister Edwards's ticket and handed it swiftly back to him. "Thank you, Mister Edwards." The ticketier, whose name tag said *Ms. Twixt*, cast her all-seeing eyes onto Annalise.

The monster within Annalise's cursed hand shifted but kept its flames at bay.

For now.

"You're next, young miss," the feathered giantess said. "Ticket—*please*."

Annalise forcibly swept her anxiousness under the lumpy rug in her soul where her bad feelings were stored and replied, "I'm sorry, I—mercy. I don't have a ticket." Annalise pinched her lips together, stomach sloshing with otherworldly rainbow candy gloop.

"Hmm." The great white crow narrowed her glossy black eyes and nodded. "I see. Give me your hand." She jutted her snow-white wing toward Annalise.

Not wanting to anger her further, Annalise held out her hand. She hoped with her entire cursed being that she wouldn't fear-vomit all over her.

"No," Ms. Twixt said. "Show me *the other*."

Annalise didn't want to take out her big, wickedly horned

hand—not now, not ever. But having no other option, she did as she'd been asked. The crow flipped Annalise's big palm over with the tip of her wing, exposing her darkly cracked heart for all to see.

The dream cats gasped; Mister Edwards yipped. Annalise stroked her hair and tried not to black out when every eye in the train car focused on her.

Tears of shame sprang immediately. Annalise wrapped her free arm around her belly, trembling with years of humiliation and pain. "I'm sorry," Annalise whispered, wiping her cheek with her shoulder. "Sometimes"—she gulped—"tears sneak up on me."

The crow wrapped a wing around Annalise's shoulders and pulled her close to her warmth. Annalise sniffed and met the black mirrors of her eyes. Within their dark glass, Annalise saw herself looking back.

"Never be sorry for showing the world who you are or who you wish to become," said Ticketier Twixt. "These struggles have brought you exactly where you need to be." The great crow licked one of her talons and riffled through a book she slid out from under one wing. Seeing the ticketier's book reminded Annalise of something. . . .

The Book of Remembering! She forgot not to forget it. Maybe it could have shown her where to find a ticket.

Ms. Twixt continued. "Your guide, Muse, instructed me to have this waiting for you on the train. The Fate Spinner's maze is tricky. Without a ticket, the labyrinth won't open— not even on the Fate Spinner's order. He felt it safer I keep it for you here . . . as your ticket, miss, is quite rare."

The white crow handed Annalise her ticket.

Annalise Meriwether, honored guest
of the Fate Spinner
Destination: the Labyrinth of Fate and Dreams

A puddle of ice water ran the flute of Annalise's spine.

Honored guest of *the Fate Spinner*?

Mercy.

"Thank you so much?" Annalise, more than a little stunned, accepted the ticket with her big hand. Another, even worse stab of pain seared though her dark mark. Annalise's eyes popped open in shock as she shoved her cursed hand back under her cloak.

"Miss Meriwether," Mister Edwards asked, inching closer to her. "Are you okay?"

Annalise squeezed her eyes shut in pain, unable to respond. Suddenly, inside her mind, she saw the Fate Spinner grinning cruelly, flashing the same sneer she wore in the picture from the book. The same sneer she gave Annalise when she'd arrived at her home years ago. Annalise had a sinking feeling she was playing right into the Fate Spinner's hands. But like the dream cat said to Mister Edwards, "Only from inside the struggle can we attempt to break free." And that was exactly what Annalise intended to do.

The moment she thought this, the pain in her hand stopped.

Just like that.

"Miss Meriwether?" the great crow asked with concern. "Dear girl, can you hear me?"

"Oh," Annalise answered, embarrassed. "Yes, thank you. I was just a bit warm, I think, but I'm much better now."

"Excellent," the crow replied. "Anything else I can get you two?"

Annalise was thirsty as a salted slug. She'd packed two jars of water, but they wouldn't last long. "Maybe. Muse mentioned there'd be refreshments on the train? You wouldn't happen to have anything to drink, would you?"

Ticketier Twixt jabbed a wing tip in the air and uttered a bit of a *caw*. "I have just the thing." She opened a drawer in an overhead compartment Annalise hadn't noticed, removed two small black birds, and offered them to the bewildered Annalise and Mister Edwards. "I know it's not winterberry juice, but these licorice rooks will do you one better." The two black licorice rooks stretched their wings and squawked before lying still on the end of the crow's white wing. "They taste terrible and won't last forever but will help keep you hydrated in the labyrinth, so you don't die of thirst."

Annalise gave Mister Edwards a grim, should-we-really-ingest-this glance. The fox nodded wide-eyed to Annalise as if the chance of death was an absolute certainty.

"They're not *alive*, are they?" Annalise asked, stomach churning.

"Heavens no!" the crow answered. "It's just an enchantment, I promise."

Annalise sighed. If it helped get her closer to her dreams, she would do it.

Annalise and Mister Edwards popped the rooks in their mouths together. Annalise blanched; she swore her teeth crunched bone. "Why are you helping us?" Annalise asked, chomping the vile black bird. The taste was unbearable— sweaty socks stewed in compost. A sudden *whoosh* of water rushed down Annalise's throat, quenching her body with cool delight. She marveled at the fox, refreshed, who nodded back the same. "Do you work for the Spinner of Dreams, too?"

"I'm a free agent," the ticketier replied. "My business is

this train: making sure it gets to where it needs to be, and that those aboard are taken care of. It's standard practice. The Fate Spinner expects it, of course." She gave a small laugh. "It wouldn't be much fun for her if people dropped dead before the real excitement began, now would it?" She gave Annalise an odd look, one loaded with kinship and pain, before she put her smile back on. "Anyway, why wouldn't I help you? If I was heading to your world for the first time, wouldn't you help me survive?"

Mister Edwards nodded quickly.

Annalise didn't have to think before answering, "Of course."

"Well, there's your answer. Now," the white crow continued, "if you'll both excuse me, we're almost at the break in the sky. Mister Edwards, Miss Meriwether, best of luck and, of course, may the magic of dreams be yours."

The crow punched Annalise's ticket—in the shape of a crow—nodded cordially, then breezed through the next door.

The skies outside lightened to cotton-candy pink. The ginormous wings attached to each car unfolded and pumped faster the closer they drew to the crack in the sky.

Out of nowhere, the train shuddered. The passengers held on for dear life as an announcement came over the loudspeakers.

Tchshht. "Next stop, the Mazelands and the Labyrinth of Fate and Dreams. Loyal passengers of White Crow Railways, may the magic of dreams be yours." *Tchshht.*

Lightning struck the heavens. Annalise and Mister Edwards peered out their window. With the crack in the sky directly above them, everything glowed red. Up close, the break was as huge as the field by her home. Spectral train tracks ran through the crack's center, and the train rode them all the way up.

"Have you ever been on the other side of the sky, Mister Edwards?" Annalise's big hand throbbed like a heartbeat the closer they came to the break. And each moment that passed, that heartbeat grew stronger, same as the horned thing inside her. Annalise stroked the length of her long blackberry hair and tried to stop thinking every bad thing imaginable.

"I have," the fox replied, clutching the seat's railing in a death grip. "I was there about a month ago, after my husband and I decided to pursue our dream of owning our own candy shop in an abandoned castle in the hills of Caledonia."

"Oh," Annalise's words shook with the train. "That is a lovely dream."

"Yes, it was." Mister Edwards smiled sadly. "I was to be the confectioner and my husband was to manage the business. Many thought our dream was silly—childish even, as

ART TK

if possessing the heart of a child was a terrible thing. But we thought, what better way to spend our lives than by doing something that keeps us young at heart? Something colorful and fun that spread a bit of childlike cheer into an often cheerless world. Something that, with just a taste of sweetness melting on their tongue, might make others feel young at heart, too."

Annalise beamed. "How beautiful, Mister Edwards. I sure could have used some of your confections over the years."

"Thank you." The midnight fur at the fox's cheeks blushed slightly to pink. "I've never been good at many things, but I am skilled at creating sweets—sculpting chocolate, sugar, flour, and cream into art so delicious that, for a moment, one's troubles melt away. That is my passion." His twinkling copper eyes fell. "It was my husband's as well. So, imagine our surprise when an oddly dressed cat raced past us in the park one day. We'd heard the legend of the Spinners like everyone else, so we followed the cat, got on the train, and were off after our wildest candy-eyed dreams."

All at once, the ruby glow outside brightened. The seats hummed. The feathered walls ruffled in a ghost-breeze. And Mister Edwards tucked his tail between his legs and yipped with fright.

"Oh, please finish your story, Mister Edwards," Annalise

said, stroking her hair. "When I'm scared, I've always found stories help."

A sudden hollowness wound through the train. Glancing around nervously, Annalise saw many of the dream cats had vanished. Only two remained—the one with the newspaper and the female beside him—both snoring and purring in their sleep.

"Really?" Mister Edwards whispered, copper eyes darting. "I've talked so much already. Are you sure you want to hear it?"

The lanterns flickered and jostled as the blinds over the windows snapped shut.

"Yes," Annalise replied while clutching her seat. "I most certainly do."

Mister Edwards smiled at Annalise with thankfulness. "Okay. Well, we took the train, this very one, and entered the labyrinth. I'm not going to sugarcoat it; the labyrinth is deadly. We were terrified the whole time, but we kept on. And, working together, we made it almost to the end."

Annalise gasped. "You've been inside the labyrinth? This is wonderful news! But . . ." Her face fell. "You didn't finish. What happened?"

Shivering, the fox curled his black tail tighter around him. The train of crows rattled and bounced. Mister Edwards talked faster and louder over the bumps. "We reached the end of the maze. The gates to Dreamland were only steps away. But before we could enter, the Fate Spinner's guards—those accursed night wolves—rushed in without warning and"— his chin wobbled—"instead of letting us into Dreamland, the Fate Spinner captured my beloved Mister Amoureux. Then," he continued, tail over his face, "she went after me."

"But why?" Annalise asked, gritting her teeth against her outrage. "Why would she do such a thing? You won, fair and square."

"I don't know." A dark flame of guilt sparked in the fox's eyes. "But I didn't go down without a fight. I escaped the wolves and ran after Mister Amoureux but didn't get far. When I got hold of him, the Fate Spinner leveled her staff straight at me and blasted us apart.." He rubbed the place where his leg used to be and forced himself to continue. "I don't know where the Spinner of Dreams was, or what happened next, because I blacked out and was left for dead. When I woke, Mister Amoureux and my leg were gone." The train car shuddered harder; they hung on tighter to the seats. "We'd survived every monster in the labyrinth. But in the end, we couldn't escape the Fate Spinner."

"That's terrible." Annalise's heart broke for poor Mister Edwards and his husband. She thought of how deeply she

116

missed her grandparents. How the space they once occupied could never be filled. Because of this, Annalise felt she understood. "I'm so sorry that happened to you."

"Thank you, Miss Meriwether." The fox's warm eyes flitted up to her. "I would have died if the train hadn't found me and ferried me home. Now that I'm healed, I'm ready to go back and find Mister Amoureux." He shook his head and sighed. "I don't even know if he's alive, but I'm determined to beat the Fate Spinner, stand before her sister, and make our dreams a reality."

A lightning bolt of inspiration struck her. "Mister Edwards, you've already completed the labyrinth!" Annalise burst with excitement. "Maybe we will beat it again!"

"Yes." The black fox gripped the armrest as the train climbed like a roller coaster heading straight up. "It was horrible. And dangerous. But"—a spark lit in his copper eyes—"I'm pretty crafty. I'm sure I can beat it once more."

Outside, the unmistakable howls of—

"Night wolves." Annalise would know their cries anywhere. "What's happening, Mister Edwards—do you know?"

The black fox tried opening the blinds, but they remained stubbornly shut. "I don't know. I can't see anything."

The train's speakers clicked on next. "Brace yourselves," said the announcer. "We're about to enter the Mazelands."

Tchshht.

Annalise and Mister Edwards shared a grim look. From the corner of her eye, Annalise spotted movement behind their backs. Two children in the adjoining train car, who appeared about her age, moved in and out of sight. Annalise wondered if they were heading to the Mazelands, too.

"Miss Meriwether," Mister Edwards asked quickly as the train accelerated. "What did you mean a moment ago? When you said that *we* could beat the maze?"

Annalise turned back to Mister Edwards. "I just thought, maybe, it would be nicer if we weren't alone on our quest for our dreams. That if we teamed up and faced the labyrinth together, maybe we'd have a better chance at beating the Fate Spinner."

Out of nowhere, the crows comprising the train screamed, the blinds over the windows flipped up, and a glaring red light flooded the car. Outside, Annalise was sure she saw eyes and teeth and wolves, but a flash and a caw later, and they were gone.

"I'd, um, like that very much, Miss Meriwether," the fox said, giving her a terrified grin. "But for now, hold on." He shouted over the caw of birds, "We're heading into the break!"

Annalise only had a moment to relish the notion that

Mister Edwards might be becoming her friend when the train lurched hard right. Annalise let go of her bag and grasped Mister Edwards's front paw. Sudden, searing pain stabbed through her hidden big hand. The beast inside her twisted and burned, but there was no time to think about that. Not as Annalise and the fox flew from their seats still holding on to each other and the train broke through the crack in the sky.

Chapter 12

Into the Mazelands

Annalise and Mister Edwards tumbled down the aisle as the train of crows rocketed through the rift between worlds. Red light blazed through the windows. The giant wings on the cars outside pumped harder, trying to balance the train twisting on the tracks. After a few seconds, the harsh light dimmed, the cars leveled, and the train of crows sailed along, smooth as silk.

They'd made it to the other side of their sky—to the Mazelands, the birthplace of fate and dreams.

Annalise landed under a chair, big hand tucked inside her cloak. "Mister Edwards, are you okay?" He'd rolled under another seat and bumped his head.

"I think so?" He blinked at her in a daze. Annalise helped him up, then led him back to his seat. They'd barely had a chance to sit down, when shadows shot past the windows, followed by a snarl and snap of wolves' teeth.

"Mister Edwards!"

"Miss Meriwether!"

Annalise latched onto the fox and peered outside. They were still far above land, riding the same train tracks through another sky. "I don't see anything," Annalise said. "But I know I heard wolves."

"I did, too."

"Could the wolves be like the crows?" Annalise asked. "Could they have magicked into a train as well? Did this happen last time you were here?"

"No," Mister Edwards answered at once. "But everything about this feels different. Like someone's trying to stop us from reaching the labyrinth." The fox's furry brow creased, and his eyes hardened to stone. "What I don't understand is why."

Ms. Twixt appeared in the next car tending to the children Annalise had seen earlier. The enormous white crow glanced over her shoulder and stared at Annalise as if trying to tell her a secret. But before Annalise could decipher what that secret was, she unfurled her great wings and dived through the train's feathered wall.

A sharp keening—like cutlery scratching across plates—sliced through the air outside. The white crow reappeared briefly before flying under the train with a shriek and fading from sight.

The air hushed. The feathers of the train's interior ruffled. The speakers *shhhh'd* with static. Then every lantern in the train blew out.

Annalise felt abandoned in space.

"Is *this* supposed to happen, Mister Edwards?" Annalise's stomach flip-flopped with worry.

Mister Edwards held tighter to Annalise. "No. It is not."

Beyond their window, the alien sky glittered with stars. Each star reflected the red light of the moon, like tiny droplets of blood splashed across the heavens. The train tracks had just spiraled downward like a strand of DNA toward a land floating in the air below, when another train on another set of tracks sailed boldly past their own. A train made of wolves—fangs, claws, leathery skin, and all.

Annalise *knew* she'd heard night wolves. When the train of wolves drew closer, Annalise thought she spotted two achingly familiar faces staring at her from behind one of its windows.

Her parents—red-eyed and haunted, huddled together in fear.

Annalise turned away and clawed at her chest—her heart, in all her years of anxiety and panic, had never beat so fast. *No*, she told herself, stroking her hair by fours. *You imagined them. You couldn't have seen Mom and Dad. It's just panic trying to trick you.*

Or maybe it's the Fate Spinner trying to make you afraid.

Beside her, Mister Edwards growled out the window. Though the train of night wolves had passed, the foreboding feeling it left remained.

"Was . . . was that what I think it was, Mister Edwards?" Annalise's big hand thrashed and fought to be free from her prison of cloak.

"My father used to say, if it looks like a duck, smells like a duck, and quacks like a duck, it's probably a duck," the black fox said with an edge of fear. "That looked like a train of wolves and smelled like the Fate Spinner." Mister Edwards turned darkly away. "I don't like the word *hate*, Miss Meriwether, but I hate her for what she's done to me and my husband." He growled and said softer, "And I hate her for what she's making me do."

Annalise's big hand burned. "I'm sorry, Mister Edwards," she said as the speakers clicked on once more.

123

Tchshht. "Our apologies," a new voice said. Listening closer, it sounded like all the crows of the train were speaking at once. "We've arrived in the Mazelands. Please prepare for landing." *Tchshht.*

"No turning back now," Mister Edwards said nervously.

"No," Annalise replied, tapping her bag the right number of times. "It's only forward from here."

Eventually, she calmed. And to her delight, Mister Edwards calmed along with her.

The two spared another glance outside. The train tracks dipped slowly downward through the Mazelands' sky. At the track's end lay a city of ancient ruins. Dark woods surrounded crumbling walls and giant statues, castles turning to dust. Annalise had seen castles in *The Book of Remembering*, but none like these. Darkling clouds expanded around them, sputtering with lightning and thunder, trembling the window glass and walls.

"Look." Mister Edwards motioned outside. "Can you see it?"

Annalise leaned farther over until a tangle of sharp passageways twisted out of the dim reddish gloom. "Is that . . . ?"

The fox nodded gravely.

Beyond the ruined city and forest was the reason Annalise had come. Her blood ran cold and hot at once. "The Labyrinth of Fate and Dreams."

Shaped like a human skull spanning miles, the ancient maze she'd seen in the book bore impossibly tall stone walls coated in the mosses of time. At the labyrinth's center stood an extravagant palace of smoky red quartz that appeared to have grown naturally out of the ground. The sketch in *The Book of Remembering* had been striking, but it was nothing compared to this.

Farther past the labyrinth, arching over the distant horizon, a beam of lilac light shone through a hole in the dark heavens, spotlighting the green lands below it. A shimmer of magic and joy rushed through Annalise—a nostalgia that reminded her of home.

"That must be Dreamland." Annalise wasn't asking but rather saying it out loud to taste the truth of it. The truth tasted like silver and gold.

"Yes," Mister Edwards answered with quiet reverence. "The home of Reverie, the Spinner of Dreams."

Rainbow birds the size of cars, and creatures that looked like dragons soared over vast rolling green meadows and sapphire waterfalls streaming into hidden pools. Pale purple sunlight encased the small world. It was the most beautiful oasis Annalise had ever seen, and she could scarcely look away.

"Does the train continue on to Dreamland?" she asked the black fox, her face alight with wonder. They were not yet over the maze, but directly above a forest, a great distance from where they needed to be.

Wolves howled from the dark woods below.

"I'm afraid not," Mister Edwards replied with a shiver. "I asked that same question the first time I rode this train. See that circle of light surrounding Dreamland?" Annalise nodded. "Try to go through that without running the maze and you'll be electrified instantly. The only way to reach your dreams is to go through the labyrinth and win."

Annalise clutched her bag tighter and counted her exhales, the breath that grew louder and louder and harder to suck through her throat. Her cursed hand ached but not in the usual way. It stung like eyes on the verge of tears.

"Miss Meriwether, are you all right?"

Annalise nodded and tried to smile. "I will be, thank—"

A blast of lightning lit the sky and shot sideways at the train. Annalise's big hand sizzled and flew from her cloak. "Mister Edwards," Annalise cried. "Look out!" She covered the fox with her body and hair and bag and good and bad hand and held tight. But it was too late.

The bolt of lightning struck the train. The cars skidded sideways and knocked off the tracks. The stench of burnt feathers choked the air. And then the train cracked.

Jagged lines like the breaks on her birthmark formed on

the walls and floors and seats. Caw-Caw-Caw-CAW! A hundred birds screamed at once as the train of crows split apart.

Mister Edwards slipped from Annalise's grip and he was gone. "MISS MERIWETHERRRRR!" the fox cried. He scrambled to grasp her hand as the sky swallowed them whole.

Wind howled in Annalise's ears as she fell. "MISTER EDWARDS!" Heart hammering, breath gone, Annalise scrambled and twisted and turned in the frigid air, grabbing wildly for the fox, but she couldn't see him in the mad fury of wings as she plunged through the darkness. All around her was the white feathers of burning crows, diving toward the ruined city below.

Long ago, the Fate Spinner had arrived at the Meriwethers' home to take Annalise from her parents, thinking they'd be overjoyed at the chance to get rid of her. Now it seemed she didn't want Annalise to reach the labyrinth at all. What sort of game was she playing? Could she be afraid Annalise might actually win?

Annalise gripped tightly to her bag and even tighter to a rogue throb of hope. She refused to let the enchantress who stole her best life beat her again. Hair in her face, cloak snapping, Annalise spoke over her fear: "I have a dream. And this is not how my story ends!"

Immediately, the cloud of crows surrounding her flew beneath Annalise and created one giant bird. The giant bird blinked at her as if to say, "What are you waiting for, human? Get on my back and fly." And as the ground crept ever closer to a gruesome death, she did.

Soaring through the sky, dark winds tangling in her hair, Annalise latched on to the multi-crow's feathers with her small hand and clutched her bag with her other. She scanned the crumbling city and woods for Mister Edwards but found no sign.

What if her new friend didn't make it?

A scourge of black-hearted leaves gusted upward from below. Night wolves howled nearby. With only one hand to grip the crow, Annalise slipped sideways and almost fell. "Mercy!" If she wanted to stay on its back, she needed both hands to hang on. There was only one thing to do.

Annalise dropped her bag to the somewhere below. She watched her memories, food, water—everything—tumble and dance into the darkness, and recited her dream: *I wish to rule my own destiny and rid myself of this curse.*

This is all that matters!

Annalise ignored the howl of night wolves and the scent of rot below. There was no sign of Ms. Twixt. Annalise hoped she was okay. "Thank you for bringing me closer to my dreams," Annalise whispered over the wind, and stroked her crow-of-crow's silky white neck. It chuffed warmly and angled to the right.

At last, Annalise spotted Mister Edwards soaring through the air ahead. Annalise cheered; her new friend had found a crow-of-crows of his own. A few wing-beats later, the forest under them ended and the labyrinth began.

More of the labyrinth revealed itself the closer Annalise came to the ground. The beast in her big hand roiled, and her panicked heart seized at the endlessly twisting walls of shadow and stone. The giant red palace in the center of the skull-shaped labyrinth had needlelike spires. The rectangular courtyard sat inside the skull's mouth, and the whole structure glowed tangerine from the torches within the palace. The crow carrying Mister Edwards soared over the high iron fence toward the courtyard. A moment later, Annalise's crow-of-crows followed.

Annalise's stomach flipped and scrambled as her crow swooped toward a massive dark silver mirror, ringed in a curving black frame, rising from the center of the court.

Her cursed hand stabbed with fresh pain.

The reflection of a spiked red throne winked at Annalise from within.

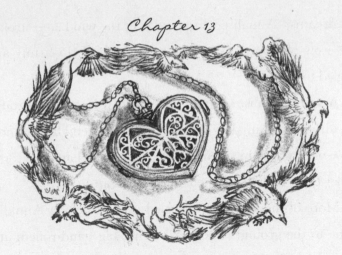

Chapter 13

THE FATE SPINNER

All her life, Annalise had tried to hide from her fate. But
no matter where she hid, Fate knew just where to find her.
She had run to her bedroom and pinched her big hand
when it was bad. Spent hours balled up on the floor, face
buried in her knees, hidden in a bramble of blackberry
hair, wishing herself someone else. Someone who wasn't
ugly and wicked, a girl who others besides her family could
love.

Annalise wished to be free. From fear, anxiety, panic, and
guilt, from her horrible destiny and the woman who gave it
to her. And now that her chance had arrived to meet the Fate

Spinner—the ruiner of dreams, murderer of grandparents, breaker of hearts, and curser of innocent girls—as always, all Annalise wished to do was hide.

But there was no hiding now.

The circular courtyard of the Fate Spinner's palace lay directly ahead. Enclosed by a wrought-iron fence the height of the labyrinth itself, the courtyard glowed in pale red moonlight. Four separate barred entrances led from the court into the maze. Skeletal trees with black-hearted leaves and face-like knots on their trunks stood on either side of each entrance. Finally, Annalise's crow-of-many landed alongside Mister Edwards. He sat on his own crow-of-crows directly before the hulking mirror that reflected a dark dais and red velvet throne.

Annalise slid from the crow's neck. The instant her feet touched ground, her big hand flailed under her cloak—begging to be set free. *Is that the Fate Spinner's throne?* she thought. If so, where was she? Annalise glanced over her shoulders. She felt watched by everything here, but she couldn't see anyone behind her.

Panic spread its black wings inside Annalise. Her heart beat-and-beat-and-beat-and-beat. She nearly jumped out of her skin. When Mister Edwards dismounted his crow, he rushed right up to her.

"Miss Meriwether!" Annalise, frozen in terror, met Mister Edwards's stare. "Thank goodness, you're all right. I was so scared for us both!" Her crow-of-crows burst apart into hundreds of birds and took, screaming, to the red-mooned sky. Annalise watched them go. "We made it," the kind black fox said, glancing far left. "And look, they made it, too."

The two children Annalise had seen on the train flew down on similar crows and landed beside them. The girl, about Annalise's age, had dark skin and spiraled black hair past her shoulders. She gazed worriedly at each locked entrance as she dismounted her crow-of-crows. The boy, taller and slightly older, resembled the girl. He had longish, wildish, tightly curled black hair and the most piercing green eyes. He nodded and gave Annalise a half smile before walking over to investigate one of the entrances. Annalise thought she might float away for all the feathers swirling up from her middle—no one her age ever smiled at her.

When the girl turned to Annalise and waved, her silver eyes gleamed inside the red moon. *She's lovely*, Annalise thought, and waved shyly back. *What dreams have they come to claim?* she wondered. *Did the Fate Spinner curse them, too?*

The four stood a few feet from the large ornate mirror, but nobody said a word.

Just because you're afraid, Annalise, she told herself, squeezing her cursed fist tight, *doesn't mean you have to be rude.*

Annalise inhaled the thick night air, turned to the children beside her, and gave them a friendly smile. "Hi," Annalise said to the girl and boy in a barely-there voice. "My name is Annalise Meriwether, and this is Mister Edwards."

"Bowie Tristle," the boy answered with a confidence Annalise admired.

"Pleased to meet you, Annalise," the girl said with the same exuberant spark as the boy. "You too, Mister Edwards. I'm Nightingale, Bowie's sister." Her grin was pure magic. She didn't even look afraid. "Good luck to you both. And hey, as they say on this side of the sky, may the magic of dreams be yours."

As they spoke to Mister Edwards, Annalise drew closer to the mirror, now pooling with charcoal smoke. Mingled scents of darkness and starlight, black licorice and rot, drifted out from within. The closer Annalise drew to the smoke-covered throne, the hotter her cursed mark became—but she couldn't stop moving forward. The dark glass pulled Annalise in with a gravity hard to ignore.

"Hey," Bowie said, snapping Annalise out of whatever trance she was in. "Look at the mirror. It's . . . *her.*"

Nightingale, Bowie, Annalise, and Mister Edwards faced the throne. The black smoke in the mirror cleared. And the

Fate Spinner appeared in the glass, clutching her staff of mirrored eyes, grinning eagerly down at them.

Black crows swarmed at the Fate Spinner's shoulders. The red palace Annalise had spotted earlier from above loomed behind her. The Fate Spinner wore a long-fitted black coat over leggings to match. Obsidian kohl on her eyelids, lips stained the same, her starlight-pale hair was half braided, half loose, and gleamed bright as her teeth. Standing this close to her tormentor made Annalise sick. She wanted to run away just as much as she wanted to fight. Finally, the Fate Spinner turned her gaze onto Annalise.

She almost heard her heart screech as it came to a full stop.

"Well, well, well," the Fate Spinner growled through the glass. "My guests have arrived at last." A spindle of fire speared Annalise's big hand. She whimpered and fell to her knees. "Welcome to the Labyrinth of Fate and Dreams!"

Mister Edwards bowed, as did Nightingale and Bowie Tristle. Annalise, still on her knees, shut her eyes, and sucked in air through her teeth, hugging her big hand to her chest under her cloak. It felt dipped in fire. She counted to four, then opened her eyes. When she did, everyone was staring at her.

"You," the Fate Spinner barked at Annalise. "Stand

before me and meet your fate." The Fate Spinner glared. Sweat prickled under Annalise's arms; her brain exploded with a string of familiar worry-thoughts.

"You're a coward."

"You will fail."

"You hurt your parents for nothing."

"Cursed things like you don't deserve an audience with the Spinner of Dreams!"

The black crows in the mirror flapped and screamed, and the Fate Spinner continued in a thunderous boom, "I said, STAND IN THE PRESENCE OF FATE!"

Annalise flinched, shaking uncontrollably. Mister Edwards slipped his paw into her nice hand and smiled. "It's okay. I'm scared, too." Nightingale and Bowie nodded at her, eyes big with similar fear. Chin trembling, Annalise gave Mister Edwards a thankful smile and let him help her to her feet.

This fox certainly did feel like a friend.

"Well now, that's better, isn't it?" the Fate Spinner said almost cheerfully. "I've waited a long time to see you again, Miss Meriwether." The enchantress leaned closer, knuckles clenched on her staff, focused on Annalise's hidden, cursed hand. "Come closer," she said, sweeter now. "Let me see your . . . *ticket*." Annalise's dark mark pulsed quickly in tune with her heart. "I must make sure it's really you."

135

Limbs rubbery, thoughts caught in a web of fear, Annalise let go of the fox's paw. She pounded her chest, trying to regulate her skipping heart. The spire behind her black mark twisted and grew as she stepped closer to the Fate Spinner's mirror.

When Annalise removed the ticket from the pocket of her cloak, it ripped from her trembling fingers, flew in through the mirror, and landed in the Fate Spinner's hand with a snap. "Excellent," the enchantress said, observing the ticket with enraptured black eyes. "Yes . . . Good. Everything seems to be in order." The ticket, clutched in the Fate Spinner's hand, vanished in a plume of gold mist.

Suddenly, Annalise's big hand burned as hot as a blazing comet. It broke free from her cloak and leaped for the Fate Spinner's face.

The enchantress flinched. Annalise fought her big hand and pushed herself back from the mirror, heart pounding to burst. "I'm s-sorry," Annalise said, choking on her words while trying to restrain her big hand. "I'm so sorry."

The Fate Spinner's ire dropped, replaced with excitement, eagerness—thrill. "No need for apologies, Miss Meriwether. Believe it or not, I know how it feels to be powerless. How it hurts being burned by those closest to you." She growled. "I know what it is to be cursed." When she flexed her left hand on her staff, the Fate Spinner's mark, the mirror image of Annalise's, peeked out on her palm. "By the way, I'm curious. Do you . . . *remember* me?"

Annalise swallowed, re-hid her big hand, and answered in a small but clear voice, "How could I forget the one who . . ." Annalise stopped herself, not wanting the others to know she was cursed. "The one who hurt me and my family." She lowered her eyes and whispered, "The one who made me a monster."

The black spire in her hand pushed farther outside her dark mark, perhaps trying to reunite with the Fate Spinner. Annalise fought against it. But it was getting harder to restrain. The others watched in careful silence.

"A monster," the Fate Spinner replied, twirling her staff. "Yes, well, we all have our fates to bear, don't we? Like your grandparents, for example, who died trying to save you." She tilted her head and cocked her head innocently. "And your parents who, even now, are preparing to die the same way."

Annalise gasped. The control over her big hand broke. Again, her big hand lunged free. But this time, it didn't hold back.

Flames shot from the shattered heart on her palm, aimed at the Fate Spinner's glass. Mister Edwards and the siblings screamed and moved out of the way. The Fate Spinner's mirror deflected the flames. The enchantress seemed almost amused.

Annalise crouched on the floor, eyes to the courtyard stone, confused and ashamed. Everyone had seen her wicked hand and what it could do. All eyes were on her. Judging. Ogling. Thinking her a freak of nature, a devil, a curse. Annalise pressed her big palm mark down on the stone, squelching the fire until it was gone.

Black smoke billowing from beneath her cloak, tears ripped from Annalise, hot, painful, and poisonous, as she faced Mister Edwards. "I'm sorry," Annalise sputtered, avoiding his gaze. "If you've changed your mind about going into the maze with me, I . . . I understand." She hid behind her thick hair, but Annalise couldn't hide her shame. As a last resort, she asked the beast inside her to please not scare away her first ever real friend.

To Annalise's surprise, her black-hearted palm cooled at once. She wondered then: If her cursed hand was an agent of the Fate Spinner, why had it shot fire at her mirror? Whose side was her big hand on?

Mister Edwards sat at her feet. "I haven't changed my mind, Miss Meriwether. On the contrary." He regarded her gently. "It is my honor and privilege to accompany you."

Nightingale and Bowie peered shyly at Annalise. Instead

of recoiling, they came over and stood with her and Mister Edwards.

Like allies.

The Fate Spinner, more serious than before, twisted her mirrored staff at her side and addressed the girl and boy and Mister Edwards. "I will enjoy watching you dreamers fail. Especially you, Miss Meriwether. One less mistake in the world will do my heart good. Now, the rest of you, bring me your tickets. The labyrinth is waiting."

Annalise's breath came fast and hot. She had called herself a mistake many times, but it hurt more when she was labeled this way by another. She stroked her hair, feeling like a failure before she'd even begun.

The tall boy with spectacularly untamed hair pushed toward the Fate Spinner. "Leave her alone, all right? I'm not going to let you talk to us this way anymore. I don't care who you are. You're being disrespectful and, frankly, a bully." He flung his ticket through the mirror. The Fate Spinner caught it, none too gently. His ticket vanished in a puff of red.

Nightingale raised her eyebrows, nodded, and gave a hearty, "Agreed." She stood alongside her brother. When she tossed her ticket through the glass, it melted in a plume of red, too. "There. You have our tickets. Now let us into the labyrinth already. We've got dreams to win." Nightingale winked at Annalise and grinned.

A thrill of joy rushed Annalise.

The Tristles seemed very kind.

Lastly, Mister Edwards tucked his tail between his legs, hurried forward, and threw his ticket at the Fate Spinner like it was on fire. When the Fate Spinner caught his ticket, it disappeared without a trace.

"Very well." The Fate Spinner's smirk lingered on Mister Edwards before addressing them all. "Dreamers"—the Fate Spinner said *dreamers* like a dirty word—"who come to the Mazelands to see my sister, the Spinner of Dreams, must run the gauntlet of fate and conquer my labyrinth first. Law states I must formally ask you: Are you ready to face your fears and fight for your most desperate, impossible dreams?" She stared at Annalise then. And inside the Fate Spinner's black stare, every darkness in the world piled in layers to create an infinite void that pulled Annalise in.

If she fell into it, she might be lost forever.

Bowie answered first. "I'm ready. Let's do this."

Nightingale next. "Let's go!"

Mister Edwards addressed the Fate Spinner but shriveled under her gaze. "I'm ready to find my partner," he said, so scared he shook. "And then t-to have our dreams come true."

The Fate Spinner gave him a curious look: half glare, half amused intrigue. "Perhaps . . ." Her attention then returned to Annalise. "And what about you, pitiful, broken thing. Are you ready to fight me like your *friends?*"

Annalise's heartbeat revved, but no panic came. She stroked the black ribbons of her braid, closed her eyes, and silently recited her dream. *I wish to rule my own destiny and rid myself of this curse.* "Yes," Annalise answered. "I am."

The black crows caw-cawed and took flight, melting into the night.

The Fate Spinner squinted at her hard, one side of her mouth tipped up in an unreadable, maybe hurt, maybe evil grin. "You remind me of someone I used to know. She was kind as well. And she too succumbed to an ill fate, just as you are bound to do."

Shrill cries rang out of the labyrinth, like someone in terrible pain.

The Fate Spinner waved one pale hand. "Ignore them. You'll be inside soon enough. And perhaps I'll see you on the other side." Without another word, the Fate Spinner vanished from behind her mirror in a puff of black smoke.

Dark hearts rained from the red-mooned sky. The black leaves danced and fell, and every entrance opened at once.

Chapter 14

THE FIRST TEST

"All you need to know about life can be learned from the trees," Grandpa Jovie once told Annalise with his usual starry spark. "The way the wind blows and the branches bend with it, this is love." Then her grandma Thessaly added in her chipper voice, "That's right. Strong trees don't stay down; they always spring back up." Grandma Frida jumped in next and stroked Annalise's hair. "The dead parts fall away, my love, and always, new shoots grow at the scar." Grandpa Hugo smiled, warm as a cat in sunlight. "Our lives are reflected in trees, Annalise. What we leave behind becomes the soil that fertilizes who we can become."

Standing in the Fate Spinner's courtyard in a gale of dead black leaves, this memory of long-lost love was exhumed from the well of time like so many restless ghosts. Annalise studied the four entrances, and the trees arching over each, and wondered if she was strong enough to become like these trees. Someone who stands strong, even in the face of the Fate Spinner.

"Ah," a craggy, deep-as-roots voice spoke. Annalise jumped. One of the crooked black trees framing the entrances sprang to life. "We, the trees, are honored that you dreamers are here."

The knotty eyes of their bark opened. Their roots ripped from the platform of stone. Blocks unsettled, shaking loose from their foundation. The eight trees stretched their limbs, herding Nightingale and Bowie, Mister Edwards and Annalise toward the center of the ancient court.

Annalise's heart beat out of control as the trees roared as one. "Inside the labyrinth's walls, all are equal!" Black leaves blustered in sudden winds. Their hair whipped and snapped with each of the tree's words. "The Fate Spinner holds no influence here. Your every decision and destiny are yours to make. For better or worse, the Fate Spinner cannot help or hinder you. Here," the trees howled, "you are on your own."

The largest tree narrowed its knotted eyes at Mister Edwards. "Even you, young fox. You've run this labyrinth before but will find no mercy within its walls." It drew closer to him, extending one sharpened limb an inch from his panicked chest. "This is your last chance. Fail . . . and you will be welcome here no more."

Nightingale and Bowie huddled together. Annalise pulled a traumatized Mister Edwards close. Everything around her shook.

Another tree, plump and bent at the middle, angled its hardwood eyes onto each dreamer. "Those who seek the labyrinth must first choose one of four paths," the tree bellowed in a childlike voice. "The first choice, the *Path of Loneliness*, faces north. The second, the *Path of Hopelessness*, south. The third, the *Path of Suffering*, lies to the east. And the last"—it giggled—"is my personal favorite: the fourth way, the *Path of Illusion*." The tree aimed a stout limb west. "The last path is the shortest, but don't let that fool you. It might prove more dangerous than the rest."

A tall, pencil-thin tree groaned slow and deep from their left. "Inside each of these paths hide four smaller passageways known as the Gates of Doubt, Rejection, Panic, and Death. They will appear to you *in this order* and contain many surprises within. You must pass through each gate in turn and defeat all that stands in your way to reach the labyrinth's end and win your dreams." It leaned closer and whispered like a secret. "Some rooms tucked deep within the maze house deadly creatures of legend, which, when defeated, bestow rewards that have never been found. Rewards of magic that will help guide you toward the labyrinth's end."

The dreamers glanced at each other with dreams in their eyes.

The shortest tree spoke next, blowing piles of black leaves when it flapped its limbs dramatically and spoke in a high operatic voice, "No matter which path you choose, be forewarned! The walls have been known to change depending on the decisions you make, and only one path leads to the labyrinth's end." The tree cackled and coughed and leaves sprayed everywhere. "Oh dear, pardon me! He-hem. MOST IMPORTANT," the tree bellowed, "if you should die within the Fate Spinner's maze, you'll become imprisoned for eternity as a ghost. Or"—it tittered in a terrible, high-pitched voice—"something much worse."

Night wolves howled, closer than before. Annalise's nerves prickled as if she'd chomped ice. Their cries reminded her again of her parents. Had she seen them on that strange train of wolves, or had it been her imagination? Were they somewhere inside this maze? If so . . . which path had they chosen?

The last tree to speak appeared to be ancient. It bore a

carved wooden beard that stretched to its gnarled root-feet, and it hadn't moved until now. "Choose your paths, young ones," the ancient tree said. "Or the labyrinth will choose for you." The trees bowed to the dreamers, and together, returned to their designated entrances.

Cold wind scourged through the courtyard like a haunted symphony, rattling Annalise's nerves and shaking her bones.

Annalise didn't like the sounds of any of the passageways, but path four would be her choice. It would be bad luck not to choose it—wouldn't it?

Mister Edwards rose on his wobbly hind legs and gestured at the third entrance—the Path of Suffering. "That's the one I chose last time." His shoulders drooped. "The one where I lost Mister Amoureux, the path I know leads to Dreamland." He lifted his muzzle and sniffed. "Yes. That's the right way."

Nightingale and Bowie, arguing quietly among themselves, stepped forward. They nodded at Annalise and the fox. "Good luck," they said, then each bounded toward different paths—Nightingale to the third (Suffering), Bowie to the first (Loneliness).

Mister Edwards tugged Annalise's sleeve nervously, leading her toward the third path. "Come on, there's no time to waste."

Annalise followed automatically, peering into every

barred pathway as the trees watched. Each entrance gaped square and black, ominous and cold. None gave any sign of what horrors it held in store.

"Wait." Annalise stopped halfway to path three; the mark on her big hand burning hotter the closer she drew. "What if you don't remember the way? What if the passageways have changed, like the trees said?"

The fox jittered and stroked his fluffy black tail. "Mister Amoureux and I studied the patterns of the maze. I know every creature that awaits us through path three. And . . . I know how to beat them." He fluffed up proudly. "Plus, foxes are excellent trackers. I can still smell Mister Amoureux's footprints from when we were here last. If the walls have changed, I'll still be able to find my way. Please, Miss Meriwether, I've done this already and I can do it again. I beg you to trust me."

Running her braid through her nice hand, Annalise knelt before the black fox. His eyes were desperate for her to believe him. "Are you one hundred percent sure, Mister Edwards?"

"Yes." He nodded quickly. "Positive."

A not-rightness wriggled in her belly, and her cursed hand struck with a sharp pain and pull toward path four—though, she didn't know if her monster was trying to help her or trying to follow the enchantress to whom it belonged.

Wait. A sudden thought struck Annalise. Maybe the book Muse had given her could tell them more about the paths? Annalise went to pull the book from her pocket—but the book was gone! She quickly checked her other pocket, but it wasn't there either.

Oh no. Did she lose it when she fell from the train? Muse told her to keep it close, but she'd forgotten it and lost it and messed everything up.

How could she be so careless?

"Miss Meriwether," the fox asked. "Are you . . . having second thoughts?"

Annalise twisted her braid, eyes darting, breath coming as fast as her worry-thoughts. She knew she should answer but didn't know what to say.

Which path should they choose? One wrong choice and everything she'd done to get here would be wasted. Like the pain she'd caused her parents. What would they think of her if she'd done all this only to lose?

Mister Edwards watched her carefully, brow furrowed. Annalise didn't want to make him upset. But four was her number. She'd never *not* followed it.

On the other hand, the reason she'd asked Mister Edwards to join her was because he knew the way out of the labyrinth. Should she listen to her instincts or her new friend? This

148

might be the biggest decision of Annalise's life and she didn't know what to do.

Annalise tapped her fingers on her thigh.

Four, four, four, four.

Four walls to break to escape her fate.

There could be no other way.

"I'm sorry, Mister Edwards," Annalise said at last." I think I need to choose entrance four—the Path of Illusion. It might be the wrong choice, but it's one I need to make or I'll feel unlucky the entire time." Annalise stroked her hair and met his grief-stricken face. "I hope I didn't upset you. And I understand if you need to go your own way."

Mister Edwards glanced at his stump and sighed. "I had four legs the last time. I'm not sure if I'd make it through the Path of Suffering alone." He paced, worrying the fur at his tail. "So," he whispered, glancing nauseously at entrance three, "if it's okay, I'd rather stay with you. Maybe with your unique gifts"—he glanced at her hidden hand—"and my knowledge of the maze, we can make it through path four and find our way together."

Annalise brightened. "Really?" She hugged Mister Edwards fast. "That's wonderful!" Her grin was infectious. "Maybe we'll do more than make it out alive. Maybe," she said, leading the black fox west toward four, "we'll get everything we've ever dreamed of."

A white blur with whiskers, a top hat, and a wink peeked through the iron bars of the westernmost path four.

Muse!

"Come, Mister Edwards!" Annalise cried, more confident than ever.

"Right behind you," the fox replied with a cautious smile.

"Remember," the trees said in unison. "Fate has no dominion here, or inside the labyrinth. You are your own captains, the sole authors of your scripts." They bowed. Their black leaves shook as the tree guardians bid them farewell. "Beware, be safe, and may the magic of dreams be yours!"

The other three entrances closed with three creaks and a clang. The eyes of the trees deadened, their feet rooted back in place, animated no more.

Annalise and Mister Edwards stepped into the Path of Illusion.

Behind them, a murder of black crows screamed.

Chapter 15

INTO PATH NUMBER FOUR

Annalise was used to darkness. Not the darkness of the perpetual night. Not the slick, sour shadows that lurked under her bed. Not the steaming black smoke that seeped from her cursed hand and did bad things on the Fate Spinner's behalf. Not these, but the darkness that grew in her mind, continually dragging her down. This sort of dark-gathering was poisonous. For once the dark thoughts began, they barreled through the channels of her brain, and there was very little she could do to stop them.

A wall of mossy stone rearranged behind their backs, locking them in. The bloodred moon cast ugly shadows over the towering walls, spilling at her feet like living things ready to grab her ankles and drag her between the stones. Sounds muted in the cold, stale air. The walls felt like they were closing in. Fear burst in Annalise like an exploding balloon of black ink and painted her insides with claustrophobic dread. She'd seen Muse before entering but couldn't find him now.

Annalise and Mister Edwards squished closer together. He seemed just as scared. The fox's ears swiveled, nose wiggling, as he sniffed the air. Annalise squinted into the darkness ahead wishing again she hadn't lost the book.

Within the endless corridor, everything looked the same.

"Was the third path this foreboding, Mister Edwards?" Annalise forced her feet forward over the ivy vines—black, heart-shaped, and razor sharp—crisscrossing the path, hoping she hadn't made the wrong choice by going against Mister Edwards. Her big hand hummed with an excited, painless energy, the thrum of a magnet that pulled.

The black fox slunk to the floor and sniffed. "This is . . . similar." Red moonlight bathed the left-side wall; darkness hid the right. All the crows, black and white, had abandoned them. Everything cinched down to silence. "I smell danger and fear—and magic. Trickles of each left behind from those who traveled this way before."

Annalise curled her hair around her finger four times.

If her mom and dad *did* follow her here, would they choose path four, knowing it would be the one Annalise would pick? "One of my dad's favorite poets wrote *the best way out is always through*," Annalise told Mister Edwards, trying to stay hopeful. "I guess all we can do is keep moving forward. Right?"

Mister Edwards cast scared glances over his shoulder. "Yes. You might be right."

After several dead ends, they arrived at a crossroads. Each way was identical. Walls tall as hundred-year oaks, stone blocks dressed in moss and ivy more barbed wire than vines, one heading left, the other, right.

"Which way do you think, Mister Edwards?" Annalise asked, stroking her hair and counting (*one-two-three-four*).

From the corridor to the right, the scent of faerie blossoms from apple-berry trees, and a hint of freshly cut grass drifted forward on a soft breeze. Annalise closed her eyes and leaned into the summery scents she never got to experience at home. It smelled divine and she relaxed instantly.

From the path to the left steeped the scents of black licorice and midnight-star spice, both embodying the earthy musk of dark magic. It smelled dangerous. Deadly.

The broken black heart of Annalise's big palm tugged and squirmed as if asking to go right. Usually, if given a choice of left or right, Annalise chose the *right* of things. Right just always seemed so much nicer than left. But her cursed hand choosing right made Annalise suspicious.

Even though it had shot flames at the Fate Spinner earlier, it had hurt Annalise for years before that. How could she trust it?

Still, she would rather go right than left.

Mister Edwards sniffed the air of each path, ears swiveling. After ruminating on the hall to the left, he answered. "Either way is terrible. But I smell a connection ahead that *might* just intersect with path three." He sighed with relief. "I'm afraid right is the way to go."

"Well . . . wonderful," Annalise said, not sure if she should be relieved or worried. She smiled anyway and cinched her cursed hand tighter. "Right has never steered me wrong before. Maybe we'll even find one of those rooms the trees were talking about? The ones with the hidden rewards?"

"Maybe," Mister Edwards answered warily. "But Mister Amoureux and I almost won without finding any rewards, so I wouldn't worry about them."

Annalise stepped into the perfumed corridor leading right, and Mister Edwards followed. As she pondered what the rewards could be, the passageway closed behind them.

Immediately, a sign wound out of the ivy overhead, strung between the labyrinth walls in a beam of moonlight: *The Gate of Doubt.*

Annalise and Mister Edwards shared a foreboding look.

"The trees mentioned this gate," said Annalise. "Have you any idea what we might find ahead, Mister Edwards?"

He shook his head. "I don't know *exactly*, since Mister Amoureux and I originally chose path three. But I imagine, since it's the Gate of Doubt, the labyrinth will try to confuse us and make us question everything we ever thought true. Make us experience different horrors, depending on our fears, and try to separate us. This being the Path of Illusion, we might each see things that may or may not be real. But no matter what happens, you mustn't believe what the labyrinth tells you," Mister Edwards said urgently. "No matter where we are in Fate's maze, something will try to stop us."

Haunted moans leaked from the corridor walls.

"What's that?" Annalise asked, peering in every direction. But Mister Edwards was too busy following his nose up the long, dappled corridor to hear her. "Mister Edwards?"

Suddenly, ghosts poured through the cracks between stones and surrounded Annalise.

"You killed us!" the ghosts screamed. "Sealed our fates."

"Stole our dreams!"

"The Spinner of Dreams *hates* people like you."

Annalise froze. She recognized their ghostly faces. They were Carriwitchet's townsfolk, those who'd died thanks to her curse.

The ghosts pushed closer. The specters' floating bodies lit the corridor with an eerie glow. They were cold as wet earth as they pushed against her. "M-m-mister Edwards?" The metallic taste of panic rose. "Where are you?"

The ghosts of the townspeople shrieked and shoved and glared. "Good thing you ate our colorful candy or we might never have found you!"

From somewhere ahead, Mister Edwards screamed. Annalise could just see him through the spectral bodies, bolting up the corridor as if possessed. Her body thrummed with adrenaline. "Mister Edwards—come back!" When she could no longer see her friend, Annalise didn't think—she ran.

The spirits laughed and gave chase.

Slipping over mossy ground and crooked stones, Annalise skidded around the next bend and found Mister Edwards. Stooped in a shaft of red light, growling and glaring at shadows, the black fox batted at his fur as if crawling with spiders. "Do you see her?" he asked frantically, eyes red with the moon. "GET HER AWAY FROM ME!"

"Who do you see, Mister Edwards?" When Annalise reached him, more specters closed in. She ignored their nasty remarks and foul stench and helped her friend to stand. "I don't know what you see, but we can't stay here. Let's go together."

They took off down the corridor, side by side. The ghosts clung to Annalise like wet blankets as they twisted through the maze. Mister Edwards thrashed as they ran, crying out in desperate pain.

"You know that fox doesn't like you, right?" said the ghost of Emanda Shoebert, with her long silver hair, rotting teeth, and bulging eyes, floating an inch from Annalise's face. "He's here to use you for your evil hand, he is."

Mort, Emanda's bald husband, pushed his hideous wife out of the way. "That's right, you devil. The fox sees the horned monster within you and wants it for himself!"

The dark thing in her cursed hand pushed closer to the surface, like it was listening, like it wanted to speak, too. The tip of the spire broke through her skin. When she looked next, Mister Edwards was gone.

Huffing and puffing, Annalise skidded around the next corner, heart throttling her chest. She'd arrived at a dead end. "Mister Edwards?" She doubled back, plowing through the nasty ghosts full speed. She took another turn, but every corner looked the same.

"Oh, sure, the fox seems innocent now, doesn't he," Emanda said, grasping on to Annalise's cloak sleeve. "But all he *really* wants is to steal your prize."

Mort got in Annalise's face. "Too bad you lost the Spinner

of Dreams's book! It could have told you the fox wants two dreams for the price of one." He laughed. "Seems he and your wicked hand had you fooled."

No. Mister Edwards wouldn't do that.

They're trying to trick you—the labyrinth is trying to trick you.

Annalise sped through the couple's cruel ghosts. They cackled inside her head and followed. Annalise didn't stop running. She focused on her feet and breath, took a right turn, and located Mister Edwards.

He stood, back to a dead end, growling low and watching her from the shadows.

"Look at him watching you," the tall ghost of Riles Murlap, the grim doctor at her birth, spat. "Can't you see he's not what he seems?"

Mister Edwards's hackles rose. His red eyes narrowed as Annalise approached.

"The labyrinth doesn't want you here," Riles continued, shouting behind her. "It hates you, like everyone else does."

"I don't believe you!" Annalise cried and approached the black fox. The closer she drew, the louder his growls became. She clenched her now-smoking fist and stopped a few feet away.

For a moment, Annalise thought he'd lunge like a wolf and bite. Doubt slipped in through the cracks of her mind.

The ghosts aren't right about him, are they?

The apparitions laughed and hovered above them.

Breathing fast, Annalise knelt at Mister Edwards's paws. "Please, Mister Edwards, it's just me, and I want to help."

The snarling fox lifted his glazed-over eyes and stared past her, talking to himself.

"She thinks she can overpower me. That she's better than me because of that thing *inside her hand. The horned creature in her hand sees—it hears, it knows!"* The dazed fox shook his head and squeezed his eyes tight. *"I can't trust her—I don't even know her! She doesn't like me, I see that now. She only brought me here as a sacrifice to the maze—to keep me from Arthur—from my beloved, Mister Amoureux!"*

Before Annalise could respond, the fox lunged forward and snapped. Annalise cried out and scrambled backward. "Mister Edwards." She choked back so many old scars of hurt, ridicule, and rejection, her voice tired with tears. "Why are you acting this way? You said not to believe them. You are my friend. Aren't you?"

Annalise crouched in the passageway's center in a shaft of crimson light. She stroked her hair by fours, clenching her cursed fist in the folds of her cloak while the ghosts laughed, waiting for her to cry. Then, as if waking from a nightmare, Mister Edwards thrust his head up and gasped.

The moonlight flushed from his eyes when he blinked

159

and set his gaze onto Annalise. "What happened?" He sank to the ground, confused. "Miss Meriwether, I am so sorry. I thought . . . I thought you were hurting me. I didn't mean to attack you." He moved closer to her, ears low. "I should have been stronger. I never should have let that happen."

"Oh, Mister Edwards!" Annalise's fear dissolved instantly into happy relief. When she glanced about, the ghosts were gone. "It's all right. Whatever you saw wasn't real. Because I do like you, and I'd never sacrifice you to this horrible place. Believe me, the last thing I would ever think is that I'm better than anyone else." Annalise lowered her eyes and stood. "You're my first real friend, and"— her heart fluttered—"I really hope you like me, too."

The shy fox smiled. "I do like you, Miss Meriwether, very much. And I'm delighted you think of me as a friend."

Annalise's face lit up like a hundred-watt bulb. "Oh. Mister Edwards, thank you." She cleared the flutter of joy from her throat. "Now, how about we get through this maze, beat the Fate Spinner, and finally reach our dreams?"

"Yes," Mister Edwards said hopefully. "I'd like that."

"Good. Let's go."

They'd only taken a few steps away from the dead end when a blood-chilling shriek ripped through the corridor on a scourge of cold wind.

Their hair and fur blew back. Annalise shivered. Mister Edwards growled, "The Fate Spinner. I don't think she's happy with us."

Annalise met his frightened eyes with her own. "It's not our job to make her happy. But it is our right to try to defeat her."

The ground shook beneath them. An echoing grind ripped through the air as the stone blocks making up the dead end fell away and revealed a new passageway. At their backs, the corridor that led them here sealed shut.

"Mercy," Annalise said, staring at the ivy-strewn archway. "Does this mean we passed the first test and defeated the Gate of Doubt?"

"You're exactly right." Mister Edwards stared into the dark entrance ahead. "This is the passageway I smelled earlier. The connection to path three that I *know* leads to the end."

The new corridor was as dark as oblivion. A sign spun out of the black-hearted ivy beneath the arch: *The Gate of Rejection*.

Annalise turned to Mister Edwards and gulped. "When you and your husband completed the labyrinth, you must have passed through each gate on path three." The fox gave a slow haunted nod. "What did you find through the Gate of Rejection, Mister Edwards?"

Mister Edwards stroked his tail and hugged it close. "We were gifted a candy shop, filled with the most beautiful cakes, cream puffs, chocolates, and pies. The candy shop of our dreams. It was so beautiful. Too beautiful. I never wanted to leave." The black fox smiled sadly. "Mister Amoureux has always been so much wiser than I am. He saw right through the enchantment. We might have died there if it wasn't for him."

Overhead, black crows appeared.

Annalise said quietly, "Your Mister Amoureux sounds wonderful. What did you do, to get so far together? How did you escape?"

Mister Edwards sniffed back emotion and cleared his throat. "Mister Amoureux found a loophole. Hopefully the trick we learned last time will work here, too." Mister Edwards motioned forward. "Shall we?"

Dead leaves blew up from the ground and vanished into the shadowed entrance. Annalise counted breaths and pushed down the growing pain in her big hand. "We shall, Mister Edwards," she answered, remembering her dream.

I wish to rule my own destiny and rid myself of this curse.

Then do it, she told herself.

As they readied themselves to step into the next gate, Annalise's cursed hand burned beneath her cloak as if dipped in boiling oil; the monster within her hand thrashed and swelled and grew. Annalise wondered what her cursed hand was trying to tell her as the two plunged into the void, utterly unprepared for what would come next.

Chapter 16

THE TERRIBLE HUNGER OF DREAMS

Annalise and Mister Edwards pushed through the darkness and into a bright ruby light. The Gate of Rejection
opened into a walled, round courtyard the size of Annalise's bedroom. Moonlight lit the circular center from high
above, sharp ivy tangled over the stones. The air smelled
as feral as an animal den layered with bones, yet the sky
was open and clear.

Right away, her big hand numbed.

Annalise hated to admit it, but she'd come to rely on the
pulse of her cursed hand to help guide her through the dark.
Sometimes she trusted the monster within her, other times,

not so much. But the farther they ventured into the labyrinth, the bigger and heavier it grew. How much longer until her monster broke free? What would happen then? How desperately she wished she had her mom and dad to lend her their confident smiles when hers were frightened and spare. Did they miss her, or were they glad she and her curse were gone? What would they tell her if they were here now?

Focus, Annalise, they'd say. *All your dreams might still come true.*

Mister Edwards sniffed the circular wall. Suddenly, an insatiable hunger and thirst grew in them both, despite their efforts to ward against that. Fear brushed Annalise's skin like cold feathers.

"I don't like this," Annalise whispered. "It feels dangerous. Like something is watching us. Like something is waiting to pounce."

"This is the Labyrinth of Fate and Dreams, Miss Meriwether. Every move we make is dangerous, and someone's always watching." He glanced at entrance through which they'd come, then ran his paw over the stones. "There should be at least one door here somewhere. . . ."

Again, Annalise chastised herself for losing the book that might have helped them. Where were the rooms with the legendary creatures hiding rewards? As much as she didn't want to find deadly beasts, she did want the magical rewards.

Something occurred to her while observing the sky-tipped wall. "Mister Edwards, did you and Mister Amoureux ever try climbing the walls? If we reached the top, we could see which way—"

"No!" Mister Edwards snapped. "I—we tried, and it nearly got us killed. The ivy's as sharp as daggers. Besides," he said, glancing at his stump. "I wouldn't attempt it anyway, with only three legs. However," he continued quieter, "if you wanted to try your luck without me . . ."

"Oh no." Annalise shook her head quickly. "It was just an idea. Don't worry. I'm not going anywhere."

He smiled. "I appreciate that. Thank you."

Unexpectedly, the feral stench of wild beasts *changed*. A whiff of sweet cake wound the courtyard of ivy and stone. "Do you smell that?" Annalise glided forward, stomach growling, pulled softly by the delicious perfume.

The fox, eyes closed and drooling, followed Annalise, nose first. "Lemon cake," he whispered. "That's new. How wonderfully odd."

The rainbow candy Muse gave her must have been making her hungrier, like he'd said it might. Annalise's stomach rumbled as loud as a lion's roar. "Pardon me." Annalise blushed. As she opened her mouth to speak, her tongue ached with thirst. "I could eat a thousand pies and the pie-maker himself I'm so hungry, then drink a small lake for dessert—couldn't you, Mister Edwards?" Stomach rumbling louder, Annalise stepped onto the round center stone carved with wolves, horns, and wings.

Mister Edwards stood beside her, rubbed his stomach, and laughed. "Clearly, yes."

Without warning, the small courtyard began to change. The gray labyrinth walls transformed from top to bottom into bricks of polished gold quartz. The ivy turned to dust and blew away, and the gate through which they'd entered sealed shut, locking them in.

They were trapped.

Annalise and Mister Edwards spun in circles. They patted the walls, searching for a way free. At their touch, four elegant closed doors, one facing each direction, emerged.

"Mercy." Annalise sighed.

New scents poured through every door; Mister Edwards sniffed each one.

Directly ahead, the stench of fire and char wafted from a black door marked: *The Road of Courage.*

The yellow door to their right smelled like the lemon cake that drew them here. The sign read: *The Road of Power.*

Children's laughter rang from the door behind them, *The Road of Friends*, splattered in colors of paint. It seemed lovely in there.

Even though Annalise preferred going right, and loved

lemon cake, when she faced the door to their left, she knew that was the one for her.

The sweet perfume of red ginger curry wafted through the lilac-painted door marked: *The Road of Dreams*. Rice and red ginger curry was one of Annalise's favorite dishes—her dad's special recipe.

Mister Edwards had been wringing his tail and pacing before the Road of Courage when the scent hit him. "Red curry," he said with a scratch of longing. "That's the smell of home—Mister Amoureux's specialty." Mister Edwards glanced at it with a desperate hunger. "This is definitely the road we're supposed to choose. The one I smelled earlier that connected to path three—the path that leads to the end."

Night wolves howled close, as if right behind the wall.

Annalise flinched. "Are you sure, Mister Edwards?" Annalise tapped her fingers on her thigh. She didn't like the Gate of Rejection already.

He twisted his tail. "Yes. My every instinct says *follow the red curry*." Black crows cawed, circling overhead. He ignored their cries. "Plus, Mister Amoureux's scent is through the door of Dreams. Why? . . . Do you disagree?" He glanced at her big hand. "Which way seems right to you?"

A tuft of long white fur swept the crack below the Road of Dreams.

They turned to each other and said, "Dream cats" at once.

Annalise nodded. "I think you're right, Mister Edwards. The Road of Dreams is the way to go." Her big hand zinged and pulled toward Muse. Annalise hoped these were good signs.

"Excellent," Mister Edwards said.

Annalise's stomach gurgled and grumped. "Then it's settled. Come on, Mister Edwards. Let's eat!"

Stomachs rumbling with anticipation, Annalise and Mister Edwards side-eyed each other with famished grins as she pushed open the lilac door.

Chapter 17

A TOWN OF SPIRITS

Through the door of Dreams, on the other side of the darkness, the labyrinth was gone. No walls, no corridors, no ugly red moon. Sunlight, warm and cheerful, shone in the clear blue sky. The sweet perfume of red ginger curry wafted toward them. The doorway they entered vanished behind them in a wisp of smoke.

They stood on a cobblestone street lined with shops, customers, and vendors selling their wares. The odd little town was celebrating something—long rectangular red flags bearing a crown of silver crows and golden horns flapped from gilded posts. All the townsfolk, dressed in red and gold, had the translucent skin of ghosts. Red geraniums grew in bright clumps between stores. Annalise recognized the town crest from the book Muse gave her, lost somewhere over the maze.

The crest belonged to the Spinner of Dreams.

"Mister Edwards," Annalise asked, moving swiftly forward, hair dancing in the spiced breeze. "You didn't mention how fantastically wonderful this road would be." Annalise's stomach practically screamed in anticipation.

Mister Edwards scanned the crowd, a growl deep in his throat, fear in his eyes. "Yes, but it's not all that it seems." The spirits milling the cobblestone street were combinations of various beasts, walking on hind legs. Lion-headed dogs in red suits, bird-alligators in skirts and big hats, porcupine-sloths in pajamas, and hippopotamus-humans in . . . nothing at all. "Hopefully we can free ourselves the way I did last time. Follow my lead."

Annalise glanced about uncertainly, clenching her agitated big hand. She nodded, looked down, and gasped, "Oh, mercy."

Annalise's clothing had *changed*. Instead of her cloak, she wore a white-and-black pinstriped dress, knee-high white socks, and black Mary Jane shoes.

Her stomach dropped.

Her big hand was exposed.

A slick scrum of panic slid though Annalise like cold black smoke. She tried to shove her cursed hand into the folds of the dress, but the horn emerged and the mark spat flames. The spirit-beasts stared. Annalise turned away from the crowd and patted her marked hand softly, as she used to do when she was little.

But it did not calm.

Stomach roaring for food and drink, adrenaline flooding through her, Annalise raised her clenched fist to her heart. "Please stop," she asked her monster.

The horn retreated, and flames died at once.

A strange surge of power filled her dark mark. A new power that felt *good*.

Her cursed hand really *was* listening to her.

More customers materialized into the street from out of the cobblestones. Toad-headed people, people-headed toads. Cats with black raven bodies and vice versa. Voices tumbled toward them, followed by the most succulent smells of food in the universe. Two non-spirit-beast children strolled out of a shop ahead. The ones they'd met at the start: Nightingale and Bowie Tristle.

"Should we say hello?" Annalise asked, stroking her hair.

Nightingale and Bowie waved, grinning ear -to -ear. Annalise stepped forward and waved back—and tripped, nearly knocking Mister Edwards down.

"Sorry," she mumbled to Mister Edwards, cheeks ablaze. Nightingale laughed at Annalise in the distance. Not in a mean way—more like she was laughing with her. "I . . . tripped."

The fox raised his whiskery eyebrows and pushed down a grin. "Yes, I saw that. I definitely think we should say hello."

Mister Edwards and Annalise (still red with embarrassment) approached the siblings at an open-air eatery at the end of the street. As they got closer, the view opened like a veil had been lifted. Beyond the eatery, green hills rolled for miles. Past the hills, the skies faded from blue to lilac. Lilac—like those over Dreamland. Maybe Dreamland and the Spinner of Dreams were just past those hills. Maybe they were getting closer?

Wolf-headed antelope waiters in vests wound through the outdoor patio of diners, holding platters overflowing with food. The two children left their seats and met them outside the cordoned-off eatery—Nightingale smiling brightly, Bowie serious and calm. "Hey," Nightingale said. "You made it!"

Annalise tried to look happy rather than anxious—not easy, with a cursed hand hidden behind her, always ready to burst into flames.

"Hi," Annalise said, fighting her hand currently trying to break free. "So good to see you again." Mister Edwards smiled shyly beside her.

"You too," Nightingale said, shielding her eyes from the sun. She wore midnight-blue leggings and a white sweater with a unicorn across the chest. Bowie raised a hand. His green hoodie read *I solemnly swear that I am up to no good.* When he smiled, his dimples came out. "Did you find special passes in the labyrinth, too?"

Annalise looked questioningly at Mister Edwards, who shrugged in confusion. The scents streaming toward them were torturous. It was all Annalise could do not to drool. "Special passes?"

Nightingale grinned. "Yeah. Free passes into Dreamland?"

All the blood drained from Annalise's face and out through her toes. "No. We didn't."

"Oh." Nightingale frowned. "We figured, since you're here, you must have. Well anyway, my brother and I took different paths into the maze, because"—she glared at her brother, who gave her a sorry-not-sorry shrug—"Bowie is stubborn. But once we got inside, we focused hard on our dream of having our family back together, and then," she laughed, "we found each other in the middle of the labyrinth! Isn't that wonderful?"

"Yeah," Bowie continued in his easygoing voice. "It was easy. Then we found this weird gothic black door. When we went through it, all we had to do was dodge these, I don't know, bone spider things, and after that, these passes were waiting for us."

Bowie held up two black and red, mirrorlike invitations:

Admit One for a Special Feast
Followed by an Audience with
the Spinner of Dreams
Ticket Holder May Receive One Dream

"Yeah," Nightingale said next. "It was so easy. Not as deadly as I heard the labyrinth could be." When she scanned the feasting crowd, her smile could've lit a dark room. "See those two being served by the snake-lady there? Those are our parents." Annalise nodded. They seemed nice—happily chatting and enjoying their meals. "When we got here, they were waiting for us."

"Really?" Annalise perked up. Maybe if their parents were here, hers were, too! She scanned the street and shops, searching for her cheerful dad and warmhearted mom, but couldn't see them.

"Really." Nightingale beamed. "But the most amazing part is"—her voice became quiet—"they died two years ago.

I know, right?" She sighed. "Getting them back was our dream, and we didn't even have to finish the labyrinth to get it. Isn't that amazing?"

The breath knocked out of Annalise's lungs. Her head buzzed, and her eyes stung. Her big hand smoldered behind her, like it understood her pain.

Why did they get their dream so easily? Why did they get free passes into Dreamland and not her? Annalise wanted them to have their family back together, of course. But why was everything always so hard for her?

A bitter skunk of a feeling heated her insides with envy. Annalise looked away, shrinking with shame.

"Annalise?" Nightingale said, concerned. "Are you okay?" When she took Annalise's left arm by the elbow, probably trying to be kind, Annalise's exposed big hand seared and stabbed and erupted in a thick cloud of smoke.

Annalise jerked her arm away and hid her cursed hand behind her back. "I'm sorry." A small bolt of black lightning burst from behind Annalise. Nightingale screamed. Bowie pulled his sister away. Every spirit surrounding them stopped eating to stare.

Mister Edwards stepped back, eyes bright with fear. "Miss Meriwether. Your hand. It's still . . . smoking."

A circle of creatures widened around her, leaving Annalise

in the center, alone. "I'm so sorry," she choked as the spiraled horn shot out and her palm spat black flames.

The surrounding spirits shrieked and ran. Annalise clenched her cursed fist tighter, the spire between her fingers, and murmured *stop, stop, stop, stop* as Nightingale and Bowie fled back to their family.

Anger pulsed through Annalise—at the Fate Spinner for making her life hard and her hand cursed, and at herself for ever believing that her monster was on her side.

Annalise was ready to run in the opposite direction when a small paw pressed into her spine. "My father always said: if you're upset, go for a walk. That the mind needs a safe place to go, a task to draw its attention. Please, Miss Meriwether, would you walk with me?" he whispered, "We're almost to where we need to be."

The horn piercing her black heart retreated and the smoke cleared. But Annalise still couldn't stop shaking. "Thank you, Mister Edwards," she sniffed. "I'm lucky to have found a friend like you."

"Likewise." The fox smiled, almost sadly, before something stole his attention.

A giant of epic proportions burst out of the eatery and skidded to a stop before Annalise. "Who, pray tell, are you? And why were you spewing smoke outside my establishment?"

The giant wore a food-splattered chef's uniform and resembled a storybook river troll. Her hair of flowing water fell over skin covered in warts. Standing eight feet tall, her voice bellowed out in a booming croak, "This is a private party given by the Spinner herself!" She thrust out her sticky frog hand. "I'll need your invitations—immediately."

"I . . . um . . ." Annalise blinked at Mister Edwards, Mister Edwards blinked back. "We don't have invitations." She recalled the large white crow on the train who'd had her ticket. "M-maybe you have some waiting for us?"

The river troll sighed. "Names?"

"I'm Annalise Meriwether." When Mister Edwards didn't speak, Annalise answered for him; that was what friends were for. "And this is Mister Edwards. Is this . . . Dreamland?"

The river troll, riffling through a book, burst out laughing. A few passing spirits did the same. "Goodness, no. This isn't Dreamland and I have no ticket for any *Annalise Meriwether.* However," she said, narrowing her eyes at Mister Edwards. "I *do* have a ticket for your terrified friend here." The troll gave Mister Edwards a wicked toady-lipped grin and handed him a ticket. "*You* are free to go through with the rest."

Annalise stroked her hair and shrank back, counting by fours. She glanced at the fox, but he wouldn't meet her eyes. "Oh, I see."

Did the Spinner of Dreams hate Annalise, too?

From the table behind the troll, Nightingale, Bowie, and their parents stuffed their faces with rice and red ginger curry. The waiter brought them starry-moon pie dripping in ice cream and a lovely lemon-zing cake. Watching their happy family, Annalise grew hot with rage—and she rarely heated with rage.

Annalise clenched her giant fist and glared at everyone stuffing their faces around them. "Did they all find special tickets from the Spinner of Dreams?"

The troll bared teeth as sharp as a shark's and growled, "That's right. *They* are not cursed. Now," she said, shooing Annalise back, "get out, go, go, go, GO!"

Annalise stumbled and fell. Her new clothes magicked into her old ones, tattered and singed. Annalise reddened with humiliation. Her anger morphed into tears.

Everyone cheered, including the Tristles—not in encouragement for Annalise to rise, but because she'd fallen.

Mister Edwards knelt beside Annalise and helped her to stand. "I'm not going," he told her with a wink. "I wasn't hungry anyway." When his stomach growled, he coughed to cover the sound. Then Mister Edwards ripped his invitation in half, threw it high, and grasped Annalise's hand. "Rejecting their gift is the loophole. Now we make a break for it."

Annalise laughed with excitement as the two sprinted past the troll.

"How dare you reject the Spinner's invitation!" The river troll lunged at them. "She'll have your hide for this, fox!"

"You can't stop people from wanting a better life," Mister Edwards shouted over his shoulder. "Invitation or not!"

"STOP, YOU DEVILS!" the river troll thundered after them. "SOMEBODY CAPTURE THEM!"

Black crows took from the roofs and shrieked. The troll and spirits gave chase.

"Where are we going, Mister Edwards?" Annalise's hair fluttered around her like wings as they ran up the empty street, back the way they came.

"Just trust me!" The troll pounded the earth behind them. "We should be back in—" Mister Edwards tripped.

"Mister Edwards!" Annalise skidded to a stop.

The black fox screamed as the troll grabbed him by the scruff. Annalise's big hand resumed burning and fighting for freedom.

"Looking for this?" The troll held him high. "We'll see how you like the Fate Spinner when she gets her hands on you," she snarled. "Eh, Mister Edwards?"

Annalise thrust her cursed hand before her and said, "Let. My. Friend. Go." Her black mark spewed black flames. Spirits scattered.

But the troll refused to move, and grinned instead. "What if I don't?"

A shock of electricity passed through Annalise's dark mark. "You'll regret it." Annalise dived forward, grasped the troll by the warty leg, and squeezed. Her flesh sizzled. The river troll screamed and released Mister Edwards. And when she did, Annalise was there to catch him.

"Come, my friend." Annalise set Mister Edwards on his feet and gripped his paw. "Lead the way."

"CAPTURE THE DREAMERS!" the troll shrieked. But the eerie beasts scattered instead. And Annalise and Mister Edwards ran. The farther they went, the more the town faded into the meadow beyond—until eventually the shops, the food, the spectral creatures, and the hideous troll faded to dust and seeped into the cobblestone cracks.

When Mister Edwards and Annalise stopped to catch their breath, charcoal smudged across the pleasant blue sky. Black crows swarmed, caw-caw-caw-caw. The heavens darkened, thundered, and swirled with ruby clouds. Behind them, Nightingale and Bowie stood at the side of the road in the recently vacated town, watching the last of their parents fade to vapor and vanish.

A cold rain began to fall, washing the city away, unearthing what they hadn't seen before. Hundred-foot-tall walls covered in ivy, deadly leaves, and black moss rose out of the rain and gloom. The labyrinth had returned.

Or maybe, it was never gone.

Annalise and Mister Edwards stood inside a large circle in the center of a four-way fork somewhere inside the labyrinth. Four ominous passageways led into the dark, with no signs, smells, or clues to what awaited them helping to guide their way.

Footsteps slapped the wet stones behind them. "You did this," Bowie shouted, racing toward Annalise and Mister Edwards. Glaring at Annalise's hidden big hand, he continued. "You made our parents disappear. We saw the whole thing."

Rain fell in buckets. Annalise stroked her wet hair, grazing her four wet ribbons. "I didn't mean to." Hot shame crept into her chest. "I swear, I meant you no harm!"

Nightingale and Bowie held their tickets in their hands. Nightingale started to cry. And it was the most horrible, hopeless sound Annalise had ever heard.

"If this is anyone's fault, it's mine," Mister Edwards said. "Come on, Miss Meriwether. We can't help them anymore. We need to keep moving."

"But they're right." Annalise regarded him and the other two in turn. Tiny-spider-thoughts swarmed and overwhelmed her brain and dropped on sticky webs and bit into her heart.

"It's my destiny to hurt people—to be alone. My whole life has been about this curse. I hate it, and I'm sorry!"

A storm of soaked, leaflike hearts plunged from the sky.

"Look," Bowie said, holding his sister and backing away. "Just stay away from us, all right? We don't need your sorries or sad excuses. Just . . . stay away." Nightingale glanced heavily at Annalise before darting into the passageway to the left and vanishing alongside her brother.

Sick with guilt, Annalise wanted to go after them. To explain she wasn't a bad person—that she wanted to be good. At the same time, she wondered who she'd hurt next on her way to her dreams. She'd hurt her mom and dad, and Nightingale, Bowie, and maybe their parents.

It'll be Mister Edwards next.

No. Annalise pushed her worry-thoughts away and remembered her dream:

I wish to rule my own destiny and rid myself of this curse.

Annalise gritted her teeth.

That's just what I must do.

Her big hand zinged in reply.

"Which way do you think, Annalise?" Mister Edwards asked, shivering, worrying his tail-fur and looking forlorn. "This fork . . . I've never seen it before. Last time I beat the Gate of Rejection, there was only one way to go. I thought—I thought once we escaped that town, we'd connect with path three, but now I'm not so sure, and I can't smell much in this rain."

Normally, this would have been Annalise's moment of panic. When all the fours in the universe couldn't pull her back from the dark flood coming to wash her away. But as Annalise scanned each entrance, she spotted something that shifted her attention. The passageway Nightingale and Bowie had entered had begun to glow.

Black crows flooded the sky.

Inside the threshold, one of the stones on the floor shone like a star. "Do you see that light?" she asked Mister Edwards.

The drenched fox squinted away from the crows, toward the opening. "See what, Miss Meriwether?"

Annalise approached the softly glowing passageway. Her big hand pulled her forward more urgently the closer Annalise drew.

"You want to go after them?" the fox asked.

"I don't know," she answered, blackberry hair shifting uncertainly in the breeze. "But I think this is the right way."

A sudden spark of power, the same she'd experienced earlier, zinged through her big hand from fingertips to wrist. Annalise's heart sped in reply.

Mister Edwards blinked rain from his eyes, shoulders

slumped in defeat. "Okay. I'm with you," he said.

"Together, then." As they moved into the corridor, the soft glow brightened. One of the stones in the floor lit like a lamp in the dark. Annalise's eyes flew wide. "Mister Edwards. Do you see the glow now?"

Annalise's cursed hand pulsed faster as she stepped on the stone. The fox had just opened his mouth to answer—when the walls of the labyrinth dissolved in a surge of sheer lemon light.

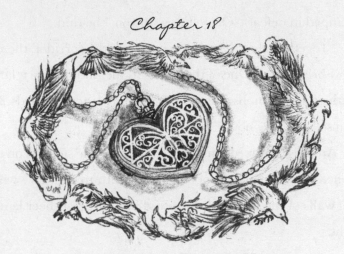

Chapter 18

INTERLUDE: THE POETS OF HOPE

The moment Annalise placed her foot on the glowing stone, a carpet of sunny green grass rolled out in every direction. Annalise curled her bare toes into the meadow as her hair and cloak fluttered behind her like wings. Summer winds tickled her skin. Annalise felt warm for the first time since entering the maze.

She searched for Mister Edwards, but he wasn't here.

Maybe he was up ahead?

The earth shook. Trees, as tall as houses, bursting with fat green leaves, sprang from the ground. Hundreds of golden butterflies fluttered from the branches and danced lightly around her. "Mercy," Annalise breathed, and spun in a slow circle. Shimmering dust billowed from their wings and glazed her in a glitter of stars. "Who are you?" Annalise asked the butterflies with a grin she felt to her toes.

"We are the poets of hope." The golden butterflies tittered in one ear and then the other. "We've come bearing a message, a sort of reward."

Annalise clapped with delight. "And what might your message be, poets?"

They landed on Annalise, gilding her cloak in fluttering wings of gold. *"Even after the longest dark night, dreams will shine. As if darkness was a spark and dreamers, the birth of the flame."* The poets took flight, circling her in a blizzard of shine.

"Oh, that's wonderful," Annalise replied, watching them fly.

And that's when she saw it. Just over the next hill stood a home like hers, except new and uncaged. Before the witch's hat house grew a garden filled with her favorite flowers— black-and-silver lilacs that smelled like starry summer nights—all perfectly alive. Birds sang. Her parents stepped out the front door, smiling into the sun. "This is my dream, isn't it?" Annalise asked them.

"This is hope," the golden butterflies replied before fracturing into wisps of gold and blowing away on a cool wind.

Annalise's delight fell as a low vibration hit the earth. Black crows loomed at the edges of everywhere, cawing a warning from the darkening sky. Night wolves howled at the edges of the field, and Mister Edwards was calling her name. The pretty scene disintegrated. The light vanished.

But still, Annalise remained covered in gold.

And even when the Fate Spinner's labyrinth returned, the poets' words wrapped Annalise in hope: *"Even after the longest dark night, dreams will shine. As if darkness was a spark and dreamers, the birth of the flame . . ."*

Chapter 19

YOU'LL NEVER GET OUT OF THIS MAZE

"Miss Meriwether?" Mister Edwards inquired. "Did you hear what I said?"

The glowing stone she'd stepped on had darkened. She saw no hopeful golden butterflies, but their message hung soft in the air.

Annalise blinked at the drenched fox. Mister Edwards didn't seem to notice she'd been gone. A flurry of wings crossed the moon and cawed.

This time, the crows were white.

"I'm sorry, Mister Edwards." She trembled inside her wet cloak, freezing cold. Golden glitter dripped from her hair. "I must have missed what you said."

"I asked if you wanted to talk about what happened." He observed Annalise warily. "With the Tristles, I mean."

Annalise took four slow breaths. "No, Mister Edwards. I just want to f-find the Spinner of Dreams, and maybe s-some food." She was so hungry and thirsty it felt as if her insides would devour themselves any minute. Her eyelids wanted to close with tiredness as well.

But Annalise wanted her dream more.

"May I ask a personal question, Miss Meriwether?"

They ventured up another, much warmer corridor. Annalise forced her eyes wide open and regarded the black fox warmly. "Sure. Ask anything you like."

Mister Edwards covered his stump and lowered his ears. "What are your worst fears?" His gaze darted every which way.

The question took Annalise off guard. She'd often longed for a friend to share secrets with. Someone to listen to what frightened her, someone who might help make those fears go away. Now, here was her chance.

"I have so many. Too many to list, really. But," she continued. "I do have one I've never told anyone." Annalise twisted her wet hair. "Even though I'm sure they're not bad creatures, I'm quite scared of spiders. I'd never hurt them, of course! Because they can't help the way they are. It's just . . . they remind me of my worry-thoughts—the way they scuttle over my brain and make me fear everything."

Mister Edwards shivered as if a million deadly arachnids were flooding the walls. "I'm not fond of them either. But I'd battle a million of them to protect those I love." They hit another dead end. Mister Edwards stood in the shadows, eyes glinting with the red moon's light. "To protect Mister Amoureux, Miss Meriwether, I would do anything."

"I understand," Annalise replied. Her cursed hand contorted painfully. Annalise clenched it tighter. "I'd do the same for my parents, to keep them from the Fate Spinner."

Without warning, Annalise's cursed hand sparked with fire and lunged for the fox's throat.

Mister Edwards ducked and ran around Annalise. "What are you doing?" he shrieked as Annalise fought for control.

But her monster was stronger than it used to be. "Stop," she cried at her cursed hand. "Leave him alone!" Mister Edwards backed away in fear. "I'm sorry," Annalise said, choking the black flames from her palm until they extinguished. "I think, maybe, the *thing* inside my hand doesn't want me to talk about *her*."

"Oh, that's—that's all right," the fox stuttered, keeping his distance. "Maybe we shouldn't speak about her, then."

Mister Edwards and Annalise started back up the corridor. "I do know she can hear us."

Annalise glared at her big hand and cursed the monster inside as they rounded the next bend. "My hand—it's getting worse. That's another one of my fears, actually." Annalise stroked her hair by fours. "Making a friend, only to hurt them with my curse."

Mister Edwards's eyes went wide. "Wait. Your bigger hand was *cursed?*"

"I'm afraid so." Annalise peeked at him from behind a curtain of hair.

He crept bravely forward. "A curse given by . . ." he whispered as if revelation just hit. *"The Fate Spinner herself?"*

"Sadly, yes." Annalise wrestled with her big hand under her cloak.

Mister Edwards mumbled under his breath, "Why would she curse you?" Then he cleared his throat and said louder, "I'm truly sorry to hear that."

Howls echoed close by—too close. They both stopped in their tracks.

"Night wolves," Annalise said. Which way were the cries coming from? The air cooled, frosting their breath. "They sound like they're everywhere."

Annalise had never wanted to believe the night wolves

belonged to the Fate Spinner—that they'd fallen through the sky at her birth. That would mean she was responsible for every person in Carriwitchet who'd died in their jaws. But now, she had a worrisome idea that the townsfolk had been right.

The howls of the night wolves closed in.

Mister Edwards kept his ears flat and his paw on the raw place where his other leg should be, and hurried faster and faster into the shadows. "Please, let's just keep going."

Annalise's stomach panged with hunger, her tongue felt made of sand, and she was sure Mister Edwards felt the same. Still, they raced ahead, stomachs grumbling and twisting in protest, and skidded around the next turn.

Dead end.

"Oh goodness," Mister Edwards said. "We must have gotten turned around. I'm sorry. Just when I think I know which way to go, the walls seem to change."

They'd have to go back. It felt like they'd be striving forward forever but never reaching the end. Annalise thought it very difficult indeed to keep chasing one's dream, with no guarantee of ever catching it.

Then, as they were about to turn around, a television screen pushed out of the ivy-strewn dead-end wall and zapped to life. "Good morning, good people of Carriwitchet," Penny

Fabius, with her frizzy red hair, thin lips, and vicious blue eyes, chirped. "Today in Carriwitchet, the air is rancid, the weather unfortunate, and the land stinking of blood." The newscaster held up her evil-eye talisman and glared at the screen. "But fair citizens of Carriwitchet, our own Richard Inglehart reports that the joyous rumors are true!" She blew a noisemaker. "At long last, the accursed child has run away for good!"

Cheers erupted in the background. Mister Edwards glanced sadly at Annalise. She looked away, not wanting to see the pity in his eyes.

"But that's not all. It seems the devil's parents"—Penny spat on the floor—"left right after her." A live-feed image of the Meriwether home appeared. The house had been burned to the ground. Only char, smoke, and the cage remained. Annalise stumbled backward, clutching her chest. "Join us for a party in the town square to celebrate our dream coming true. Stay tuned to Channel 7, the Eye on the Sky, for updated Meriwether reports." The television pushed back and vanished into the ivy and stone.

Tears, hot and horrible, dripped down Annalise's cheeks. Her parents *had* left.

Did they go after her on the strange train of wolves? Or did the townspeople chase them out? Or worse? Were her parents *dead*?

The wolves were getting closer, their cries hungrier. Annalise's gaze darted from the fox to the tops of the labyrinth walls.

"Miss Meriwether?"

She shook her head. "Please don't touch me."

Panic curled around and inside her like an old friend. She wanted to close her eyes, to fall, to hide. Walls on three sides, wolves and a fox in her path, her parents gone; Annalise heaved in breath after breath, body buzzing with a rubbery numbness. She twisted her braid, trying to count her worry-thoughts away. But her breath kept coming faster and her heart kept beating stronger until her fears scrambled like spiders over her brain. Until Annalise was a girl-shaped bundle of fear, pulsing at the edges of time and space, no trace of hopeful Annalise left.

"Miss Meriwether!"

Annalise could barely hear Mister Edwards over her scuttling spider-thoughts—so many that they blurred into a cacophony of sound. A sound that had weight, wrapped her body in ropes, and squeezed.

"Miss Meriwether!" Mister Edwards's voice echoed from far away. He said something else about walls and ivy and then screamed, desperate for her help.

Hang on.

Her friend needs help.

Annalise's panicked thoughts cleared at once.

"Mister Edwards?" Blood pumping with adrenaline, Annalise scanned the dim corridor. She couldn't see him. Annalise had the shakes but wasn't cold. "M-mister Edwards, answer me."

Thunder clapped. The ivy at her feet moved. Clouds sheathed the red-light moon. Annalise dropped to her knees, calling her friend's name.

No answer.

Her big hand shot forward and skimmed the labyrinth floor, searching for the black fox. "Mister Edwards, if you can hear me, answer!" Laughter fell from the sky on a cold wind. With it, familiar black hearts rained around her. Grazing her skin. Nesting in her hair. While batting them away, she heard something mutter from behind the ivy-strewn wall. Annalise drew nearer. An eye blinked from the vines in the dark. "Mister Edwards!" Her cursed hand lit with gold flames yet didn't hurt. She held it up to the wall to better see the fox. The ivy curled tighter around him. "Hold on!"

His fur was matted. Drops of blood dripped from his belly and arm. He struggled but couldn't escape. Twin vines, working like a spider's legs, wrapped his body in a web and dragged him up the wall. Annalise thrust her small hand into the ivy, ripping at the plants. "Save yourself," he mumbled before his face went slack and his eyes closed.

"No." Annalise pulled at the vines, steering clear of the sharp leaves. But the more she pulled, the tighter the vines squeezed. "Mister Edwards, you have to fight back—for your dream—for Mister Amoureux!"

At the mention of his Mister Amoureux, Mister Edwards's eyes popped open. He thrashed like he'd never thrashed before. He bled and hurt but didn't stop fighting. But it wasn't enough. The wall took him deeper and deeper. If she didn't do something to help him, she'd lose her only friend.

After losing Muse—twice—she would not let that happen.

Annalise considered using her big hand and the flames within, the currently sparking gold light reminding her of the poets of hope. Annalise hoped her big hand didn't hurt the fox this time as it had hurt so many others before. *Be good to him*, she asked her cursed hand. *He is my friend.* And Annalise thrust her burning big hand into the ivy after him.

Golden flames burst from Annalise's black mark in a *whoosh*. The ivy screamed like a hurt animal, curled inward, and died. Sparks of ash and flames coughed from the wall and spat Mister Edwards at her feet.

Annalise grinned with surprise.

Her plan had worked!

"Mister Edwards, are you okay?"

The fox lunged from a cloud of smoke and hugged Anna-lise. "Thank you," he half choked, half laughed, wiping blood from his mouth. "Thank you for rescuing me."

Whatever accursed thing lived within her left hand had saved Mister Edwards's life. She'd been unsure if it would help her, but she'd tried anyway.

Maybe I can use my big hand against the Fate Spinner, too. Use my curse to set myself free.

A livid scream swelled through the labyrinth, shaking the walls.

"The Fate Spinner," Mister Edwards growled.

Annalise's big hand seared. She clenched it tighter. "We're getting closer."

Mister Edwards smiled a bit sadly. "She's getting worried."

The clouds moved aside and undressed the moon. The labyrinth shone in bright ruby red. The dead end where the television had been rearranged itself. A small black-and-white-striped gate pushed through the charred ivy, bearing a sign that read: *The Gate of Panic.*

The view past the gate was darkness. A chill froze Anna-lise's blood to slush. "That doesn't sound good."

"No good whatsoever." Mister Edwards sniffed the gate,

then peered up at Annalise, face bloodied, body weakened, fur damp. "I've seen a gate like this before, Miss Meriwether. And if it leads to the place I think it does, I'm sorry, you're not going to like it."

The sounds of snarls, yips, growls, and claws skidding on stone exploded at their backs. When Annalise swung around and faced the moonlit corridor, night wolves galloped toward them, teeth gleaming, seconds away.

Panic made Annalise fast. She threw open the gate, grabbed Mister Edwards's paw, and crossed the threshold as four red-eyed wolves lunged into the dark after them.

Chapter 20

THE MYSTERIOUS REYNARD

Annalise slammed the Gate of Panic behind them. The fox toppled into her as the labyrinth sealed at their backs. Mister Edwards screamed as the four night wolves ran into the other side of the gate at full speed.

"Mister Edwards, are you okay?" It was so dark, Annalise could barely see. She got up and brushed herself off. Beyond the barred barrier, the night wolves snarled, barked, snapped, and cried.

"I'm here," Mister Edwards said behind her. "Those— those wolves. They almost got me." Annalise crawled toward him, following his eyes, bright as moons. "Thank you for saving me. Again."

The poor fox looked so guilty and ashamed, Annalise wanted to hug him. When she held out her arms, he fell gratefully into them. "Of course, Mister Edwards. But I should be thanking *you* for accompanying me." Annalise let him go. "You've helped me so much. Sometimes my panic and anxiety make me forget why I'm here. But you help me remember. And your love for Mister Amoureux reminds me of my own dream. You may not realize how important that is, but it's essential." Annalise stroked the four black ribbons atop her braid. "Helping you is my pleasure."

The black fox lowered his gaze. "Thank you, Miss Meriwether. I truly hope, in the end, all your dreams come true."

The night wolves' howls grew softer as they slunk back into the maze.

Instantly, the skies brightened, and light increased around them. They'd landed in a circle, no bigger than Annalise's kitchen, which opened onto four tunnels. The entrances weren't covered by doors or gates, but rather, were blocked by elaborate mirrors. Annalise glanced at each mirror in turn. Not only did she see her dirty, singed self, but also the long strange halls of infinity staring back. Mister Edwards hunkered on all threes, sniffing each entry, while Annalise studied them all.

To her left stood a mirror edged in gold. When she stepped before it, writing suddenly scrawled across the glass:

1: Everything You Cannot Have. A rising crescendo of hurt ripped through the black heart on her palm as the palace of the Spinner of Dreams appeared. Annalise instantly felt at peace until her cursed hand thrust from under her cloak and pressed to the mirror palm first. A pulse of heat shot up her arm and shocked her heart. A voice she didn't recognize spoke through the glass, *"Reynard, please, find her! I beg you, find her, and then—find me!"* Annalise pulled back her hand, palm smoking and burning, and tucked it away.

Mister Edwards rushed to her, gaze haunted. "What happened? Did you see something . . . frightening?"

Annalise nodded, trying to squelch the heat in her big hand.

"Yes," Mister Edwards said, grimly turning away. "I'm afraid there's plenty more of that to come."

The mirror to the right, framed in glittering black, read: 2: Demons at Your Heels. When Annalise stood before it, the autumnal scent of Carriwitchet wafted through the glass—of death, rot, cemeteries, yesterdays gone by. Nightingale and Bowie materialized, crying over their parents' graves. "Bring them back," Nightingale cried, facing Annalise. "You killed them. But if you come through the mirror, you can bring them back." Bowie placed his palms flat to the glass. "Please, Annalise. This is the right way. Don't trust . . . lead t . . .

dreams." His voice was breaking up, turning to static. ". . . Don't . . . t . . . the f . . ." His voice cut out.

Annalise's cursed hand flared in agony and punched the mirror, wanting to shatter their reflections. Annalise backed away, restraining her hand and shaking her head. "I'm so sorry—I can't help you." Annalise wasn't sure if what she was seeing was real or a trick of the labyrinth. Without Mister Edwards's expertise, without the book Muse had given her, how was she supposed to know what to believe or what to do?

The third entrance, edged in a black-and-red frame resembling reptilian scales, read: 3: There Be Dragons. The primitive screams of animals in battle drifted outward. Next came the slashing of talons and gnashing of teeth, followed by the stench of charred meat. When Annalise stood before the third mirror, her cursed hand stopped hurting and smoking, and gave a familiar zing. It pulled forward, and immediately, the Fate Spinner's red palace materialized in the glass. A white cat appeared on the other side of the mirror. Muse. He tipped his hat and winked at Annalise. When she waved back, Muse and the palace blinked from sight. In their place, an image of a golden dagger appeared for a snap, before it vanished too.

She thought back to the trees that spoke of legendary beasts and magical rewards. What if the dagger was one of the things she needed to find to help her to the end?

Mister Edwards paced in front of the fourth and final entrance. The oval mirror bore a frame carved from bone and read: 4: The Spinner of Fear. Again, Annalise's big hand whipped into a fury. Spiderwebs crossed the shattered black mark on her palm. Annalise screamed and shook them away. A reflection of the labyrinth rose in the glass. Her mom and dad ran through the corridors, calling her name. Giant white spiders the size of cars chased after them. "Annalise, where are you?" they cried. "We can't find you!" Their voices grew louder and louder as she gulped her breaths by fours.

Were these visions real? Or an illusion of the labyrinth?

What was she to believe?

Annalise observed the black fox, standing transfixed, fidgeting with his tail before the Spinner of Fear. "Mister Edwards," her voice shook. "What do you see in there?"

Mister Edwards gave the mirror a wide berth. "That path holds a nightmarish and deadly monster that I never wish to meet. Luckily, we don't have to go that way." He motioned to the mirror of dragons but didn't take his gaze off the first mirror. "Mirror three leads to path three, which leads to the end, I'm almost sure of it." He finally faced Annalise. "I can smell the dragon Mister Amoureux and I battled behind this very mirror. We were almost to Dreamland when we found it. But," he continued, a new level of horror on his face, "the Fate Spinner got to us first."

Caw-caw-caw-CAW!

Before Annalise could comment on her friend battling a dragon, Mister Edwards drifted back to the first mirror and mumbled under his breath, "If this way is wrong, why do I smell him so strongly through here?"

Suddenly, the stranger Annalise had heard crying out from the first mirror echoed through her mind: *"Reynard, please, find her!"*

Everything grew quiet. Annalise swore, in the sudden hush, her big hand whispered, *"Ask his given name."*

A rush of energy soared out from her dark mark.

Her cursed hand had spoken.

"What is it, Miss Meriwether?" Mister Edwards backed away from the first mirror, breathing fast.

Annalise clenched her cursed fist at her side—four times. "Mister Edwards? What is your given name?"

The fox's tail swished. He answered guarded and slow. "My first name is Reynard. Why do you ask?"

Reynard.

"Miss Meriwether," he asked quicker, desperately. "Did you hear something in one of the mirrors? It might be important!"

Annalise swallowed the burning pit in her throat. "I heard

someone calling your name through the first entrance."

Tears fringed the fox's eyes. He hurried back to mirror of *Everything You Cannot Have* and placed his ear to the glass. "You heard Mister Amoureux?" He laughed. "He *is* here!" He hugged Annalise tightly. "Nobody else calls me Reynard. But . . ." His joy slipped into worry. "We're supposed to take the mirror of dragons. That's the way to the end." Mister Edwards muttered, "Maybe he's right inside waiting for me? Maybe I don't have to . . ." Mister Edwards ran his paw over his ears. "Maybe we don't have to fight the dragon at all." He furrowed his brow and shook his head. "But if we don't go the right way, terrible things will happen, just like before." He paced. "What if it's a test? What if we fail and the Fate Spinner hurts Mister Amoureux? I'm scared to make the wrong decision." He sobbed angrily. "I'm scared of her!"

The Fate Spinner. It always came back to her.

Annalise knelt beside Mister Edwards as black crows screamed. "I am too. Mister Edwards, I'm scared of a lot of things." Annalise unclenched her fist. The tip of the spiraled black horn poked through more than an inch. Smoke curled up in a pale gold stream, swam into the entrance of dragons, and vanished.

Whether Mister Edwards took the first path or not, she needed to trust the signs pointing to mirror three.

"Mister Edwards, I think you were right the first time. I

206

think we need to go through the third mirror. I always choose the number four of things so I'm nervous, too. But," she said, stroking her hair, "the third path is the only one that didn't make my big hand lash out and burn with pain. And I don't know why, but maybe that means something." She glanced at him shyly. "Maybe the thing inside my big hand wants us to beat the labyrinth, too. Maybe it can help us beat her. It did help save you earlier."

Mister Edwards sighed. "You're right. It does seem to be looking out for us. And we know we can't trust anything on the Path of Illusion." He nodded and stood. "Going through the mirror of dragons will get us to Dreamland." He glanced wistfully at the first entrance, then nodded. "Yes. We should stick with the plan."

Annalise released a held breath. "I couldn't agree more."

The two stood before mirror three, side by side. Mister Edwards held his head higher, more confidently. He leaned closer to her and whispered, "The Fate Spinner made a mistake leading me to you. And if she's angry about us taking her on together?" He snarled, "So be it."

Laughter gusted through the glass before them on fiery winds. Annalise's hair whipped in ribbons of purple, Mister Edwards's fur blew this way and that.

The bitter stink of char and smoke wafting out from inside the mirror stung Annalise's nose. The cries and screams of the dragons thumped the glass, walls, floor. Worry-thoughts swarmed, trying to suck her confidence away.

You're going to fail.

Die.

Burn.

The dragons will rip you apart—

Stop.

Annalise clenched her big fist and remembered her dream: *I wish to rule my own destiny and rid myself of this curse.* Then she put on a brave smile for the trembling fox. "Please, after you."

White crows appeared and cawed comfortingly high overhead.

The glass before them thinned to a curtain of smoke. Mister Edwards regarded her nervously but walked through the entrance head high. And Annalise followed.

As she stepped through the smoky veil, a shimmer of magic caught her eye. The writing on the mirror had changed.

There Be Dragons morphed into The Spinner of Fear. Annalise had just enough time to think *the labyrinth tricked us* before the Fate Spinner's voice, so loud it rattled the earth, howled, "Inside the Path of Illusion, nothing is as it seems!"

The Fate Spinner's laughter followed them to the other side.

Chapter 21

THE SPIDER TAKES THE FOX

The red moon had tucked itself behind clouds, the world darkened to cinnamon and black. Annalise couldn't see her hand in front of her, and the air was as thick as earth. She stumbled forward, feeling her way.

In the silence, screams of agony echoed from someplace below the labyrinth. Tiny sounds followed. The scuttling of many-legged creatures scraped by her feet in the dark.

Only one thing makes that sound, Annalise thought. A thing with too many eyes and legs and fangs, like her dark worry-thoughts. A thing like—

Spiders.

"Mister Edwards?" The scurrying grew louder. Her skin

ignited with squirming nerves desperate to run. She scanned for any sign of spiders or her friend, but it was too dark to see. *This is wrong. You've gone the wrong way. Go back!* Annalise turned, hand out, searching for the way they'd entered, and felt solid wall.

The entrance had already sealed.

Tiny legs brushed past her ankles. Annalise jumped. She cried out and darted ahead through the blackness, almost too heavy to move.

"Mister Edwards!" The scraping and scuttling grew louder and more numerous. Things squirmed in her hair. She sprinted faster, shaking her arms and body and batting around her head.

"Mister Edwards. WHERE ARE YOU?"

Annalise ran, arms out, straight into a wall. Both hands broke her fall. And both flared in pain.

Cradling her hands at her chest, Annalise staggered right. Whispers of tiny monsters rushed past her feet. Suddenly her big hand throbbed with sharp lashings of pain—each step forward made it hurt even more. "Mister Edwards!"

Then softly, "Miss Meriwether?"

"Mister Edwards?" Annalise skidded to a halt.

"I can't see you!" He sounded frantic and too far away. "The Fate Spinner tricked us. She—" His voice cut off at the end.

"Tell me where you are." Annalise rushed along the slippery, moss-covered corridor, following his voice. The stones got slipperier and slipperier; the horned creature below her dark mark stretched and grew.

"Something's got me—" He sounded closer. "Keep going—you'll find the mirror . . . I'm . . ." He screamed. "Hurry!"

Breathing heavy with adrenaline, Annalise pitched ahead in the rusty dark, chasing his voice, until she couldn't run anymore.

Gauzy strings dangled from above—sliding over her face, sticking in her hair. The farther she drew up the corridor, the thicker the strings became.

Webs. The word spun through her mind.

"Mister Edwards?" Water dripped somewhere close by. The damp tang of swamp clung to her skin. Annalise gulped and licked her lips; she'd never been so parched or famished in her life. "Mister Edwards, keep talking so I can follow your voice."

"You're almost there." He sounded so close, but she still couldn't see him.

Annalise brushed sticky webbing from her clothes. The pulse of the beast in her hand quickened and thrashed. "I'm coming, Mister Edwards—hang on!"

The red moon suddenly returned to the sky. A pink blush

illuminated the corridor. Annalise found herself at another dead end. And there, strung up in the shadows against the hundred-foot wall, was the largest spiderweb Annalise had ever seen.

"Mercy," Annalise said as her heart sped and as too many yellow eyes opened in the dark.

An enormous spider the size of a car, half in moonlight, half in shadow, moved forward atop a gargantuan silver-rose web. Her body—like the ones she'd seen in the mirror, chasing her parents through the maze—was pure white. The spider's legs moved swiftly in the shadows, spinning something Annalise couldn't see. Annalise's heart slapped her bones hard, again and again. She wanted to cry. To quit and go home. To wake up from this nightmare in the arms of her parents, in a world where they were safe and sound. But until she finished what she started, her world would never change. And if that meant fighting this monster to beat the Fate Spinner, so be it.

But where was Mister Edwards?

"Greetings," the spider hissed from the shadows. Her voice was warm and inviting, like a mother's, like a friend's. Annalise's marked hand burned and pulled forward. She had to restrain it before it got her killed. "I know who you are," the goliath cooed. "Your name is Annalise."

The beast pushed her head and front legs into the red moonlight. She wasn't an ordinary spider but a skeleton, made of mirrors and bones. She had slim multi-jointed legs—many, many legs. Her shell bore not a hint of hair. Her hollow skull-eyes held mirrors, each reflecting a frightened Annalise. At the bone spider's feet, the meal she'd been spinning came to light.

Held between her skeletal front legs was a lifeless, three-legged black fox. "Mister Edwards!" His tongue lolled from his muzzle; his eyes wide, stared blankly, unconscious. Annalise stiffened. She forced herself to take four steps forward. "What are you doing with my friend?"

I need to free him, but how?

I wish I had the Book of Remembering!

The spider's mandibles snapped. "That is the wrong question," she said with a grin. The spider's breath stank of carcasses too long in the sun. "Ask the right question, and maybe I won't suck your friend dry—*yet*." Spin, spin, spin, spin. "Here's a hint to get you started. I knew your grandparents once. Shame, don't you think, what happened to them?"

My grandparents? Annalise grazed the four ribbons on her braid.

They'd left on a train. *Did they end up here, too?*

"How do you know my grandparents?" Annalise asked the bone spider. Its mirrored eyes drew closer, staring straight through her soul. "Did the Fate Spinner put you up to this?"

"Delightful," the bone spider hissed, scuttling down from her web. Annalise took several steps back. "Those are the right questions." A creeping grin slipped up her skull as she wrapped the fox's face in another layer of silver webbing. "I shall answer your last question first." Spin, spin, spin, spin. "The Fate Spinner cannot control me but *does* know I rather enjoy trapping deliciously plump little foxes." Its mirrored eyes flashed. "And those who think themselves *better* than their given fates."

The spire beneath Annalise's dark mark pushed against her skin. Her monster had helped her before, and Annalise felt it wanted to help her now. *Not yet,* she whispered in the quiet of her mind, hoping her horned monster heard her.

Her black mark zinged in reply.

Annalise hid a smile, counted to four, and forced herself to meet the spider's eyes. "I feel everyone deserves a chance to figure their fate out for themselves, don't you?"

The spider sprang forward, mandibles snapping a foot away from Annalise's nose. "I can see right through you, Annalise! You're a child. Too weak for this labyrinth. Too kind to sacrifice this useless fox to get to your dreams. Too

214

sentimental to accept the offer I'm about to make you."
Annalise wanted to run from the terror before her but forced
herself to stand. And after the right number of seconds, the
beast finally moved.

The spider hung the cocoon holding Mister Edwards like
a decoration from the top of her web, dangling in the pale
ruby light. The air pushed in close—thick enough to taste:
moss, humidity, death, the sudden chill of ghosts.

"What sort of offer?" Annalise asked.

The spider grinned. "I will return the black fox to you
and let you pass. But, you must give *me* something in return."

Pulse whipping a fury through her veins, Annalise forced
her gaze from poor Mister Edwards and onto the spider.
"What would you want?" Annalise asked.

The spider gestured one long, thin leg toward Annalise's
hidden big hand. "Something you don't want anyway," she
hissed. "Your cursed hand."

Night wolves howled inside the labyrinth, always just out
of sight.

They'd wanted her big hand, too.

Annalise's black mark seared angrily. She assured the
creature hidden behind it that it was almost time. "What do
you want with my curse?"

"Wrong question." The spider toyed with Mister

215

Edwards's cocoon. "I, too, am a prisoner of fate. I can't answer that question, same as I can't rip the hand from your body and suck the life from it, as I'd like to." She snapped her mandibles and perched them before the cocoon. "I'd crumble to dust if I tried, thanks to the old magic governing the labyrinth. So, if you do not surrender your large hand willingly, you will go no farther and you'll never see your friend again. That is my price."

Movement from Mister Edwards's cocoon caught Annalise's attention. His front paw slipped from the webbing and flexed. He was alive!

A thrill of power shot through Annalise from her dark mark to her heart. All of her seemed to electrify. She'd never felt so powerful and brave. "And if I refuse?"

The spider pinched her mandibles hard against the cocoon. Mister Edwards screamed, then wilted like a dying black rose. "The fox is mine." Snow-tipped mountains, blue sky, caves, and seas reflected in her ocular mirrors. "You're not the only one with dreams, you know. I've always wanted to travel. To live a life of peace in a distant land. And if I give your cursed hand to the Fate Spinner"—Annalise's big palm jerked forward like a dog on a chain; Annalise held it back—"I'll be granted freedom from this prison of fate." The bone spider left Mister Edwards and faced Annalise. "From one dreamer to another, let me take your curse off your hands and set your beloved Mister Edwards free. What say you, ill-fated child? Do we have an accord?"

Annalise tapped her leg by fours, remembering the kindnesses of the fox, the first in her history to truly be her friend. She thought about how she'd feel betraying him, leaving him to die. She couldn't do it. That wasn't her. Not only that, but she'd never reach the labyrinth's end.

The spider clicked her bone legs on the stone floor. Her mirrored eyes narrowed onto Annalise. "Choose, Miss Meriwether." The spider salivated and moved inches from Annalise's cursed hand. "My hunger for dreams grows."

"No." Annalise took a few steps back, stomach churning. "I won't surrender my hand or the life of my friend, and I won't dishonor or surrender our dreams by giving in to you and the Fate Spinner."

She knew what she had to do.

"If that's what you want," the beast growled, engorging to her full height—twice as tall as before. The bone spider shrieked, "May the best Spinner win!"

Annalise shouted to her cursed hand in the quiet of her mind, *now!* and thrust her big hand from her cloak. Fire flared from her marked palm. The sharp spire ripped free, longer than ever.

And the bone spider lunged forward to bite.

Annalise gripped the spider's front leg; her horn stabbed straight through. Power flooded through her hand—big and bright as angels, sizzling with golden light. The spider shrieked and thrashed her legs, tossing Annalise into the air.

Then Annalise let go.

"How dare you!" the thing shouted in warbled speech as Annalise crashed to the ground. The stench of burnt skeleton filled the cavern-like room. The spider's bone feet smacked the ground around her so hard, each strike cracked the stone.

Annalise dodged while whispering to the one within her big hand: *Now show me what else you can do!*

Annalise darted around the enormous spider after Mister Edwards, dangling from the web. Hundreds of tiny skull-and-bone spiders scuttled over the walls after her. Another shock of power surged through her black mark, followed by a stream of gold flames. The swarm of spiders screamed but didn't stop coming. Annalise spun in a circle, aiming the fire-blast at the unnatural beasts until they scuttled over the wall, exoskeletons ablaze.

The giant spider hissed, raised her front legs, and jumped through a cloud of flames. Annalise watched the giantess fly toward her in slow motion. In each of the giantess's mirrored eyes, Annalise saw the Fate Spinner's face grinning back at her. Annalise glared and took aim. "I guess," Annalise shouted, not unkindly, "the best Spinner is me." And with one clean shot, Annalise blew the giant bone spider away.

Seconds before the poor creature crumbled to dust, her mirror eyes reflected blue skies and mountains, caves and seas of faraway lands. Annalise watched respectfully as the spider's dreams went up in flames. "I'm sorry you didn't get your dream," Annalise told the sad beast with remorse, and reined in her flame. "Wherever you are, I wish you peace."

The spider's spirit rose from her ashes. No longer a beast of mirror and bone, the giant was covered in golden fur and had lovely dark eyes. "Thank you for freeing me," the spider's spirit said. "Not in the way I'd imagined, but a better one—a freedom outside of fate. Enjoy your reward, dreamer. I was going to gift you a truth but felt you needed this more."

Lying atop the spider's bone dust rested an item illuminated in gold. Annalise hurried over and grabbed it, grinning from ear to ear.

The bone spider had found her lost book.

"This book is the first of three magical items hidden within the labyrinth that will help guide you toward the labyrinth's end. When next you open this binding, clues to an ancient mystery will be revealed. And when you pass through the door after the next, a memory will return you'll need to survive. Fight well, Warrior of Dreams. And may the magic of dreams be yours." The spider's spirit vanished in a burst of sheer golden light.

With a shy, proud sort of grin, Annalise slipped *The Book of Remembering* into her cloak pocket and scrambled to the top of the web. She sliced Mister Edwards free and climbed down with him cradled in her arms.

The black fox she'd come to love hung limp against her. He wasn't moving or breathing. "Mister Edwards, wake up!"

Suddenly, the spiderweb blocking the dead end shriveled and disappeared, revealing a small door painted in rainbow glitter. Upon it scrolled four words: *The Room of Secrets*.

"Stay with me, Mister Edwards. Something wonderful is inside, I can feel it."

Chapter 22

A FEAST FIT FOR A QUEEN

The fox out cold in her arms, Annalise shouldered open the door and crawled inside. The second Annalise entered, the small door vanished in a *whoosh* of black flame. Gone were the stone blocks of the labyrinth, the sharp-leafed ivy, the red moon, the dark, the grim. Annalise found herself in a sunlit room the height and length of a couch. Four tiny doors on each side were decorated with mirrors of shimmering gold, though they reflected nothing within. A floor of lush grass below, a skylight framing a lilac sky above, the room was so short that Annalise could barely sit up straight. But it felt safe.

She'd won back her lost book.

But it would have to wait.

Mister Edwards squirmed in her arms.

Annalise set the white bundle holding her friend on the grass and broke through the sticky web of the bone spider's cocoon. His sleek black fur stuck up willy-nilly. Sticky threads clung to his eyes, sewing his lashes together and webbing his ears shut. Annalise cleared them while counting to four.

"Mister Edwards, can you hear me?"

No answer, no breath, no sound.

The poor fox lay slack on the grass, front paw bleeding, one of his claws shorn free. Annalise stroked his forehead, smoothing the downy fur at his ears until slowly he came around.

"What happened?" he asked, squinting around the brightly lit room.

Annalise grinned and pulled him into a hug. "You're okay! Mister Edwards, you're okay!"

He sat up on his own and regarded her with gratitude, and a sheepish sort of love. "I am, thanks to you." A pale purple sun ray drenched him in light. "What is this place? I've never seen it before."

Annalise twisted uncomfortably and glanced up at the window. "I'm not sure where we are, but it feels safe, don't you think?" Her big hand smoldered outside her cloak. When she caught him staring, she blushed and hid it away. "What happened to you, Mister Edwards? How did the bone spider get you?"

He shivered, ears flat to his head. "The walls must have switched on us. When I stepped through the mirror, the spider was waiting for me. I tried fighting it off. Mister Amoureux and I had beaten something like it before, but I couldn't do it alone. I tried calling you, but you didn't hear me." He shook his head and stared at his broken claw. "I thought reaching the end of the labyrinth would be easier this time, but clearly I was mistaken. I'm sorry, Miss Meriwether, for not being a better guide."

"And I wish I could have gotten to you sooner." Annalise stroked her long blackberry hair, some of which was burnt. "The path to one's dreams isn't always all it seems, is it?"

The fox hung his head and closed his eyes. "No, it certainly is not." He stroked the sticky fur of his tail. "Look, Miss Meriwether, I need to tell you something. Something I should have told you long ago. I—"

A wisp of onyx smoke puffed out from the mirror facing east. Four words blossomed on the gold glass in curling black script: There Be Dragons (Honest).

"Mercy," Annalise said with a sigh. "The entrance that tricked us earlier is back."

A new level of horror on the fox's face, he mumbled, "I

don't know if I'm ready to face what awaits us there. . . ."

"Mister Edwards," Annalise cried excitedly when another mirror image swam into view. "Food!"

The golden mirror door to the south resembled the front counter of an old-world bakery. Bixx-cakes with whipped caramel frosting under glass. Mugs of autumn-spiced pumpkin tea with savory curls of steam. Puffed rolls stuffed with avocado, pimiento, and cucumber on white china plates. Cubes of black anise cheese speared with toothpicks, and pink lemonade in a pitcher dripping with cool-water sweat.

A feast fit for a queen.

Practically drooling, Annalise pressed her small hand to the glass. When she did, the mirror shouted back. "There is a key!" the mirror declared in a screech. "You have exactly four seconds to use it properly. GO."

Annalise and Mister Edwards stared at each other agape. *A key?*

What key?

One second.

A voice whispered from inside her big hand, "The thing that sets you apart."

Two seconds.

Mercy. Did my cursed hand just answer me?

Three seconds.

My big hand. Not everyone has a big hand!

A black cupboard-like hole opened in the glass, big as a bread box.

Four seconds.

Annalise whipped her cursed hand from her cloak and stuck it inside. Her dark mark prickled and tingled and zinged, and then—

"Ahhhh," the mirror sighed. "It *is* you. . . ."

Heart flapping like a manic bat, Annalise removed her big hand from the opening and stroked her still tingling cursed palm.

Again, her big hand had helped her.

Thank you, she thought to her monster. *Very much . . .*

An overwhelming and sudden remorse filled Annalise for having wanted her big hand gone the same way everyone had always wanted *her* gone. For hating it as her town hated her. For fearing it as Annalise had always feared her curse.

The broken black heart on her palm warmed but said nothing more.

Annalise thought of her cursed hand a bit differently after that. Less of a cursed big hand and more like a great one.

Sweet scents wafted toward them from the dark space in the mirror. Annalise and Mister Edwards drooled. "And now," the mirror said, "you may feast!"

A shelf holding two plates loaded with mouthwatering food drew forth. Annalise had been ravenous for hours. She and the fox almost cried.

"Oh-my-glop," Annalise mumbled with an overstuffed mouth. "This ish ermazerng." Her great hand felt no pain. She and Mister Edwards were racing toward their dreams. Though she did worry for her parents, and feel anxious about those suffering in Carriwitchet, in this moment, Annalise was happy.

Mister Edwards shoved cupcakes and fancy sandwiches into his muzzle like nobody's business, his eyes swirls of hypnotic joy. He sloshed down the raspberry lemonade and passed it to Annalise with a burp. "Pardon me," the fox said with a bashful grin.

Annalise bowed. "You are forever pardoned, good sir."

The two laughed and ate and burped until they were full—until they'd swallowed their last bites and sips, and the skylight dimmed overhead.

The room submerged in sudden twilight.

Annalise and Mister Edwards turned to each other, still licking their lips, and then scanned the miniature room. Of the four gold-glass mirrors, only the one that read There Be Dragons (Honest) had conjured a view. The glass reflected a wide corridor, and inside the corridor, she spotted her cat—Muse.

"Do you see my dream cat, Mister Edwards?" Annalise gestured toward the light. "Just there."

The fox shook his head and turned away. "No. I see only . . . fear. But whatever you see, I trust you. I suspect you may know the way to Dreamland better than I." He smiled with a desperate sadness Annalise wished she could take away.

It's hard to love a friend, Annalise thought. To wish so hard that their dreams came true only to watch them suffer again and again.

Annalise hoped, with whatever power she possessed, that she and her friend both found their dreams at the labyrinth's end.

A roar from behind the eastern mirror shook the walls, red ash puffed out through the glass. Muse tipped his hat to Annalise. When she waved back, he disappeared, just like he'd done before.

"Um, Miss Meriwether?" Mister Edwards said, gaping at Annalise's cloak. "There seems to be something rather *glowing* in your pocket?"

The book. She'd forgotten about her reward!

When Annalise pulled *The Book of Remembering* from her pocket, it lit the room in a sunny glow. "The book I lost," Annalise said, her face bathed in soft light "The magical one my dream cat gave me I never thought I'd see again."

Mister Edwards leaned over and squinted anxiously at the light. "A book, Miss Meriwether? Is it very tiny?"

She narrowed her eyes. "You really don't see it?"

The black fox rubbed his paw over his forehead. "No. All I see is light."

"How strange," Annalise said before images bloomed on the page.

The king and queen, the parents of the Spinners of Fate and Dreams, reappeared. The dark-skinned king wore a cloak of white feathers and a crown of crows and wolves. The pale queen, dressed in a red velvet cloak and a crown the same as her husband's, smiled up at her. Something came undone in Annalise's chest.

They reminded her of her parents.

Annalise's great hand pulled toward them. Her dark mark sparked flecks of gold, which skittered across the pages. As the magic melted into the book, the king and queen spoke:

"We are lost somewhere in this labyrinth," Queen Saba said. They stood inside a great courtyard before two elaborate thrones.

"Find us," continued King Noll, "and you will be rewarded with items that have been lost with us for thousands of years."

"Items you will need to defeat our daughter of fate and find our daughter of dreams."

"Set us free," King Noll continued, "and your enemy will fall."

"Good luck, child of dreams," Queen Saba said with gentleness warm and rare.

They bowed. "And may the magic of dreams be yours."

The book snapped shut. The glow fell away. Annalise stared at the fox expectantly. But he still appeared confused.

"Did the magical book show you something?" He worried the fur on his tail. "Because it looks like you saw something *surprising.* And if that something was about me, I'd like a chance to explain."

Reeling from what the king and queen had told her, Annalise almost hadn't heard him. She returned the enchanted book to her pocket and furrowed her brow. "What do you mean, Mister Edwards?"

The fox sighed and brushed his paw over his stump. "Before we go, I need to tell you something. Something I'm not proud to admit, but must get off my ch—"

A rumble wrenched the room. Immediately, the walls began closing in.

If they didn't leave now, they'd be squished.

"Tell me later, Mister Edwards," Annalise said. "We need to go."

A twinge of electric excitement pierced her great hand.

On instinct, Annalise pressed her shattered black heart to the mirrored door that read, There Be Dragons (Honest).

The glass dissolved into golden smoke, and a dim entrance appeared.

"Yes. Later," the fox said, as the room folded with a *pop* behind them.

Chapter 23

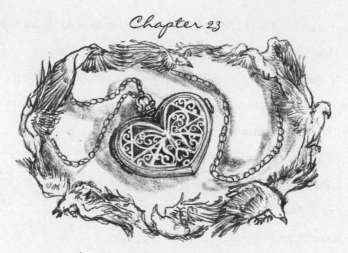

ANNALISE BATTLES A DRAGON

Somewhere ahead were dragons.

As Annalise and Mister Edwards squeezed out the small door of the Room of Secrets, her reward for besting the giant bone spider slipped from Annalise's pocket. She grasped *The Book of Remembering* before it fell.

At the binding's touch, the second -half of Annalise's reward came. A memory from years earlier replayed in Annalise's mind in vivid detail, as she and Mister Edwards stepped into the light. . . .

"How many types of dragons are out there, Grandpa Hugo?"

Annalise asked. A book of dragons lay open before them as she sat in his lap: Horrific Mythological Beasts through the Ages.

"Until the Fate Spinner stole them all for herself? There were so many, the world was overrun with them," her grandfather answered.

"Mercy." Annalise blinked in surprise.

"This one is a water dragon—a Hydra. See all its heads?" Annalise nodded gravely. "When those trying to defeat it cut one off, two more grew in its place."

Annalise gasped.

"Oh, and see this one." Grandpa Hugo pointed to a dragon with spiked wings, red eyes, dark feathers, and a razor-like beak. "That type of dragon is a cockatrice. It has a magical gaze that turns enemies to stone, and it has only one weakness. Within the silver spike at the tip of its tail lies its heart. One blow with a strong enough weapon will take it down. However, if the silver spike cuts you, you will turn to glass and shatter, and your spirit will be trapped in Fate's labyrinth forever."

Annalise placed her small hand on her grandfather's cheek and peered into his tincture-black eyes. "Why do such dangerous creatures exist, Grandpa Hugo?"

Her grandfather smiled. "So brave girls like you can grow up and tame them."

Annalise shrank against his warm-sweatered chest and clenched her cursed hand tight. "Do you think . . . someone like me could ever do such great things?"

"Oh," her grandfather replied. "I think you're just the girl for the job. The perfect candidate for greatness is often the one who feels least qualified." He patted her big hand with love. "Never doubt your greatness, Annalise. You are the very definition of the word."

As Annalise emerged into a familiar red light, her memory faded. She and Mister Edwards stood in a sprawling courtyard of gray stone. Black-bladed ivy twined the walls. The scent of smoke clung to the air, burning Annalise's lungs. The sky was as dark as death's shroud, the winds cold, cruel, and disturbed. In the distance, the Fate Spinner's palace rose sharp as stalagmites, glowing ruby against the night.

Directly before them, crumbling quartz statues littered the courtyard in various states of disarray. Sculptures of animals, women, children, and men; their pained and fearful faces pointed helplessly at the red moon. Studying the lifelike statues, the memory of Grandpa Hugo and the dragons returned.

He'd mentioned how the cockatrice turned its victims to stone.

Mercy, Annalise thought, when she realized the memory of her grandfather was the second half of the bone spider's reward. The memory was a clue. They wouldn't be confronting just any ordinary dragon. They'd landed in the den of a cockatrice. A cockatrice that turned its victims to stone.

Annalise made a silent vow to the stone dreamers before them, lost on the way to their dreams: *If I reach the labyrinth's end, I'll ask the Spinner of Dreams to break the cockatrice's spell and bring you back to life.*

No, not if—when.

Mister Edwards darted from statue to statue with tears in his eyes as if searching for a familiar face. Annalise wondered if he'd lost other loved ones to the Fate Spinner's maze? Friends or family who'd left seeking a dream and never made it home? Annalise hoped that whoever Mister Edwards was searching for wasn't here but somewhere safe and happy, living their greatest dream.

Annalise turned her focus to the twin thrones near the far wall and suddenly remembered what the book showed her about the Spinner King and Queen. *"We are lost somewhere in this labyrinth,"* Queen Saba said. *"Find us,"* continued King Noll, *"and you will be rewarded with items that have been lost with us for thousands of years."*

"Items you will need to defeat our daughter of Fate and find our daughter of Dreams."

"Set us free," King Noll continued, *"and your enemy will fall."*

Maybe one of the items they needed was here?

An enormous mirrored door hung on the wall directly

ahead, glittered with falling snow.

Another to the left cascaded with endless black feathers.

The towering wall to the right had no mirror, only a yawning black entrance resembling the mouth of a cave, pluming with dark crimson smoke. The cockatrice must be inside that cave.

"Mister Edwards?" Annalise's pulse rose to a soaring crescendo. "You mentioned this place before, didn't you?"

The fox, tail looped between his legs, studied the mirrorless arch. "I did."

The courtyard trembled. The blocks surrounding them shook.

"And we're nearing the labyrinth's end?"

"Yes. We're three-quarters through the labyrinth." He faced her and trembled something fierce. "Prepare, Miss Meriwether, for the battle of your life."

BOOM-BOOM-BOOM-BOOM.

Footsteps pounded toward them. A shriek ripped through the air. Fire roared from the darkened entrance, and a twenty-foot cockatrice emerged.

The dragon had black-feathered wings. A forked tongue slithered from its sharply curved beak. Spikes the length of Annalise's legs lined the sides of its body, crown, and throat. It moved carefully toward them in a blaze of fire and smoke.

"Don't look it in the eye!" Mister Edwards shouted, pointing at the statues. "It'll turn you into one of *them*." She'd never seen him so scared.

Annalise moved in front of the fox, blocking his way from the beast. "I know, Mister Edwards. Stay behind me. I'll keep you safe."

The traumatized fox resumed his place at her side. "No. I'm really scared after what happened last time I was here, but you've done enough for me already. I—I want to fight."

"Okay." She grinned nervously. "Then we fight together."

Annalise focused on the cockatrice's lower half as the dragon pounded forward, wings flared, talons scraping stone. She couldn't see its eyes, and with its eyes, its intentions.

When would it strike?

A thick slime of dread slipped down her spine. The horn in her great hand had yet to show, and no fire had gathered in her dark mark.

Where was her power?

Where was her monster now that she needed it?

If her great hand didn't help fight, what would she do?

There weren't enough fours in the cosmos to count her panic away completely. Still, Annalise removed her great hand from her cloak, aimed it at the dragon, and mentally recited her dream.

I wish to rule my own destiny and rid myself of this curse!

Annalise and Mister Edwards ducked behind the statues of two children holding hands. The cockatrice lifted into the air, flapping its colossal wings and roaring flames. "How did you beat the cockatrice last time?" Annalise asked, ducking from a rain of cinders.

"I had Mister Amoureux with me," Mister Edwards squeaked, peering around the statue. "He's an expert marksman. He blinded one of its eyes with a shard of quartz. An exit opened, and . . . we managed to escape."

The cockatrice obliterated the statue before them with one swipe of its wing. Annalise grabbed Mister Edwards's paw and jerked him toward the mirror of snow. The cockatrice swung around and lunged as they ran toward the winter glass.

"How did you escape?" Annalise shouted over the dragon's roar. "Maybe we can get its other eye and leave the same way?" They dodged another round of fire and hid behind the black throne.

"No!" Mister Edwards stared fearfully at the mirror raining black feathers. "That dark door led to . . . to—Oh, Mister Amoureux . . ." Mister Edwards cried, reliving his worst experience.

Annalise needed to stop running and get them out of here.

She locked eyes on the dragon's tail. *Within the silver spike at the tip of its tail lies its heart,* Grandpa Hugo had said. *One blow with a strong enough weapon will take the dragon down.*

Its tail was the key.

The cockatrice rushed forward, shooting flames. Annalise and Mister Edwards jumped back, patting cinders from their hair and fur. The dragon pinned them against the mirror of white. They were trapped.

If the dragon roared now, they would burn.

Suddenly, Mister Edwards darted forward and around the dragon, scooping up shards of quartz, screaming like a warrior through angry tears. "Get away from my friend!" He pitched stones at the cockatrice, aiming for its eye. The dragon shrieked and whipped its tail straight at them.

In a wild burst of heat, the horn twisted through Annalise's great hand. A zing of power radiated through her mark—whatever lived within her was awake and ready to fight.

Annalise sprinted to her friend and shouted—to the cockatrice and perhaps to the one in her great hand, "I wish to rule my own destiny and rid myself of this curse, so show me what you've got!"

She thrust her great hand toward at what she hoped was the cockatrice's face. A blast of golden flame surged from her dark mark. The cockatrice shrieked and stumbled backward. A shock of hot wind exploded from the dragon as its cry drew farther away.

This was her chance.

Eyes low, Annalise ran at the cockatrice. When it flung its tail forward, she grabbed for the tip holding its silver heart—but missed. The cockatrice roared a stream of red flame and whipped a wing at Annalise.

"Miss Meriwether—look out!" Mister Edwards jumped toward her too late.

The dagger-sharp claw of the dragon's wing sliced into Annalise's great hand.

Her vison wavered. Dark blotches bloomed in her eyes. The monster in her great hand writhed. Breathing fast, mind frothy with poison and panic, Annalise forced herself up on shaking legs and leveled her horn at the cockatrice. "We are dreamers," Annalise shouted. "And we will never surrender our dreams!"

The cockatrice thrust forward with a booming screech, but Annalise and her monster were ready.

Gold lightning blasted in a fury from the tip of her horn, obliterating the dragon's fire with her own. Black spots obscuring her vision, Annalise shot again, striking the dragon's right wing. The cockatrice howled and blew backward in

ART TK

an epic boom, striking the black mirror. Glass shattered out in a spray. The cockatrice cried humanlike whimpers of pain. When it fell, it did not rise.

Mister Edwards cheered. And Annalise fell to the ground.

"Miss Meriwether!" Mister Edwards helped Annalise up, gaping at her great hand. "Oh dear. You were cut?"

Annalise's vision swam in and out of focus. She was dizzy and disoriented. "I'm afraid so." Blood dripped from a gash across the knuckles of her great hand and dripped to the stone. Annalise and Mister Edwards blinked at her blood, transfixed.

Her blood was gold. And each place it dripped, shadowshine berry trees sprouted and grew. *Shadowshines—said to be a gift from the Spinner of Dreams.*

Up through the floor shadowshines rose, between the statues of quartz and bricks, fat with black-and-gold berries, yet bearing no thorns. Soon, the courtyard looked like an enchanted forest.

But how had these trees come from her?

And why was her blood gold?

Woozy, Annalise's legs dropped out from under her, but Mister Edwards caught her before she fell. "I've got you, Miss Meriwether," he said, little fires smoldering in his fur. "And I'm not letting go."

Annalise decided then: no matter what happened from here, Annalise loved the little fox for life.

Blobs of darkness pooled in Annalise's vision. Her body went numb.

Her world faded away and another appeared.

Chapter 24

FROM POISON AND DREAMS

Inside her poisoned delirium, a dream expanded around Annalise like a living entity. In the world behind her eyelids, she stood at the beginning of a long hallway of black doors. All were closed but one.

A ray of sunlight beamed inward from the door at the end. Through it, a lilac sky glowed. A crowd milled about on green grass. A delicate spring perfume blew toward her, drawing Annalise forward. When she started toward the crowd, they parted like a sea of colored dust, revealing a large table, with name tags on each fancy plate.

This is the place. The one Mom said was waiting for me through the door to my dreams.

The crowd raised their drinks and waved Annalise forward, welcoming her. No one was running away. Her dreams were close enough to taste.

Without warning, her great hand stabbed through with pain, the door slammed, and a dark mirror rose in its place.

The Fate Spinner's face appeared in the glass. "You think you're better than me," the white-haired enchantress growled through lips black as her soul. "Such vanity to think you're stronger than fate. You're just a broken child with an ugly hand, banging on the door of a dream that will *never let you in*."

Annalise glanced at her great hand, the one that made her strange—the one that made her powerful. "You're wrong," Annalise replied with a smile. "Thanks to the life you gave me, I've grown used to darkness, monsters, panic, and pain. Maybe the power I've gained will get me through anything. For that, I thank you, Fate Spinner." Annalise stared into the black eyes of Fate and saw her true self looking back. "Perhaps the hardness of my life is just what I need to achieve my dreams."

"You won't escape me," the Fate Spinner snarled, glaring at Annalise's great hand. "And when I finally get rid of you, everything you love will die, too."

A voice rose from inside the horn.

Her poison runs through us, it whispered. *Breathe deeply and wake.*

A flash of fear crossed the Fate Spinner's dark eyes. Black licorice and lemon perfumed the air before the Fate Spinner vanished in a whirl of black smoke.

And, from the other side of the hall, Mister Edwards called Annalise's name.

Chapter 25

A SECRET. A STORY. A TRUTH.

Annalise gasped in a deep breath and woke.

When her eyes popped open, Mister Edwards was leaning over her, face tense with concern, holding a cluster of ripe shadowshine berries to her nose. Annalise lay beside a wall. He must have dragged her away from the cockatrice. The poison from the dragon's sting streamed from the gash on her great hand in plumes of black smoke.

"Miss Meriwether, you're alive! Thank goodness my mother taught me the healing properties of shadowshine berries," he said, glancing at the hurt dragon in the distance. "You blacked out. I thought—I thought you were gone. I'm so happy you're all right!" The fox hugged her tight.

"Me, too, Mister Edwards." She grinned. Annalise tried to stand but was too weak. The horn in her great hand had retreated, the wound the dragon made had sealed, but the cockatrice wasn't done yet.

A weak stream of fire blew across the courtyard. A wing slashed through the trees and nearly struck them. "You stay," Mister Edwards said, stuffing her pocket with shards of sharp quartz. "If it attacks, try to blind it with one of these. I'll find us a way out. Be right back."

Mister Edwards darted off in a streak of black before Annalise had a chance to protest. She sat up after a bit of a struggle and peered anxiously through the shadowshine forest as Mister Edwards threw shards of crystal quartz at the cockatrice—and hit. The cockatrice stumbled, let out an unholy cry, and staggered back against the wall.

Annalise stood as the cockatrice fell.

Mister Edwards arrived at Annalise's side, huffing and puffing with pride. "You're up—how wonderful!" He grinned, tail tip on fire. "I blinded it, Miss Meriwether! Did you see me? We can look at it now. I did it. I didn't let it turn me to stone!"

Annalise grinned. "Mister Edwards. That's fantastic. I'm so proud of you!"

A glow of light, brighter than before, shone from the pocket of her cloak. Mister Edwards and Annalise noticed it at the same time. But this time, when Annalise removed *The Book of Remembering*, she wasn't the only one who saw it.

"Miss Meriwether? Is that . . . ?"

"The book from my dream cat, yes," she laughed, feeling so amazingly alive.

Beyond the thrones, the cockatrice whimpered and flapped its tattered wings. Guilt crushed down hard. The poor thing. She hated hurting any creature, especially one set up by the Fate Spinner. It lay by the far wall, weak but not dead.

"What does the book say?" Mister Edwards asked, worrying his tail.

The book flipped open at his question. The page showed a sketch of the cockatrice's tail, and the silver heart within. Beneath, words appeared in a golden glow: *Take my heart and then my reward.*

"It says the cockatrice has a reward we need to win."

She told the fox about the message from the king and queen.

Mister Edwards breathed out a sigh of relief. "Then that's what we do," Mister Edwards said, new grit in his voice. "We take it down, claw our way to the end, and get what we came here for."

The creature inside her great hand had grown larger. "Good plan. But we'll need to subdue it first."

The book flipped the next page on its own; more words bloomed in black: *Shadowshine thorns create an unseen barrier protecting dreamers from harm. The berries bring death to those who ingest the fruit.* The book snapped shut so abruptly her bangs blew back in the gust. The glow died.

Annalise put *The Book of Remembering* away and stroked her braid four times: if she could get the cockatrice to consume the berries, they could easily take its heart.

Ten feet away, inside the forested court, the cockatrice released a mighty shriek. "Follow my lead, Mister Edwards. I think I know what to do."

Annalise plucked a handful of black-and-gold berries from the shadowshine trees; Mister Edwards did the same. They snuck around the side of the poor creature, gasping, eyes bleeding, wings mostly bone. And when it opened its beak to cry, Annalise pitched the poisonous berries into its mouth.

"Yes!" Mister Edwards cried, and followed Annalise's lead.

The cockatrice thrashed and choked, turned in their direction, and launched its spiked tail at Annalise. Thinking fast, Annalise yelled, "Jump!" And when the tail passed, they skipped over it. "Good! Now hold my small hand, Mister

Edwards. And hold tight." "Okay," he said, clasping on.

Are you ready? Annalise thought to the one inside her great hand.

Her horn pushed through her great hand. *Always*, her monster replied.

Again, the cockatrice lashed its tail toward them. Heart thundering, Annalise narrowed her gaze to the tip of its tail and wrapped her first and second fingers around her horn, wielding it like a weapon. "Now, Mister Edwards, pull!" The dragon gave one last scream. Annalise grabbed for the silver tip of its tail while the fox held her in place. It passed before her and Annalise latched on. Her horn seared straight through the dragon's scales and into the cockatrice's silver heart.

The cockatrice thrashed, ripping Mister Edwards free of her hand. But Annalise didn't let go of the dragon's tail. A familiar surge of energy rushed through her. The tail limped and fell. Annalise landed alongside the dragon, on her feet.

She pulled her horn free from the tail and took several steps backward. "I'm sorry," she shouted over its terrible cries. "You left me no choice."

The cockatrice shifted its mighty head toward her, its eyes twin black holes, and growled, "And you have left me the same."

Annalise gasped. It sounded more human than beast.

"Miss Meriwether," Mister Edwards said, hurrying to her side. "I think you might have done it!"

The cockatrice laughed low and deep. "Until you take my heart, I cannot let you pass."

Annalise's great hand burst with pain and before she could stop it, the cockatrice snapped its tail forward. Not at her, toward Mister Edwards.

A swish. A thud. A keening cry echoing high overhead, "Miss Meriwetherrrr!"

The cockatrice struck Mister Edwards from behind.

"Mister Edwards!"

Her small friend soared toward the mirror of black. Annalise moved in slow motion. The spiraled horn in her palm retreated. Blood rushed in her ears. Words bloomed from the mirror of black feathers in a shimmer of red: *A Fox's Just Rewards*. They appeared just a second before the mirror slurped Mister Edwards like a noodle and ate him whole.

"NO!" Annalise's scream ripped from her throat and attacked the air with sound. She raced to the mirror, but when she got there, the glass had turned to labyrinth stone. The doorway was blocked, and Mister Edwards was gone.

Oh no. What nightmare was he stuck in? Would he ever find his way out? Would Mister Edwards survive without her?

Would she survive alone?

Panic clamped on to her shoulders with lead hands. Annalise cried through the stones, heartbeats tripping over each other too fast. "Mister Edwards!" She banged the wall with closed fists. "Can you hear me?" But all she heard was her pulse raging through her skull. "Mister Edwards—come back . . ."

"The fox is gone," the cockatrice groaned, all sign of fight gone. Annalise swept her gaze over the ruins of this ill-fated place and fixed it on the cockatrice. It lay before the twin thrones on the opposite end of the court, twisted shadow-shine trees and broken statues of defeated dreamers scattered between them. Thick clouds of ash, spark, and reddish-black smoke coughed from the dragon's beak. "He may never return."

Both sides of her broken heart beat out of sync—half in fear, the other sorrow. All of her hurt. Annalise pulled up her large plum hood to ward off the falling ash and approached the dying beast. "Where did the black-feathered entrance lead?" she asked, stepping through the tangled wood.

Shadowshine trees bent gently toward her as she passed, whispering soft words she couldn't quite hear, soothing the ache in her great hand. But all she could think about was Mister Edwards. *I need to go after him. I can't leave him behind.*

To which a deeper instinct within herself answered: *What about your own dream? Would you trade it for his?*

"That I cannot answer," the cockatrice wheezed. "The fox must find his own way." A surge of pity filled Annalise from a deep place. Maybe *The Book of Remembering* knew where the black-feathered entrance led. Almost to the beast, Annalise opened the book. But all the pages were blank. "As for you, child of dreams, you have beaten me fairly. Come closer and you may have my reward."

Annalise's great hand surged with power and her mind with fragile new hope. She stopped just out of the dragon's reach. "What sort of reward?" Annalise asked cautiously, hopeful it was the sort mentioned by the trees.

"A secret. A story. A truth," the cockatrice wheezed. "Something the Fate Spinner doesn't want you to know."

Could she trust the creature that separated her from Mister Edwards? Maybe it wanted her closer, to take her great hand?

If it tries, my monster and I will fight it off together.

Annalise took four deep breaths and knelt at the beast's side. "I will hear your secret, cockatrice, and thank you for it."

A sudden shock struck her great hand. It pulled toward the cockatrice and grazed its crimson-scaled neck.

A bolt like lightning passed between them at her touch.

The cockatrice and Annalise gasped.

The current that moved between them felt like *love.*

"I wasn't always one of the Fate Spinner's monsters," the cockatrice said with awe. "Once, the Spinner of Dreams and I were very close. So close, I know many of her secrets." Another shock struck Annalise's great hand. The horned creature within her churned. "And even though the magic of the Mazelands prohibits my revealing the way out of the labyrinth, I can give you a clue to finding it yourself. A clue hidden inside the truth of what happened the night of your birth."

Annalise's mouth opened, and her eyes grew as big as plum stars. "How do you know about my birth?"

"That is unimportant. But this is most important of all: every truth comes with consequence. With every word of your story I speak, the last exit out of this courtyard—the mirror of snow—will grow smaller. If you agree to hear my truth, you risk losing your only chance to leave. Then, when I die, you will become a trapped beast like me—forced to hurt others on the path to their dreams." The massive cockatrice shrank with each spoken word. "Choose."

Annalise had given up her parents and lost her only friend. She'd hurt Nightingale and Bowie, the spider, and the cockatrice. Until she came here, Annalise had always loved with her whole heart and put others first. And maybe it was wrong, and Annalise was as wicked as the townsfolk said, but she wouldn't rest until she finished what she came here to do—or everything she'd done to get here would be in vain.

"I choose the story," Annalise answered quietly, hugging herself close. "I choose the truth." She glanced at the snow-white mirror—her last chance to escape. Annalise swore she saw Muse dart past in his hat and monocle. The one behind her dark mark shocked her lightly—four times. She took this as a sign. "I have a good feeling, cockatrice. Maybe the mirror of snow will wait."

"Very well," the cockatrice groaned, and shrank another size. "Place your marked hand over my shattered heart, and I'll show you what I can before I die. What you do with the information is up to you."

White crows filled the night sky. The cockatrice slid its tail forward and laid it at her side. Annalise hesitated, but only for a second, before placing her shattered black heart over the hole she'd made in its tail.

The ground rumbled. The white crows flooding the skies caw-caw-caw-CAWED. And a flash of lightning forceful enough to rival the gods shot through Annalise, into the cockatrice's silver heart.

The cockatrice cried and flailed. Annalise released her

grip. "I'm sorry," she said, and curled her great hand to her chest. "I didn't mean to hurt you—"

"You are freeing me." It smiled as if seeing the most heavenly sight. "Never be sorry for choosing your dream." The cockatrice shuddered. Its body shook the floor before it shrank, and the cockatrice was a dragon no more.

A dark-skinned man in a cloak of white feathers and weathered black robes lay in the cockatrice's place. He was old, silver hair intertwined with black. He resembled the king she'd seen in the book, but aged. A gold crown of crows and wolves circled his head. His hands rested on his chest. Within them, he clutched the dragon's beautifully carved silver heart, a hole puncturing its center.

Annalise, still on her knees, shuffled backward, trying to catch her runaway breath. She thought she knew who he was, but she needed to be sure. "Who are you?"

The man gasped in a breath, smiled brightly, and opened his eyes. "Once upon a time, I was a king, and a father to twin daughters—both different, both kind."

Annalise brightened. "You *are* the Spinner King—the father of Kismet and Reverie."

"I am," he answered, blinking his golden eyes, wet with tears. "You freed me. I only hope my reward is payment enough."

"The truth of the night I was born?"

"The truth of the night you were born." The king offered Annalise the cockatrice's shattered heart. "Take this into your hands, and I will show you much more than my daughter's book ever could."

Heart racing, great hand bursting with excited energy, Annalise cupped the heart. A rush of light exploded within her great hand—the same golden shine that glowed from her book. Annalise's stomach dropped. Dizziness came next. She squeezed her eyes shut.

In the darkness, a light wind tickled her ear. "Goodbye," the Spinner King whispered. And when Annalise opened her eyes, the shadowshine court and king were gone.

Chapter 26

THE MEMORY SPELL OF A DEAD KING

Green hills rolled out before her to the horizon. Annalise sat on a white velour throne on a golden dais. A palace of polished white crystal quartz, tipped in spires of gold, rose at Annalise's back. A pathway of multicolored stones wound out from the dais to a great gilded archway at the base of a gentle hill. A bright sun shone from a lilac sky. Cottages and huts with smoking chimneys dotted the landscape. And far, far in the distance, the twisted labyrinth rolled on without her. This was not the Fate Spinner's domain. This was the palace of the Spinner of Dreams: *the Court of Dreamland.*

She'd seen it sketched in *The Book of Remembering*, marveled at it from the sky when she fell from the train, and spied it through the door after she was poisoned. Annalise would've known it anywhere. Color burst from every direction. Creatures big and small made noise from land, sky, and trees. Everything shimmered—including her.

Annalise wore a luxurious gown of gold and white feathers, and a crown of golden horns and silver crows. She'd been so busy drinking in the sights she hadn't noticed the white cat in a top hat and monocle in her lap.

"Muse?"

The cat nodded and angled his gaze northwest. She stroked his fur, thinking this a very strange dream, and followed his gaze. On the opposite side of the labyrinth rose the Fate Spinner's palace of spiky red quartz. Annalise's skin froze like she was chomping on ice. She was almost certain that even inside the king's vision of truth, the Fate Spinner was watching her now.

"Stay very still," Muse whispered to Annalise. "You're seeing events as they happened in the Mazelands the night you were born. Remember, even when you can't see me, I am here." Muse faded, along with his final words, *"You are not alone."*

The Fate Spinner appeared below. She glided through the

259

golden gate at the end of the path, fire in her eyes, anger in her soul. "How dare you defy my wishes again, Reverie?" She climbed the pathway of rainbow stones in a fitted black jacket, vest, and leggings, hair half up in plaits, staring straight at Annalise, mirrored staff at her side.

Annalise glanced about in confusion.

Reverie?

Wait. Clothes, Dreamland, crown. Annalise stroked her hair—her hair was . . . wrong. Rather than long and blackberry, it was black and shoulder length.

Was Annalise seeing through the eyes of the Spinner of Dreams?

Black crows fluttered behind the Fate Spinner as she stopped at Reverie's throne and glared. "Are you even listening to me, sister? Or are you lost in one of your worthless daydreams?"

White crows funneled from the lilac sky, a winged army that flocked to Annalise's side.

Did they see the real her?

"So that's it? You're not going to speak to me anymore?" The Fate Spinner curled her hand tighter around her staff. When Reverie's white crows dived at the Fate Spinner, Annalise—or rather, the Spinner of Dreams—raised her left hand, calling them off. "I see how it is," the Fate Spinner snapped. "So typical. Our people may love you, Reverie. But they don't know you as I do—a selfish dreamer with a head full of nonsense." Her voice thinned, fine as dust. "All I wanted was your help. For you to make our people love me, the same way they love you." Tears she tried to hide rimmed her black eyes. Suddenly, the Fate Spinner didn't sound like a young woman but like a girl no older than Annalise, lost, afraid, sad. Annalise empathized. She knew those emotions well.

"You know the laws, dear sister," the Spinner of Dreams finally replied. "You cannot change my fate. Nor can I alter your destiny or grant you your dreams, even if I wanted to."

"Nonsense!" the Fate Spinner cried. The checkerboard of crows scattered and cawed. "We are enchantresses, aren't we? We shouldn't be subject to any laws—we should be the ones making them!"

Annalise's heart pounded—a herd of gazelles on the upside down of her chest. Yet she didn't move.

"Kismet, please," the Spinner of Dreams said. "You must stop this. Mogul decreed these laws at the time of our births. The rules are set. *It is done.*"

Annalise wasn't sure what was happening, or why she was inside the body of the Spinner of Dreams, but listening to the Spinners now, Annalise knew one thing for sure: she

261

could love the Spinner of Dreams and still understand the Fate Spinner, too.

The Fate Spinner knelt at her sister's feet, clasped her hands at her chest, and begged, black eyes glittering bright with hope. "We were friendly once, don't you remember?"

The Spinner of Dreams leaned forward, radiating the same sympathy Annalise felt encapsulating her. "I remember, Kismet, fondly. We were—until you banished our parents to the labyrinth and turned them into monsters. I *did* love you. Even now, I love you still."

The Fate Spinner took her sister's hand. "Then help me. I'm on my knees, begging like a servant. The people cannot stand me. They curse my name—even when I'm generous with blessings, bounty, and love, they can't see past their hatred of me for the hardships I'm forced to give. Can't they see I'm trapped in a cursed fate, too?" Her lips trembled. "Just once, let me trade places with you, sister. Break the rules for a day. Let me feel what it's like to be loved and accepted. Please, I beg you!" She wiped her cheeks, streaked with dampness and black kohl, eyes brimming with all the hope in the world. "If you are as kindhearted as our people say, please, have mercy."

Annalise sensed the horned beast within her left hand breathing and growing. Felt the pulsing beat of her monster's heart, like a ghost.

"I am sorry, Kismet, I truly am. But we are both bound by the laws of who we are—one born of fate, the other of dreams. This can never change."

The Fate Spinner dropped her sister's hand like it was infectious. She pushed herself up by her staff; every mirrored eye opened wide. "I thought you, of all people, were capable of thinking for yourself. But I see I was wrong." The Fate Spinner wiped her eyes on her sleeve and spun her glare into a grin. "I, too, have a dream, did you know? Can you guess what it might be, *Dream Spinner*?"

A tingle of electricity hemmed the wind. White and black crows warred overhead. Night wolves sprinted toward them from the direction of the labyrinth. Reverie stayed seated on her throne and spoke as if nothing out of the ordinary had happened. "If you have a dream," she said with warm grace, "I'd like to hear it."

Annalise spotted Muse behind the Fate Spinner, sadder than she'd ever seen him. Still, he held his head high while peering out from behind the Fate Spinner's long skirts.

"My old dream was so simple," the Fate Spinner said to her sister. "To be respected and loved by our people. But thanks to your selfishness, I have to conjure a new dream." Four night wolves drew to the Fate Spinner's side, ears flat and snarling.

A flurry of crows took to the air.

"And what might that dream be, Kismet?" the Spinner of Dreams asked kindly.

The Fate Spinner growled, "I wish to rule my own destiny and rid myself of this curse!"

Annalise gasped: that was her dream, too!

Reverie froze as she stood to comfort her sister. Annalise's great hand flared in a hot blast of pain. Her vision exploded in black and she fell through the bottom of the world.

Annalise opened her eyes in the courtyard of stone. The shadowshine trees stood proud, but the Spinner King was gone, along with the dragon's broken heart. Annalise blinked into the forest surrounding her, underneath the bright crimson moon.

In the spot where the king's body had been moments before was the most beautiful, intricately carved dagger Annalise had ever seen. The handle and cross guards were made of black dragon hide. The silver blade, inlaid down the middle with gold wolves, crows, and broken hearts, rested alongside a black scabbard wrapped in the same soft leather of *The Book of Remembering*.

It was the very dagger she'd seen in the mirror that led to the cockatrice—*There Be Dragons (Honest)*.

A note written in black char scrawled across the courtyard stones:

*This dagger, forged from a cockatrice's
heart, yields the power to shatter illusions
on the path to one's dreams. Use it to find
the demon queen past the mirror of snow, a
quest more painful even than this, and the
third item is yours. Thank you, Annalise.
May the magic of dreams be yours.*

The mirror of snow led to the next reward!

Annalise bowed her head. "Goodbye, Spinner King, and thank you. Wherever you are, may the magic of dreams be yours as well."

Her great hand twisted and pulled toward the white mirror, which had shrunk considerably.

Mercy. Annalise jumped up, strapped on the scabbard and blade, and hurried to the glass, now two-by-two-feet square. A layer of ice coated the mirror. Behind it, snow swirled against a backdrop of night. Annalise got on hands and knees and readied herself to enter, when—tap-tap-tap-tap from behind the drifting white glass.

"Miss Meriwether?"

Annalise thrilled from head to toe. "Mister Edwards?"

Annalise placed her small hand to the frosty mirror; it sank through to the frigid other side. Her fingers numbed instantly. Snowflakes whipped against her skin as she reached for her friend. But she couldn't find him.

"Where are you?" She laughed with relief. "Are you okay?"

The mirror shrank even more. It was now or never.

Annalise made herself small and thrust both hands through the frame. A paw shoved her hands back. "You can't come in here," Mister Edwards snapped. "It's a trap." Beyond the glass, howling wind and high-pitched screams. "Find another w—" His paw and voice tore away in the gale.

"Mister Edwards!"

The mirror shrank around her arms. Beyond the glass, her great hand fought to get to her. Panic kicked her heart into overdrive.

Right or wrong, trap or freedom, Annalise had to go.

This was the only way left.

"I'm coming, Mister Edwards!" Annalise squeezed through the small frame and plomped directly into a drift of snow.

Chapter 27

THE MIRROR OF SNOW

Before she left home, if someone had told Annalise that she'd battle a dragon that turned out to be a king who'd taken her inside the past and given her an enchanted dagger made from his enchanted heart, she'd have insisted, "That could never happen to someone like me. I'm not strong enough to handle such things." But as Annalise plopped face-first into a moonlit wonderland of falling snow, she thought, maybe she *was* strong enough. Maybe the battle to prove herself worthy had readied her for this labyrinth all along.

Shivering, Annalise stood. Snow glittered and swirled.

The heavens blinked with stars. A silvery moon shone overhead, casting the field surrounding her in a bath of arctic blue. On either side of the field were pine woods coated in white. The snow, already to her knees, was rising fast, and the mirror through which she'd entered, and all other signs of the labyrinth, had been erased the second she'd landed here.

Where am I? Her teeth had begun to chatter. *Is this like the last illusion? Am I still in the labyrinth?* She spotted no footprints; the snow and wind must have washed them away. Where was Mister Edwards?

Another fresh spear of pain sliced through her great palm. Annalise cradled it to her chest and scanned the woods for her friend—but she found no sign.

"Mister Edwards?" When Annalise called into the blizzard, the wind stole her voice. She peered into the dense thickets of trees. Her hair whipped and danced at her shoulders—wild blackberry in a sea of glistening silver. Tiny flurries of wind and ice bit her skin with sharp winter teeth. Annalise called again over the frozen gusts. "Mister Edwards, can you hear me?"

Winter winds howled in reply. Annalise wrapped her charred cloak tighter around her and trudged deeper into the night.

She'd only gone a few feet when the dragon-heart dagger

hummed at her side, and she spotted movement ahead. Four pitch-black skeletons as tall as the trees emerged through the whirling snow, blocking Annalise's path. Their limbs were as long and slender as a spider's, their bodies as dark as an endless void. Their eyes, tiny mounds of chipped ice, were backlit by the pale moon. They resembled four-legged daddy longlegs—but eviler by far.

Why do spiderlike creatures keep trying to stop, fight, and defeat me?

She'd never seen anything so terrifying.

One-two-three-four—repeat.

Eyes wide and scared, her great hand contorting in pain, Annalise watched as the long-limbed humanoid monsters closed in on four sides. They leaned down and stared at Annalise so thoroughly, she felt observed by the darkest part of the world.

"Go away!" she shouted into the wind. But they kept coming. Annalise tried counting her quick, pounding breaths to calm her wild-beating heart, but none of her usual methods were working. The skeletons' burnt-looking skulls grew closer. And Annalise's terror reflected at her within their glossy black eyes.

"Hello, Annalise," the first charred skeleton spoke in her grandma Frida's kind voice. "You were always a disappointment to us, you know." The impostor pushed its charred skull a foot from her face; Annalise smelled her grandma's baby-powdery perfume. "We didn't have the heart to tell you. But after you turned us into monsters, we don't mind breaking your heart." The midnight skeleton grinned with broken black teeth, and the others grinned, too.

Annalise looked away. *These are the Fate Spinner's lies—and I won't listen!*

"You were an embarrassment," another said with Grandma Thessaly's signature sass. "What with that hand and the devil inside it, and you being so depressing and weird, and too selfish to think of anyone else." The other skeletons formed a tight circle around Annalise, their sharp limbs closing in. "We always knew you'd fail at whatever you tried to do."

Annalise steeled her heart, and breathed, breathed, breathed—breathed. The dagger felt hot at her side. The Spinner King's message said the dagger had the power to shatter illusions. *If I strike them with its blade, maybe they'll go away.*

If I strike them down, maybe I'll find the queen and the next reward.

Her frozen feet stung with cold, her heart galloped with fear, but she would do what she needed to anyway.

I wish to rule my own destiny and rid myself of this curse.

Annalise dug under her cloak and freed her blade from

270

its scabbard. She held it before her, hand shaking. "You're not real," she told the bone skeleton wearing her grandma Thessaly's face. Then she struck it in the ribs, where its heart should have been.

And hit bone.

The dead thing laughed. "Oh, sweetheart." It ran one icy finger along her cheek. "We are most definitely real. Sorry to disappoint you, but no enchanted dagger can kill us, and we hide no magical reward."

So, this place was a trap, like Mister Edwards said?

Breath chugging fast and hot, Annalise pulled her dagger from the charred skeleton's bones, pushed through the drifts past the darkly towering things, and searched for a way out. There's always a way, her grandpa Jovie used to say. Keep your eyes open. Keep going. Eventually, you'll find a way free.

"Aww, my beautiful granddaughter," the blackened skeleton of Grandpa Hugo murmured into her ear. Its limbs bent at wrong angles. Its skull tilted like a curious bird. "So brave to keep going, even though you can't leave." The white moon shone through the impostor's ice eyes as it focused on her great hand. "This is a prison. One way in, no way out." It rose to its full height, bones popping as it stood and bellowed over the treetops, "LONG LIVE THE FATE SPINNER!"

The skeletons shrieked—louder than the winds, louder than every noise anywhere. Annalise shoved past them, sheathed her dagger, and trudged quicker through the snow, cradling her great hand, still shooting with fire and pain. The horned creature behind her dark mark was growing steadily bigger in its attempt to break free.

Annalise had the startling realization that perhaps, like her, it had a dream, too. "Now you've gone and done it," Grandma Frida's shadow skeleton said. Slinking up on her right, it unhinged its jaw and howled, "You've always been a disobedient and wicked girl, and nobody, not even your family, ever liked you!"

Snow and wind howled from the creature's mouth. Annalise's hair shot back in a torrent. Her grandparents would never say such things!

These aren't their thoughts. These are the Fate Spinner's words. She's scared I'll win. This is the Fate Spinner trying to break me. And I won't listen!

The last charred skeleton jumped before Annalise. It reeked of fires long dead and of Grandpa Jovie's cedarwood soap. "You should have known you wouldn't make it," Grandpa Jovie's impostor said in his gentle voice. Annalise's knew it wasn't really her grandfather—a man who would never say such a thing to her—but her heart broke a little hearing him say so. "Not even your parents believed in you or your dreams. Give up, Annalise. Deep down, you know you're not worthy of anything good."

Her parents. All this time she'd barely thought about them. She should have been trying to find them since she'd first seen them on the train of wolves. She was a terrible daughter and an even worse friend. She had failed. She had killed. She had been selfish, and maybe she didn't deserve to win. Annalise tried, she really did, not to let her grandparents' words in. But her panic had a mind of its own.

The monster inside her great hand fought and writhed, and maybe even spoke. But whatever it said, it wasn't as loud as the scrabble of thoughts swarming her mind. Poisonous notions released within her like black balloons in a gale. Darkness welled up. Cold seeped in. Annalise's breath came faster. Hot ugly tears streamed down her frozen face, and oh, how they burned! All while the Fate Spinner's monsters looked on. Annalise was spiraling, down, down, down, down, into a bottomless darkness.

Suddenly, she didn't feel so strong.

The black skeletons towered over her on every side. Annalise stumbled backward and tripped over the snow. She fell flat on her back. Blinking away tears, her face hot, her heart broken—as broken as her hand, her sky, her beautiful, improbable dream—Annalise didn't even try to get up. She was so tired. How had she even made it this far? What was she doing here, in this place, so very far from love, warmth, home?

Annalise let her burning eyes close.

"There now, child," the Fate Spinner said, her voice echoing across the heavens. "Let my labyrinth take you. Let the snow cover you until you are still." Soft blankets of shimmering snow coated Annalise until only her left eyelid showed through. Her soft-spoken words settled into Annalise's spirit and spread. The four dark and burnt skeletons curled over her like the petals of a black daisy, reaching for her great hand.

Annalise sighed beneath the snowdrifts, pain and worry and fight melting away.

Her journey had been so long. So dark. So cruel, desperate, and cold. The weight of her life sat upon her, attempting to crush all the power and will and strength she'd gained. The snow-blankets wrapped her in a mother's gentle arms as the Fate Spinner whispered, "It's all right, Annalise. Give your curse to me, and you'll finally be free of all those foolish dreams."

Annalise's eyes snapped open.

Foolish . . . dreams?

Her father in a green-grass backyard building longboats in the sun.

Her mom writing by a fire, smiling triumphantly at an award on the wall.

Mister Edwards and his love crafting sweets in Caledonia in peace.

And Annalise free of her curse, the sky healed, her town prosperous and its people content; the architect of her own destiny.

These were not foolish dreams. They were true, and lovely, and real.

And they belonged in the world.

A twinge of heat kindled within her dark mark. Not pain, but flame. Annalise pushed herself through the snow. And as the skeletons were about to reach her great hand, a stream of golden butterflies caught her attention.

The poets of hope drifted from the trees to her right and fluttered back the way Annalise had come. As one, they formed a gold-winged frame in the middle of the clearing, where the mirror through which she'd entered had been.

"You're almost there," they twittered. *"In the dark, your fires spark. In the light, your dreams take flight!"*

With each word they spoke, the frame glowed brighter, lighting up the deep blue night. And finally, an image of mirrored glass within the butterfly frame appeared. Within it, her parents waved her forward, calling her home. "Come on, Annalise," her father said. "You can do it."

"We love you, sweetheart," her mom said with a proud smile. "Finish the maze, beat the Fate Spinner, and come home."

Annalise's heart warmed at once. The icy spell the Fate Spinner had cast over her cracked and fell away. Annalise trembled, small and cold, in the center of a circle of monsters.

The Fate Spinner's laughter rattled the sky. "We know what you are, Annalise Meriwether," the skeletal creatures screamed in the voice of their mistress. "And we will never let you leave!"

The blizzard grew thicker, darker, colder. Annalise no longer felt her great hand or her own monster within, but the horn twined steadily out from within. There was no visible end to this wasteland of ice and space—but she couldn't give up now.

Annalise lunged from the snowdrift, horn first. "I am a girl with a dream," she shouted over the howling gale. "And that makes me stronger than you!"

A flash of power rushed through her. Annalise spun toward the giant bone monsters and took aim. Fire raged through her. The creatures shrieked and hissed. Their charred bones contorted in pain as they swatted the gold and black flames shooting from her great hand.

"Get back!" The spiraled black horn through her hand was as long as a sword, and her hand bigger than it had ever been. The energy surrounding her doubled, tripled, quadrupled. The enchanted wood seemed to gather strength.

Or maybe, the power was coming from her.

"I don't want to hurt you, but I will!"

The skeleton closest to her screamed and grabbed for Annalise's great hand; she blasted it so forcefully, it flew backward and scorched the trees. The charred skeleton landed and galloped off on all fours, screeching into the night. The others bounded after it, and soon, they were gone.

Annalise crouched in the snow—frozen and heaving, adrenaline supercharging her blood. How many times had her great hand helped her? Even though she'd spent most of her life wishing it away, how many times since she started treating it kindly had it fought valiantly at her side?

"I see you for what you truly are," Annalise said, cradling her great hand. The creature shifted beneath its horn. "You are a gift—a strength I didn't know I had, and I swear, I will never take you for granted again."

Maybe that was another reason the Fate Spinner wanted her great hand. Maybe the power growing inside her exceeded her own.

"You can't escape me, Annalise," the Fate Spinner

howled through the trees. "No matter what you do, you cannot escape your fate. . . ."

The winds slowed and fell with her voice. The snow tapered and died. And from out of the enchanted field of snow, four familiar walls rose—the one directly before her held the flutter-winged mirror of gold, her parents waving her forward. Annalise grinned so hard at her monster, the high dimple on her left cheek appeared. "Let's go show the Fate Spinner what we've got."

Annalise's stomach twisted. *And hopefully find Mister Edwards along the way*, she added to herself.

With each step that Annalise ran, more snow melted, and the more defined the walls became, the brighter the butterflies glowed. The midnight-blue darkness lit with their wondrously warm shine. Annalise hurried toward the golden butterflies, braid waving behind her, confident all she'd have to do was walk through the mirror into the labyrinth. But by the time she arrived, the mirror had turned to stone.

"No." Here came the trembling *thump-thump-thump-thump* of her heart, the anxiety fighting her body for control. But Annalise fought back.

She shot fire at the wall, hoping to melt it; but nothing happened. She tried pushing it—but it wouldn't budge. The Fate Spinner's laughter crawled across the skies but that only fueled her on. "Annalise," she whispered to herself. "You mustn't give up."

The poets of hope opened their wings. Words written across each wing, when read in sequence, created a poem:

Even after the longest dark night, dreams will shine. As if darkness was a spark and dreamers, the birth of the flame.

"You're r-right," Annalise said, the cold seeping in deeper. "D-dreams will sh-shine."

A light grew and grew from the pocket of her cloak.

The book.

Fingers numb, Annalise lifted the book from her pocket with her small hand and it flipped open on its own. The pages glowed, lighting the frozen, dark night. A picture of her real grandpa Hugo emerged on the page, along with his real voice, *"Never doubt your greatness, Annalise. You are the very definition of the word."* He looked right at her, eyes sparkling with pride. *"Find her, dear Annalise. Find her and make all your dreams come true."*

Hugo's image faded. The Spinner King appeared in the book next and spoke directly to Annalise, *"This dagger, forged from a cockatrice's heart, yields the power to shatter illusions on the path to one's dreams. Use it to free the demon queen and the final reward is yours."*

The book snapped shut. The dagger hummed in its

sheath. And Annalise brightened with hope.

Maybe if she stabbed the wall with her dagger, the illusion, if that was what this truly was, would break? "Thank you, Grandpa Hugo and the Spinner King, thank you!"

Behind her, a murder of black crows screamed. Hundreds, heading straight for her. Annalise faced the wall ahead.

"The only way to escape these four walls is to break one of them down." Annalise removed the silver dagger from her scabbard, cried like a warrior, and thrust it deep into the crack of the stone.

The Fate Spinner's scream shot across the night.

Black fire, ash, and spark exploded from the place the blade penetrated the wall. Crows cried. Night wolves howled. Annalise didn't see any demon queen appear, but slowly, the blocks rearranged. They pushed back until the last of the wall made way for Annalise and her dreams, and only the frame of wings around a veiled entrance remained.

A sign hung over the winged frame. *The Gate of Death.*

Annalise remembered the words of the thin tree in the beginning of the maze. *"Inside each of these paths hide four smaller passageways known as the Gates of Doubt, Rejection, Panic, and Death. They will appear to you in this order and contain many surprises within."*

This was the final gate to Dreamland.

Mercy.

Annalise was almost there.

A thick haze of silver-red smoke obscured the tunnel ahead. The cheers of a large audience or mob drifted out from the opening and glued to her skin. It was the sound of spectators pumping fists, hungry to see someone fall. Of creatures out for blood. Annalise inhaled four deep breaths, but they did not clear her dread.

"Together," Annalise said to her monster—to her friend—and stepped forward through the frame, ready to fight her way free from this labyrinth once and for all.

"Together," her monster answered—but not as a thought in her mind. Though the reply came from beneath her monster's horn, it spoke with a voice of its own.

Annalise froze. Her great hand contorted and grew—and grew and grew and grew. Her eyes and mouth popped wide, as a lightning bolt of pain stabbed though her great hand. The spiraled horn pushed farther outside of herself, the skin of her hand on fire. Annalise screamed in horror and agony and dropped, knees to the ground.

The Monster Born from a Curse

All her life, Annalise had abhorred her big hand. It was the villain that made life hard for her parents, killed her grandparents, and kept Annalise hidden from the world. Until entering the labyrinth, she'd blamed her marked hand for every pain, hardship, and sorrow bestowed upon her by the Fate Spinner. But she hadn't realized that by vilifying it, by wishing it gone, Annalise had made her great hand a monster, when maybe all it needed was to be wanted, treasured, accepted—loved.

She wasn't just a girl with a curse. Annalise was a being of strength, will, fire—magic. A force capable of growing a mythical creature inside her, a power born from misfortune. Annalise was a girl with a dream bigger than fate— powerful enough to change the world.

When Annalise landed on the other side of the golden frame, she fell to her knees in the dirt, screaming in agony. An audience she couldn't see stomped and cheered from every direction. Land of snow gone, red haze surrounding her, Annalise shuddered as the horn twisted up and out, higher and higher from the black heart marking her great hand.

What's happening? Tears streamed down Annalise's cheeks. Hair hung in her face, grit dug into her knees. Eyes squeezed shut, teeth bared, Annalise watched as her great hand stretched and distorted—and grew—until finally, it became too heavy, and dropped to the ground.

Spiraled black horn pointed at the sky, a blast of golden fire rocketed from her great hand and the monster within. Annalise screamed so loud, she silenced the raucous crowd— as a creature of myth, magic, and flame propelled from her great hand, horn first.

Annalise's monster charged into the crimson mist and vanished. The second her monster was free, the pain in her great hand died, and the Gate of Death through which she'd come shrank and disappeared.

The unseen crowd broke their stunned silence and erupted in wild applause. Annalise's great hand had reduced to the size it was before she left home. The skin of her dark mark where the beast leaped free sealed as if nothing had happened. Not only that but the shattered black heart of the Fate Spinner was no longer broken.

Annalise grinned. The heart on her palm was whole.

And something new had appeared. A long golden thread, thin as a spiderweb, drifted out from her black mark and into the smoky air. She couldn't see where it ended, but Annalise felt sure that the monster she'd come to know as her friend was tethered at its end.

Annalise had seen the creature as it leaped free, but she still couldn't believe it.

"Mercy," Annalise whispered into the haze.

A black fire unicorn had been inside her all along.

Still shaking, Annalise pushed off her knees. As soon as she stood, the vicious crowd booed, and the haze running the ground cleared. Annalise recognized where she'd landed at once. She'd read many stories of grand colosseums where lives were sacrificed for sport—where gladiators and gladiatrices battled for their lives, and only one walked away. But never in Annalise's wildest imaginings had she thought she'd be one of them.

Until now.

A caged arena spread out before her. Massive black bars domed high overhead. A towering oval wall rose from the hardscrabble ground, joined with the barred dome, and locked her in. Two solid iron doors stood on either side of Annalise, embedded in the side walls. A thick haze still veiled the spectators shouting from the stands. Annalise searched the smoke for her unicorn but found only vague blurs of gold light shining out from the mist.

When Annalise took a step, the grinding of a rising door screeched to her left. A winged creature, twice the size of the cockatrice, emerged. The top half of its body resembled a tawny lion with a mane of black flames. Dark scaled wings stretched at its sides. Glowing red mirrored eyes and sharp black horns decorated its massive skull. Its back legs were hooved like a Minotaur's, and its tail took the form of a writhing fanged snake, hissing and biting the air. It carried a gold box in its massive fangs.

Was this the demon queen the king mentioned—the one that held another reward as powerful as the last?

Could the demon queen be the lost Spinner Queen?

Shackled to the ground with the thickest chain Annalise had ever seen, the lion-headed Minotaur fixed its ruby eyes on her, dropped the box with a clatter, and roared. Fire blew from its jaws. A blast of flames crossed the arena toward Annalise. She hurried backward and ducked. The tops of her black ribbons scorched. Annalise lost breath at the whip-beats of her heart as she squelched the flames in her hair. The chimera leaped and strangled at the end of its chain.

She'd had Mister Edwards to help her last time.

How could she do this without him?

The invisible crowd, so loud only moments ago, silenced. The hairs on Annalise's arms stood. When she turned, her black unicorn of fire and horn charged like a winged demon out of the shadows, straight at her.

Purple eyes giant with fear, Annalise stumbled over her feet in awe.

"Climb on," the unicorn said in a familiar voice, skidding to a halt before Annalise. Sparks of cinder rose with each beat of her bone-and-leather wings. The unicorn's sleek black head was that of a horse, but with one spiraled black horn between her eyes. Her tail, mane, and hooves flamed out in fires of gold. Overlapping black-hearted scales, matching Annalise's dark mark, armored her body. The golden thread trailed from the unicorn's chest and anchored inside Anna-lise's marked palm.

They were joined, even when separate.

"Hurry!" The enormous unicorn lowered a wing to her

feet. Without hesitation, Annalise climbed up onto her back. "Now," the fire unicorn said as the chimera blasted another torrent of flames, "let's show the Fate Spinner what we can do!"

The unicorn pumped her wings and pushed off the dusty ground.

Annalise's thrill spoiled quickly as she slipped sideways on the unicorn's scales. She fought to stay on. With the unicorn's wings thrashing up and down at Annalise's feet, and her flames licking up around her, there was no place to hold that wouldn't burn her.

"Grab my mane," the unicorn said as she circled the ring. "And don't worry." Her gold eyes met Annalise's purple ones. "Nothing on me can hurt you."

Annalise grasped the unicorn's mane—to her amazement, she found it cool. A zing of energy filled Annalise upon gripping the unicorn's mane—lightning, thunder, magic, a universe spinning inside her. The thread connected them brightened and glowed.

"You're beautiful!" Annalise said past the lump in her throat and wrapped her arms around the unicorn's neck. "You're a beautiful and mighty unicorn." A glitter of golden ash flew out behind them, dusting the arena below. Annalise laughed. "And you came from me!"

The chimera strained at the end of its chain as they passed. The audience screamed for blood. Still, as Annalise soared atop her unicorn, blackberry hair snapping out behind her, she experienced a moment of peace. Annalise wished Mister Edwards was here and that he could feel it, too.

"My name is Esh-Baal," her unicorn said. "It means *Fire of the Ruler*." Esh-Baal took a slow curve, galloping faster. She climbed the air toward the bars covering the arena and the white crows circling above the dome. "You brought me to life, Annalise—and my fire is yours!"

Esh-Baal flew closer to the chimera. It shrieked and flapped, pulling at its constraints. The rectangular gold box the size of a traveling chest lay on the dirt before its hooved feet. Esh-Baal drew nearer. The hidden crowd stomped and hollered.

"What do you think it's guarding?" Annalise asked Esh-Baal.

Maybe it was the final item she needed to beat the Fate Spinner.

"I can't tell," her unicorn replied, soaring around the beast. "But that's not all its protecting."

To the right of the chimera, a giant ornately carved mirror rose from the dirt. Inside the glass, upon a dais, the Fate Spinner sat on her red throne. Black crows shrieked above her.

Her whole sky churned with wings as she watched Annalise and Esh-Baal curiously. Her staff of mirrored eyes gleamed at her side. Her red quartz palace towered a distance behind her.

"What do you think she wants?" Annalise asked Esh-Baal, guts twisting with sourness. She dug her dagger from her scabbard.

"To watch us die," Esh-Baal replied, eyeing Annalise's blade with respect and a hint of a smile.

The Fate Spinner narrowed her gaze onto them and watched them come. But no more would Annalise let Fate intimidate her. Annalise collected her breath in groups of four and forced her head high—for the child she once was who never would have dreamed she'd have the courage to stand where she stood now: ready to stare down the Fate Spinner, grab hold of her destiny, and change her life. Annalise's nerves jangled like change. But she wouldn't stop fighting toward her dream. *For myself, and every child who's ever been cursed, told they are worthless, broken by another. For those who don't know they are more than what the world claims them to be, I will fight.*

The spectators silenced when the Fate Spinner spoke. "Greetings, Miss Meriwether. How good to see you again." Her gaze lingered on Esh-Baal before returning to Annalise. At the sight of the dagger, the Fate Spinner looked ready to hiss but held back and growled out instead, "I had my doubts you'd make it this far, what with your . . . various insuffi-ciencies." Annalise clenched her fists. Esh-Baal's fires flared. "But now that you're here, bravo." The Fate Spinner gave a slow clap and stroked her luminous hair. "You've made it to the last part of the labyrinth. *And the worst is yet to come.*"

The hidden spectators shouted, "She'll never beat you, Fate Spinner!" Followed by, "Look at her, weak bit of a thing, all spindle and worry—the devil and her demon horse won't last a second, they won't!" The mob sounded like the townsfolk who'd villainized Annalise so often she'd grown up believing their words.

When the Fate Spinner raised her staff, the crowd silenced at once. Her black eyes glittered at Annalise like midnight seas. "I've decided to give you another chance to offer your-self to me before anyone *else* gets hurt."

Annalise's heart froze to her ribs. "What do you mean, *anyone else?*"

Esh-Baal skidded to a stop on the ground as close to the Fate Spinner's mirror, and as far from the thrashing chimera, as she dared. Annalise did not dismount.

The Fate Spinner folded her long white fingers over the head of her staff with a coy grin. "I may have no authority inside my labyrinth, but I can offer choices. And thanks to my newly acquired prisoner, I'm able to offer you one now."

The Fate Spinner leaned forward from her throne. "If you step through my mirror and give yourself and your horned beast to me as sacrifice, I'll let this frightened prisoner go. You will save them from being devoured by my hungry chimera here, who hasn't eaten in some time. You also won't have to keep fighting my monsters, of which I have an endless supply. Of course, you'll never leave my labyrinth, but that's a small price to pay for such a *compassionate* and *kindhearted* dreamer like yourself, wouldn't you agree?" The Fate Spinner, overcome with delight, laughed. "Oh, did I forget to mention, the prisoner in question is someone you care for and couldn't bear to see hurt?"

Esh-Baal pawed the dirt with one hoof and snorted angrily in a shower of sparks, every muscle tensed. Annalise scrambled, trying to figure out who the Fate Spinner had taken prisoner—Mom? Dad? Mister Edwards? She might even mean Nightingale or Bowie, as she had begun to care for them, too. "Who is your prisoner?" She squeezed her dagger four times. "Which someone I care for is in pain?"

The box before the chimera moved. Esh-Baal tensed at her side like she wanted to eat the Fate Spinner's face. Annalise rested her great hand upon her, and her unicorn calmed.

The Fate Spinner's smirk grew. "Surrender yourselves and I'll tell you."

The box rattled harder. Something inside it cried.

"What have you done?" Annalise asked, stepping closer. The chimera tugged harder at its chain. "Tell me, please."

"This is your last chance. If you do not take my offer, Miss Meriwether, you'll have to live your life knowing you sacrificed another to me, so you could have your own dreams. Could you live with yourself, knowing this?" The audience hushed. Annalise's knees noodled terribly. Her whole body buzzed with the instinct to run. But there was nowhere to run to, and running wouldn't get Annalise her dream. "Tell me what you choose."

"I am with you," Esh-Baal whispered. "Whatever you decide, I believe in you." The spiral of her unicorn's horn lit with a twist of golden starlight; the thread between them blazed. Annalise's face crinkled with thankfulness and love.

The chimera roared. Liquid fire dripped from its mouth and sizzled upon the golden box. Whether this was a trick of fate or not, Annalise couldn't live with herself if she didn't see what—or who—was inside the box. But she would do it on her own terms. She wouldn't ever take the Fate Spinner's deal.

She would trick her instead.

Esh-Baal nickered softly. A nicker that sounded like, *Yes*.

"You know what I think?" Annalise told the Fate Spinner in a warbling but persistent voice. "I think this is another of your tricks to try to control me." The chimera lunged and snapped at the end of its chain. Esh-Baal spread her wings and flew, and Annalise shouted over the crowd. "But dreamers are more powerful than you'll ever be, Fate Spinner. And even those broken by fate can pick themselves up and rise!"

The faceless crowd hissed and jeered.

The Fate Spinner stood. "How powerful you think you are—how brave and clever. Well, I've seen it all before." Something like love softened the Fate Spinner's face; she blinked rapidly and lowered her haunting eyes. "I more than anyone know how weak dreams are in the face of fate." She moved closer to the mirror, her face an inch from the glass. "But I see you, *Annalise Meriwether.* And I know exactly how your sad story ends: with the death of your dreams."

Annalise held on tighter to Esh-Baal and her dagger.

Let her come. I've beaten her monsters before, and I can do it again.

Annalise leaned close to Esh-Baal's ear. "Together," she whispered, wearing a shy grin of her own, "we go for the box and fight for our dreams."

"And together," Esh-Baal cried, galloping higher, blazing a path through the air, "we rise!"

Annalise hung on tight with her great hand, weapon high in her right, her cloak, frayed and charred, undulating out behind her. The unicorn flapped her great wings and charged at the chimera, horn first.

"So be it." The Fate Spinner growled.

The chimera bellowed and lunged and finally broke free of its chains.

The box at its hooves shook.

"And now," the Fate Spinner shouted. "The real fun begins."

Chapter 29

FRIEND OR FOE?

Annalise did not enjoy being unprepared. She liked to
know what she'd be doing so she could prep for any surprises. She liked right better than left. She liked the number
four better than three. She liked order and structure and
knowing which way to go. But right now, as she soared
above a gladiator's arena on a dark unicorn tethered to her
great hand as the winged, lion-headed Minotaur chased
after them, Annalise realized that there were some things
in life for which one could never be prepared. That sometimes it was the surprises that showed someone who they
really were.

The Fate Spinner watched from her mirror, knuckles

clenched on her staff and throne. And when her chimera roared an inferno of fire and attacked, Annalise and Esh-Baal were ready.

They dived straight toward the chimera, into the wall of flames. Esh-Baal faked right and slipped under its hooves. The chimera swung midair and swooped after them. Annalise's eyes stung, and her hair was singed, but her heart soared. She and her unicorn were a well-oiled machine—one power in two parts. Every move Annalise wanted to make, Esh-Baal made without being told. Annalise clung to Esh-Baal's mane with her great hand and her dagger with her right, planning the right time to strike.

Esh-Baal was pumping her wings north when the chimera whipped its snake tail at her flank and bit. Esh-Baal tore away with a cry. Annalise could feel Esh-Baal's pain through their connective thread as if it was her own.

Esh-Baal was hurt but fine.

And her leg bled drips of gold.

A few drops landed on the parched earth below. Each drop bore a shadowshine tree, just as Annalise's blood did in the Spinner King's court. Except these, rather than berries, bore tiny black thorns.

Annalise marveled as Esh-Baal went in to strike.

Esh-Baal soared behind the chimera, concealed in a thick cloud of smoke. Before the beast could turn, Esh-Baal burst from the haze and speared it in the side with her horn. The beast arched its spine and screamed. The Fate Spinner slid to the edge of her throne, teeth clenched, snarling as her monster struggled to fly.

Right before the chimera fell, its eyes, humanlike in their recognition, focused on Annalise's dagger. Maybe it sensed the magic of the blade—the magic that, with one slice of the Spinner King's heart-forged dagger, could take it down.

The chimera's eyes closed, and it crashed to the ground.

The arena shook with its fall. The hidden crowds booed and stomped their feet.

Esh-Baal skidded to a stop in front of it, and Annalise recalled the Spinner King's words spoken to her from *The Book of Remembering*: *"This dagger, forged from a cockatrice's heart, yields the power to shatter illusions on the path to one's dreams. Use it to free the demon queen and the final reward is yours."*

If this was the demon queen he spoke of, Annalise would have her reward.

The beast landed behind the golden box it had been guarding before their fight began, and fought to stand. "Fight!" the Fate Spinner shrieked beyond the mirrored glass. "Take. Them. Down!" The beast flailed its wings and whimpered like a hurt child.

Esh-Baal approached the chimera's side slowly. This was their chance.

Pulse roaring in her ears, Annalise readied her dagger, vowing not to hurt the chimera too much. Almost to its shoulder, it raised its tail to strike. Annalise sliced into its tawny hide without hesitation—just enough for the dagger's magic to work. "I'm sorry," Annalise told it, but the damage was done.

The beast's eyes flooded with darkness. The dagger hummed in her hand as the chimera sighed a soft breath of swirling ash and did not breathe again.

A nervous energy rippled through the audience. The Fate Spinner rose from her blood throne, face simmering with rage. "No!" she cried, voice echoing past the stars. "Get up, you useless creature—get up and bring them to me!"

But whatever illusion had been cast over the chimera had already begun to break. Annalise and Esh-Baal watched in amazement as a spirit rose from its chest—a woman dressed in regal red, white, and black robes, wearing a crown matching the Spinner King's. She curtsied to Annalise and Esh-Baal, gratitude bright in her eyes.

Annalise exhaled her next words with wonder. "You're the Spinner Queen, aren't you?" she asked. "You are Saba, Mother of the Fate and Dream Spinner."

Inside the dark mirror a few feet away, the Fate Spinner's muscles went slack. Her chest heaved, old sorrows made new on her face. The grip on her staff loosened, and the shattered black heart on her palm was exposed.

"It can't be," the Fate Spinner said.

"But it is," the Spinner Queen replied coldly before turning back to Annalise. "Thank you for freeing me," the beautiful woman-spirit said. A large heart-shaped silver locket gleamed at the Spinner Queen's neck. If it was black, it would resemble Annalise's new dark mark exactly. The Spinner Queen's motherly expression made Annalise ache for her own parents. "In return, I may reveal something you've lost. Someone my daughter took prisoner when that prisoner risked themselves for a friend."

The Spinner Queen motioned to the shuddering box. "I leave the Fate Spinner's prisoner for you, dreamer, to do with as you will." She kissed Annalise's cheek, then removed her locket and strung it around Annalise's neck. A zing of energy rolled up from Annalise's toes. "My locket, in our family for centuries, sealed shut the moment Kismet cast Noll and me into the maze, and hasn't been opened since. This is the last reward to help guide you to Dreamland—the final lost item of the labyrinth. Deliver it to the gates of Dreamland and they shall open for you."

"Mercy," Annalise breathed, touching the silver heart, which warmed at her touch. "Thank you. Thank you so much." Esh-Baal and Annalise bowed.

"Farewell, Annalise," the Spinner Queen said with a snap of her fingers. "May the magic of dreams be yours." The locked box clicked open. And when Annalise and Esh-Baal raised their heads, the chimera's body withered to ash, and the spirit of the Spinner Queen vanished in a puff of red smoke.

The crowd rose up in a rage—booing and shouting, "TRAITOR TO THE FATE SPINNER!" and "DEATH TO ALL WHO BETRAY HER!"

Annalise gasped and covered her mouth, but not because of the audience—because of what she found inside the golden box when the red smoke cleared.

"Mister Edwards!" The shackles on his wrist and ankles broke with a clatter. The cloth binding his muzzle disappeared. And there, lying limp, curled at the bottom of the broken box, was the friend she'd lost in the maze—one small black fox.

The Fate Spinner twirled her staff of mirrored eyes, shook every nostalgic emotion from her face, and set her sights on Mister Edwards, her expression as hard as stone.

Annalise knelt at Mister Edwards's side, beside herself with joy, and hugged the scared fox tight. "Oh, my friend, it's so very good to see you!"

Mister Edwards gaped in shock and confusion, his copper eyes bouncing frantically back and forth between Annalise and Esh-Baal. "Miss . . . Miss Meriwether." He choked back tears of his own. "You shouldn't be here. You shouldn't have gone into the mirror of snow. I warned you!" The fox rubbed his bleeding wrist where the shackles used to be. "I'm so sorry. Please. You should leave me and go."

"Mister Edwards," Annalise stated excitedly, taking his paw. "We'll figure a way out." She smiled kindly at her friend. "We won't leave you behind."

"No!" Mister Edwards struggled against her. "You don't understand. You *must* leave me and save yourself." Mister Edwards shrank under the dark unicorn's hard gaze. "I didn't want to abandon you, I swear it. I . . . oh merciful gods," he sobbed harder. Annalise brushed the tears from his cheeks, furrowing her brow. "I didn't want to lose you." He squeezed his eyes tight and mumbled softly, "I never wanted to lead you here."

The crowd of specters booed. The moon brightened onto the Fate Spinner's mirror. The arena filled with the night wolves' cries.

"Now, now, Mister Edwards," the Fate Spinner interrupted with a lazy smirk. "You know as well as I do, that is a lie."

Mister Edwards winced. Annalise regarded him curiously.

Thunder cracked above the arena's domed bars. The shadowshine trees dotting the arena shook.

"After all," the Fate Spinner said with a proud grin. "You did agree to lead Annalise to me, *did you not?*"

Nobody moved.

The breath hissed from Annalise's lungs. Her face burned as she stared at the fox. "M-mister Edwards?" Annalise stuttered. The thread between her and Esh-Baal reddened into a strand of spun fire. Feelings old and new, of hurt, betrayal, and loneliness gathered inside her and swelled like a dam ready to burst. "You made a deal with the—with the Fate Spinner? To lead me . . . to *her?*"

The veiled spectators applauded and cheered—and laughed. Esh-Baal cantered nervously around Annalise and the fox. Smelling the winds, the unicorn's attention moved to the forty-foot-tall iron door to the right, and the dull thuds echoing behind it.

Esh-Baal stood before Annalise and said, "You should get on my back—now."

But Annalise was barely listening. All she could do was stroke the length of her hair—four, four, four, four—and hug herself tight. "This whole time?" she asked the crying fox.

"Since the train?" Her mind crawled in too many directions, and her frantic heart would not calm. She'd trusted him. She'd truly thought that he was a friend. "Was this your plan all along?"

The fox's cheeks sagged, his ears hanging like silken black socks. Finally, he nodded. "I'm ashamed to say it's true. When I beat the labyrinth last time, the Fate Spinner was waiting. I lied about Mister Amoureux finishing with me. How could he have. When her cockatrice had already turned him to stone." Annalise gasped. Mister Edwards lowered his eyes. "I was devastated and scared. I couldn't take him with me. My only option was to leave him in the courtyard and reach the end of the maze. To find the Spinner of Dreams so she could make him whole. But Fate captured me before I had a chance." He dropped to his knees, shaking his head. "I only wanted to get back the love the Fate Spinner stole from me. She told me she'd give him back if I guided you—a stranger then—through the labyrinth so she could get rid of you for good. But I couldn't go through with it. You'd become my friend—and I didn't want to lose you, too. I tried to help you, but by then, it was too late."

Annalise gripped her silver dagger in one hand and twisted the Spinner Queen's locket in the other. She knew how it felt to love someone the Fate Spinner had stolen. She'd have done almost anything to have her grandparents back—and even then, she'd still had her mom and dad. Mister Edwards was alone. After going through this maze and giving everything for her dream, she wasn't that same girl who left home scared of everything.

Only yesterday, she wouldn't have harmed a living creature for all the love and confidence and uncursed hands in the world. But now she was a dragon slayer—a defeater of giant arachnids, chimera, and skeletons—a girl with a fire unicorn—a friend to another brokenhearted soul. They had changed here, in this labyrinth. And that meant something to Annalise.

"Do you mean what you said, Mister Edwards?" Annalise asked him, staring at her boots. "That I—I mean, that you consider me a friend?"

Chin trembling, he nodded and met her eyes. "Yes. That's true too. I agreed to help her before I knew you. That still doesn't make it right. But"—he wiped his eyes and smiled defiantly at the Fate Spinner in the glass—"while the Spinner of Dreams may never grant my dream after what I've done, I promise, no matter what happens, I'll help you reach the Dreamland gates."

Esh-Baal lowered her head to Mister Edwards, sniffing him, golden eyes blazing. "He is telling the truth."

Annalise smiled at Esh-Baal, then at the sad black fox.

"I know." She felt no malice for Mister Edwards. How could she, when she'd betrayed her own parents by sneaking away after her dreams and leaving them behind? "No need for sorries, Mister Edwards. I understand." She looked over at the Fate Spinner, staring with haunted eyes at the locket around Annalise's neck. "Fate and dreams make us do desperate things, especially when they involve those we love. Besides," Annalise continued brightly, "you didn't lead me here, not really. I'm the one who left home to face her. With a little help from my new friends, I found my way here on my own."

Mister Edwards exploded into a grin and rushed Annalise with a hug. "Thank you, Miss Meriwether. Thank you!"

The creature behind the iron door shrieked loud enough for them to rush to cover their ears. From the way its voice carried, it sounded as tall as the door.

Esh-Baal lowered her wing for Mister Edwards to climb aboard. He looked at Annalise uncertainly, tail between his legs.

"Her name is Esh-Baal," Annalise said with a small laugh. "Her flames are cool, but her scales are slippery, so be careful." Reluctantly, Mister Edwards scrambled up Esh-Baal's bone-and-leather wing. "And hold on tight."

Annalise sheathed her dagger and tucked her locket under her cloak. Then, blackberry hair wafting gently in the hot, dry wind, heart screaming with fear in her chest, Annalise climbed up Esh-Baal's wing after him.

The Fate Spinner applauded, unfazed. "How touching. So noble of you to forgive him, when you're both seconds from death." The spectators stomped and cheered when the Fate Spinner stood. "Not that it matters," she said with a smug grin. "You won't survive what comes next." The Fate Spinner drew closer to the mirror and motioned to the obscured crowd. "When you are defeated, this is what you will become."

And the fog over the spectators cleared at last.

Chapter 30

You Must Believe

There once was a girl with the most beautiful dream anyone could ever imagine. Annalise, born with one hand twice the size of the other wanted her dreams to come true. But the Fate Spinner did everything in her power not to let that happen. And no matter how kind the girl was, or how much she loved or tried or gave, the world spat Annalise Meriwether out.

At least it had until now.

Thousands of glowing white wraiths occupied the stands circling the gladiator's arena. Like the chimera before them, the spectators were shackled in place. They snarled and lunged at their chains. Thrusting evil-eye talismans before them, their eyes shot blades at Annalise and Mister Edwards, atop the fire unicorn's back. "KISMET!" they chanted. "LONG LIVE THE FATE SPINNER!"

Esh-Baal turned in a circle, fires glowing with rage. Annalise stared at the spirits head-on.

"You don't deserve a dream!" one shouted. "If we can't have what we want, why should you!" another howled. "Go back, you freak!" the wraiths screamed. "Back to the maze where cursed dreamers belong!"

The monster hidden behind the gigantic door to their right battered the iron, denting the metal, shaking the trees and walls. But the Fate Spinner kept her polished onyx eyes on Annalise. "The wraiths in the stands were just like you once. Delusional dreamers, loyal to my sister. Now they're dead to the world, and their dreams are dust on my floor. There's no hope for dreamers like you." The Fate Spinner shifted her gaze onto Mister Edwards atop Esh-Baal's back and continued. "And no redemption for traitors like *him*. Your fates are set. Give up. You will never have your dreams."

Annalise gripped her dagger tighter, burning the wraiths' faces into her memory. Their words swarmed around her, trying to bite their way into her heart, to make her bitter like them. Yet all Annalise felt for them was pity.

She'd come too far to become one of them.

Strange noises erupted from beyond the arena wall at their backs. Not the starving cries of a bloodthirsty monster like the one behind the iron door but the happy cheers of—

Children?

Esh-Baal and her riders turned.

A grinding rumble echoed as the wall opened near where Annalise and her unicorn had entered the arena. Two dreamers leaped through the opening, cheering excitedly, as if they'd just burst into the green fields of Dreamland. Once through, the labyrinth stones rearranged, and the opening vanished.

Nightingale and Bowie.

"Ah!" the Fate Spinner said, relaxing deeper into her throne. "Right on time. How delightful."

Annalise and Mister Edwards dismounted Esh-Baal and hurried to greet them.

"What are you two doing here?" Annalise asked. Her mouth went suddenly dry. Their skin was covered in dirt and cuts; their jeans and leggings, shredded; their hair tossed with debris. Annalise wondered what horrors the Fate Spinner had put Nightingale and Bowie through.

"We could ask you the same thing," Bowie said. "How did you get here?" He glanced between Annalise and

Mister Edwards, the wraiths and Esh-Baal, with a mixture of disbelief, anger, hurt—and awe. "And *where* did you find a unicorn?"

Annalise smiled gratefully at Esh-Baal. "I didn't," Annalise answered. "She found me."

Nightingale circled Esh-Baal, eyes sparkling despite her worried expression. She reached out to touch Esh-Baal's neck and laughed when the dark unicorn leaned into her hand. Nightingale's enchanted grin quickly fell into dismay. "This was supposed to be the end of the labyrinth." She faced the Fate Spinner's reflection. "This was supposed to be Dreamland. I don't understand."

Bowie glared at the Fate Spinner. "We won our final challenge. We beat the cyclopes and the red-eyed wolves. We made it to this big, elaborate, white-framed mirror, and we saw the arched gates of gold in the reflection. Crows even flew down and gave us tickets to see the Spinner of Dreams. But when we went through the mirror to Dreamland, we ended up here."

Nightingale nodded. "It doesn't make any sense."

"What color were the crows that gave you tickets?" Mister Edwards asked quietly.

"Black," Bowie replied. "Why?"

"They belong to the Fate Spinner," Mister Edwards answered. "The white crows are loyal to the Spinner of

Dreams, and though they may watch over dreamers from above, they are not permitted inside the labyrinth walls."

Nightingale shook her head, blinking around her in disbelief. "We thought we'd be seeing our parents. We—" Her voice jagged. "We thought we'd won our dreams—but again, the Fate Spinner stole them away?"

"Fate tricked us." Bowie clenched his fists and approached the Fate Spinner's dark glass. "How could you trick us again?"

"Wait. What if this arena *is* the end?" Nightingale asked. "What if this entire labyrinth is a trap?"

Gooseflesh rippled Annalise's neck. *That can't be true, can it?*

The creature behind the large door threw itself against the iron harder and shrieked in frustration.

Bowie gaped at his sister, revelation dawning. "Oh, you've got to be kidding me. What if Dreamland doesn't even exist?"

The Fate Spinner stood and applauded, shouting, "Bravo, Mister Tristle! You and your sister have discovered what very few are privileged to learn. That there really is no hope left for dreamers. And more important," she added with an innocent pout, "Mister Tristle is right." The black crows screamed. "Dreamland died years ago."

Mister Edwards stroked his ragged black tail and blinked up at Annalise. "Miss Meriwether? That can't be right . . . can it?"

Nightingale, Bowie, and Mister Edwards looked hopeless.

They looked tired. They looked done. Only Esh-Baal, breathing flames and pawing the earth, still looked prepared to fight.

Annalise stood before the dreamers and spoke. "No. It isn't true, and you mustn't believe her." Annalise remembered Reverie and Dreamland from the Spinner King's memory—vibrant, lovely, and very much alive. "This is her trick. Her lies are the true curse of fate. The illusions, the slivers of fear, the doubt she puts in dreamer's heads? They're designed to lead us astray."

"Sorry to disappoint," the Fate Spinner replied, all trace of humor gone. "But it is very much true. I may be a lot of things, but I am no liar."

The Book of Remembering.

Maybe the book would show her the truth—images, clues, information that proved the Fate Spinner was lying about Dreamland.

As Annalise reached for the book, the Fate Spinner continued. "If you need more proof," she said, motioning to the wall to her right with an excited grin on her face, "my labyrinth has something to show you that might convince you. . . ."

An odd, small mirror, set between two shadowshine trees, opened in the wall and a horrific image swirled into view.

"Mom and Dad!" Nightingale threw her hands over her mouth and ran to the mirror where her parents appeared inside the Fate Spinner's red palace. They were guarded by twin dragons—one black, one white. Their parents' hair was smoking, their clothes burnt. The two squatted in the corner in fear as the dragons bore down. "They look alive. Bowie . . . are they alive?"

Bowie lunged at the Fate Spinner's glass without answering her and screamed, "Let them go!" He banged his fists on the mirror and flew back in a blast.

Nightingale ran to her brother.

Mister Edwards stayed by Annalise's side.

"I won't let them go. Not unless Annalise agrees to work with me," the Fate Spinner purred sweetly. "Isn't that right, Annalise?"

A chaos of black crows screamed at her shoulders. Annalise's unicorn reared, flaming hooves kicking the air, blazing with all the fires of the underworld.

But at that moment, an unexpected pain drew Annalise's attention. The dark mark Annalise thought was dormant sizzled with energy—like static building before a storm. Mister Edwards stared at Annalise's great hand and smiled with a sliver of hope.

"You're a monster," Nightingale growled at the smug Fate

Spinner. "A monster—without a heart!"

"Well, that may be. Nonetheless, it doesn't look like they'll make it, does it?" She shrugged and batted her eyes. "A shame, since I just gave them back their lives. Oh, speaking of parents. Look who I found, Annalise. You will be so pleased."

The view in the mirror changed.

"Annalise!" Mattie Meriwether shrieked behind the mirror, pounding the glass.

"Mom?" Annalise rushed in front of Nightingale and Bowie and gaped in horror. Her mom was trapped in a dead end of the labyrinth. Four enormous night wolves snarled behind her.

"Save me!" her mom shrieked. "Don't let me die!"

Black smoke rolled through the mirror, and her dad appeared next.

In another dim corridor, her dad stumbled through the labyrinth, bleeding through ragged clothes, ivy twining his body, dragging him down. He kept falling and getting up, but each time, the ivy pulled tighter. "Annalise," he groaned, meeting her gaze. "Be a good girl. Let your dreams go." He fell. The wall opened like a mouth. The ivy dragged him inside. "I beg you—GIVE YOURSELF TO HER!"

Annalise heaved in breath after breath, mind scrambling.

Her parents would never ask her to do those things. Would they? Were these images real, or was the Fate Spinner playing them for fools?

"However," the Fate Spinner went on, twirling her staff of mirrored eyes, "I am a generous enchantress, so if you walk into my mirror now, I'll agree to let your friends and their loved ones leave my labyrinth unharmed." The Fate Spinner motioned to the black-smoke mirror. "As a bonus, I'll even restore the traitor's husband to flesh and blood."

A new image bloomed on the glass.

"Mister Amoureux!" Mister Edwards uttered a forlorn cry. The statue of a silver fox, hung by a chain in a dungeon, twisted slightly. A devil-like beast with rose-red skin, black eyes, and curved horns pushed the stone fox back and forth with an ominous laugh. One hard swing would shatter him against the wall. Mister Edwards fell to his knees before the Fate Spinner's mirror. "I beg you, please. Let him go."

The Fate Spinner clicked her pointed black nails on her staff. "Traitor. You only have yourself to blame for any hurt your fox endures. If Annalise doesn't comply, your husband will end up shattered on the dungeon floor. Or, if I'm generous, I'll restore his life—only to have him spend eternity as my servant. Every day I'll remind him why he's here. When I use him as a stool or my monsters' plaything. When he's crying and alone. When I work his tender paws to the bone, I'll remind him he's suffering because his partner chose to help a cursed stranger over him." The Fate Spinner turned to Annalise. "Give up, and I'll free them. Fight me, and they die with you."

Nightingale and Bowie whimpered quietly, sneaking desperate glances at Annalise. Mister Edwards wiped his tears on his arm, eyes low and ashamed.

"No!" Annalise shouted. All eyes turned to her. "We mustn't listen to her. Instead of believing in those fighting to keep us from our dreams, believe in the cats that led us to the train and the bravery it took to follow them. Believe in the strength we've built within us to get where we are now." Annalise stroked Esh-Baal's black scales with care. "Believe in your parents' love and in the love of Mister Amoureux. Because the end of the labyrinth isn't a place many live to see, and I believe we're almost there." Annalise paused. "Believing you're worthy of your dreams is where the magic of the Spinner of Dreams lives. That's the secret the Fate Spinner doesn't want you to know. That's the reason we dreamers are here together."

"That's enough," the Fate Spinner spat with disgust. "It's over. *This is your end.*"

The white crows drew closer to the domed bars.

Their cries sounded like cheers.

Annalise turned her back on the Fate Spinner. "If we believe in the Dreamland outside the Fate Spinner's gates, she cannot defeat us!" In a quick thrust, Annalise raised her dagger to the sky. A blast of fireworks shot from the tip of the blade, lighting the dark in gold.

No, not fireworks—butterflies.

The poets of hope.

The golden-winged butterflies poured from her dagger, eclipsed the bars, and circled higher than the white crows. In the magic of their fluttering wings, the dark sky lightened. *"See your world as your dream, you will live, as you deem . . ."* they sang.

A shimmering dust of sunlit mica fell from their wings, and suddenly, the view began to change. On the horizon, the golden spires of a grand palace of clear crystal quartz arose. Four tattered flags bearing the profile of a woman in a crown of crows and horns snapped from the turrets. Annalise, Mister Edwards, Nightingale, and Bowie blinked at the heavens, reflections of Dreamland in their eyes.

The crowd sighed and calmed. The monster behind the door quieted and stilled. The poets' magic dusted the arena in glitter.

Dreamland exists for those who don't give up.

But her friends still didn't look convinced. They turned back to the small mirror where they'd seen their family, where the stone fox still dangled now, uncertainty clear on their faces.

The Fate Spinner fumed behind her mirror, glaring at Annalise, a cloak of shrieking black crows at her back. If she had seen the poets of hope and the images of Dreamland their magic produced, she didn't let on.

"That was quite a speech, Annalise," the Fate Spinner said like a calm before a storm. "Too bad every word is a delusion born from your broken dreamer's mind." The images of Dreamland drifted away, but the butterflies remained— soaring over the spectators who trailed the tiny poets in awe. The Fate Spinner's voice rose in a boom. "I HAVE YOUR LOVED ONES BEHIND MY WALLS! And if you do not give yourself to me, you will end up like those fools in the stands. Believing in my sister and her dreams will not get you anywhere but dead!"

Annalise's dagger hummed in her white-knuckled grip.

Her dagger.

If the images were illusions, and her dagger *shattered* illusions. . .

Esh-Baal glanced at her intensely, horn blazing with new fire, the thread linking them shining bright. Annalise's dark

318

mark pinged with an electric charge she recognized as a signal of rightness. A signal that her instincts were true.

"What say you, Annalise?" The Fate Spinner leaned forward, a flash of annoyance crossing her face when Annalise raised her dagger high.

One-two-three-four.

"I say you're a liar!" Annalise lunged at the small mirror.

The blade struck. The glass wavered and a new image—a true image—appeared: the devil alone in the dungeon, chained to the ground, asleep.

Annalise and the others grinned. It wasn't real. Annalise couldn't tell if the Fate Spinner saw what they'd seen or not. But before she could find out, the arena shuddered.

The shackled wraiths gasped, then silenced. The creature behind the door screamed like a demon. Annalise's great hand shocked with pain when the forty-foot-tall iron door began to rise.

Esh-Baal lowered one wing. "Everyone—get on." Nightingale and Bowie glanced at each other and scrambled up Esh-Baal's black wing behind Mister Edwards. Annalise went last and sat in front.

"Her name is Esh-Baal," Annalise told the Tristles. "Hold on tight."

As they rose, someone in the crowd caught Annalise's eye.

In the first row nearest the ground, a white cat in a top hat and monocle tipped his hat to her as they passed.

Muse!

"Good luck," he shouted as Esh-Baal soared past. "May the magic of dreams be yours!" Muse vanished from sight as quickly as he'd appeared.

But that's okay, Annalise thought. For in her heart of hearts, she knew he was here somewhere. And soon, she'd see her Muse again.

Annalise gripped her dagger and flew.

Chapter 31

THE DEMON WITHIN

A monster emerged from the dark cave behind the iron door, more terrifying than the cockatrice and chimera combined. The audience of wraiths jumped up and cheered, rattling their chains. The Fate Spinner watched closely from her throne as a living nightmare emerged into the crimson moon's light.

The demon, as tall as the bars doming the arena, had long bruise-dark tentacles that lashed out in a frenzy of slippery whips. Four giant tarantula heads atop the creature hissed in unison. Spiders. Annalise couldn't seem to get away from them. Red mirrored eyes with slit pupils capped each tentacle, all aimed and staring at Annalise—and Annalise could not look away.

Horror, bright as a million flares, lit inside her.

Panic wasn't far behind.

At the sight of the goliath demon, Annalise's throat closed. Her heart swelled. Lightning bolts shot through her. An army of anxious black thoughts scuttled over her brain, and behind Annalise's back, Nightingale, Bowie, and Mister Edwards screamed—maybe in fear, maybe fighting to hang on as Esh-Baal darted in and out of lashing tentacles, and dived.

Hot wind raging past her ears, Annalise forced her gaze from the monster and focused on her dream:

I wish to rule my own destiny and rid myself of this curse!

She repeated her mantra until it sank into the dark soil of her mind—until it seeded and bloomed. And as the armored fire unicorn borne from her curse reared before the demon, Annalise stared the fiend down and shouted into the dusty red wind, "Now, dreamers—we fight!"

The audience cheered. Esh-Baal charged.

And the demon lunged.

Tentacles lashed out around them—staring, reaching, grabbing, brushing past Annalise's skin. Esh-Baal dodged into a dive. Mister Edwards clung tighter to Annalise as Annalise ducked and slashed with her blade, but the tentacles were too fast—they grabbed and pulled at her while her friends screamed and fought behind her.

The demon was everywhere, and they couldn't escape.

"Give up," the demon hissed from the dark corners of Annalise's mind. "Let go, little weakling, little freak, little helpless, foolish girl. You know you always fall, so fall!" Annalise's breath came hot. Her heart sped. Every eye on its writhing body was staring her down.

Suddenly, Annalise wanted to run—to curl into a ball in the corner and hide from this demon, from her dreams, and fear, and her fate, and the whole world. Annalise counted to four, and four, and four, and four, struggling to hang on to her darting unicorn as worry-thoughts tunneled into her mind deeper and faster and uglier than ever before.

Behind her, Nightingale and Bowie shouted her name. Arms grabbed at her back. Mister Edwards called over the roar of the crowd. Annalise slipped and couldn't hang on. Before Annalise knew what was happening, the air *whoosh*ed out from under her and she fell.

The crowd broke into nervous cheers and staggered applause as Annalise plummeted. Hair and cloak and four black ribbons rippling upward, tears of defeat in her eyes, the dagger flew from Annalise's hand. Before it hit the ground, the demon caught it in one of its mouths.

The Fate Spinner's surprised laughter rang through the arena.

Annalise landed in a soft copse of shadowshine roots. Esh-Baal skidded to a halt beside her, gold lightning blazing from her horn. "Annalise, get back on!" Esh-Baal lowered her wing. But Annalise wasn't fast enough.

The tentacle demon wrapped its many-eyed limbs around Annalise's body and lowered its tarantula heads so close that Annalise could see down their throats.

Mister Edwards, fangs bared and growling, scurried down her unicorn's wing, ready to bite anything that moved. Nightingale and Bowie followed right after, but the demon shoved them away.

"Annalise, you are determined, I will give you that." The Fate Spinner's voice rang out from the mirror. "But determined isn't a pretty look on a girl like you. Are you finally ready to give yourself and the unicorn to me? Or shall I have my tentufear break you and your friends in the most violent and painful of ways?"

Nightingale and Bowie screamed. Mister Edwards darted in and out of the monster's limbs, trying to grab Annalise's dagger.

Then the demon turned to face them.

The closer she looked at the tentufear, the more she saw.

Its limbs were not solid at all but consisted of millions of tiny bruise-colored spiders, crawling over its body. transferring worry-thoughts onto her. *No, it's an illusion. Don't look*, she told herself and forced her eyes away. *Focus on getting your dagger away from this horrible creature.*

Esh-Baal, who'd stood quietly observant until now, reared and charged at the Fate Spinner's mirror, smashing it with her horn. Sparks exploded, but the glass remained intact. The Fate Spinner glared at the dark unicorn, and Esh-Baal glared back.

"You cannot get to me nor I to you, as you well know," the Fate Spinner said to Esh-Baal. "I will get you and the girl, one way or another. And when I do, neither of you will live or dream much longer."

The unicorn of fire and dark-hearted armor shook with rage. "You don't deserve to stand in the presence of Annalise Meriwether," Esh-Baal said. "And despite what you think of us dreamers, we will always be stronger than your fates made us out to be."

The Fate Spinner leveled her cold gaze onto Annalise.

Annalise did not break the Fate Spinner's stare—she would not look away first, even if her eyes froze until the end of time. The locket the Spinner Queen gave her gleamed in the red moonlight. And even as the tentufear squeezed, a powerful strength buzzed beneath her skin. Annalise let it fill her and steady her breath—one-two-three-four. Her body buzzed with the fire of determination.

Annalise gave the Fate Spinner a confident grin.

"That's right," Mister Edwards said, trapped by the tentufear alongside her. "We'll fight you together, and together, we will win. Then," he shouted loudly for the anxious crowd, "WE WILL HAVE OUR DREAMS!"

The arena remained silent. None of the spectators made a sound. The tentufear stood by, all eyes on the Fate Spinner, as if holding back was the hardest thing to do.

Annalise eyed her dagger determinedly, lodged in one of the tentufear's fanged jaws.

The Fate Spinner raised her staff and rose. "Have it your way. Battle my demon. I shall enjoy watching you fall."

Dark winds rose. The tentufear released the dreamers.

White crows by the hundreds poured into the sky above the bars—caw, caw-caw, caw! The poets of hope soared overhead, singing their bard songs. Annalise glanced up at them all with a smile, with a new impenetrable hope.

Right before she rose to her feet, Annalise lifted the Spinner Queen's locket outside of her ragged plum cloak and spun it four times.

The silver flashed gold only once, but the wraiths

saw. They snapped their heads from the white crows and enchanted butterflies and onto Annalise. And when Annalise, Mister Edwards, Nightingale, and Bowie stood and brushed themselves off, the wraiths in the stands sprang to their feet—bleary-eyed and blinking as if waking up.

Then they cheered a new name. A name Annalise never thought she'd hear cheered *for*, rather than against. "Annalise, Annalise, Annalise, ANNALISE!"

The crowd applauded and pumped their shimmering fists.

For her.

Blackberry hair and ribbons whipping fiercely in the icy wind, Annalise shouted at the Fate Spinner over the rising storm, tears of triumph in her eyes. "We did not come to your labyrinth to give in to your threats, Fate Spinner. We are all dreamers here—those in the stands and in the labyrinth—even you. Each of us has come for our dreams. And I, for one, will not give up UNTIL I CLAIM THEM!"

The wraiths went wild. Nightingale cheered. Bowie pumped his fist high in the air and said, "Annalise, you are the coolest girl I know!"

Annalise didn't know it was possible for her whole body to blush.

Golden butterflies swooped in and fluttered madly

around her as Nightingale scowled at her brother. "What am I, moldy headcheese?"

Bowie didn't have a chance to reply.

The tentufear rose to its full height and snapped its tentacles forward in a burst, grabbing both siblings at once. It laughed low and wild, then launched them high and far over the labyrinth walls. The wraiths stopped cheering. Nightingale and Bowie screamed as they flew. Lightning struck from all points in the sky, and the cries of Annalise's new friends died.

Night wolves howled in the distance.

But Annalise howled loudest of all.

"NO!" A familiar power crawled under her skin and burst. Pulsed. Raged. Black fire licked behind her eyes, emboldening the fire inside her.

Mister Edwards slipped his paw into her great hand and squeezed four times. "They'll be fine," the fox said, nodding fast. The poets of hope fluttering overhead mirrored in his eyes. "I'm sure of it. Maybe they'll even find their way to Dreamland before us?"

Annalise forced herself to focus on her dream.

I wish to rule my own destiny and rid myself of this curse.
I wish to rule my own destiny and rid myself of this curse.
I wish to rule my own destiny and rid myself of this curse.

I wish to rule my own destiny and rid myself of this curse.

Breathing hard through her nose, chin tucked to her chest, Annalise narrowed her gaze onto the dagger gripped in tentufear's maw as it moved slowly toward her.

She needed that dagger.

And she would have it.

Suddenly, the tiny black thorns on the shadowshine trees sprouted long and sharp as sabers. *Shadowshine thorns create an unseen barrier protecting dreamers from harm.*

Annalise grinned and gritted her teeth. "Yes, Mister Edwards. A dreamer must always have hope." She ripped a thorn free and handed it to the fox. "Take this and use it as a weapon. It'll help protect you."

The Fate Spinner banged her staff. Red lightning flashed across the black sky. "Dreamers," she bellowed, "prepare to die!"

"Get on!" Esh-Baal called, lowering a wing. Mister Edwards took the foot-long shadowshine thorn with a grin and scrambled onto Esh-Baal's back, wrapping the dark unicorn's long fiery mane around his body, securing him safely so he had his paw free to fight.

The moment the fox wielded the thorn, his body shone with a golden glow.

As Esh-Baal galloped from ground to sky, the Fate Spinner

gripped her staff so tightly the mirrored eyes directly beneath her fist shattered. Black blood leaking between her fingers, she leveled her staff at the glass as they swooped past. "May the best Spinner win," the enchantress said.

The crowd cheered Annalise's name.

Chapter 32

THE FINAL BATTLE

The wraiths in the stands went wild when the dreamers soared over the arena and the tentufear lunged after them. Esh-Baal rounded the far wall. The demon whipped its spider-coated arms at Esh-Baal, but the fire unicorn wove in and out of its reach.

Annalise set her sights on the tarantula head clutching her dagger in its fangs, and cried over the cheers of the crowd ("Annalise!" "Mister Edwards!" "Esh-Baal!" "DREAMERS FOR THE WIN!"), "Esh-Baal, take me to my dagger!"

The black heart of Annalise's great hand zinged with sudden gold flames. A new power had sparked within it—her great hand wanted to fight.

She leveled her black-hearted palm at the tentufear and blasted it with firebolts of gold. The spider-heads hissed and screamed and thrashed. Several arms severed and fell. Esh-Baal cheered and took a quick turn. She galloped higher, hooves blazing, shooting her own golden flames. When her head was turned, the tentufear swiped a large tentacle from the right. Annalise slipped. Mister Edwards clamped his shadowshine thorn between his teeth and grabbed her before she fell.

"Thank you, Mister Edwards!" Annalise hollered.

Mister Edwards slashed tentacles left and right with his poisonous shadowshine thorn, leaving trails of gold shine in his wake. Each of the demon's arms that he hit thrashed and pulled away. "Anytime!"

Esh-Baal rose amid whipping tentacles. She aimed her horn and dived at the tentufear. Before Annalise had a chance to strike, Esh-Baal pierced the tarantula head holding Anna-lise's dagger. Its ugly face lit on fire. The tentufear bellowed and screeched. And the dagger slipped from its maw.

Annalise caught the dagger midair and laughed. "Hello, old friend," Annalise said under her breath.

Mister Edwards cheered, "Yes!"

The tentufear came at them harder—lashing out, it wrapped Esh-Baal's legs in its arms. "Oh, no you don't,"

Annalise said as Esh-Baal dropped from the sky.

Without missing a beat, Annalise slashed the tentacles binding Esh-Baal's legs with her blade. The creature shrieked and let go, arms smoking. The crowd broke into applause. And the dreamers went back for more.

The tentufear reappeared, avoiding Annalise's dagger. Mister Edwards hit its arms again and again, until he jabbed the tentufear so hard his thorn snapped. "Oh dear," he shouted over the moans of the crowd. "I lost my weapon!"

The golden aura surrounding him vanished.

"Take these." Annalise pushed her hair from her eyes and checked her left pocket. She still had the sharp rocks he'd given her from the Spinner King's court. "You blinded the cockatrice. I believe you can get this demon, too."

Mister Edwards beamed. "Good idea, Miss Meriwether!"

Fate's demon of eyes and arms, venom and fangs, attacked from behind, thrashing and shrieking, trying desperately to bite. Esh-Baal took hit after hit, and Mister Edwards kept slipping. They wouldn't be able to keep this pace up much longer. "Esh-Baal," Annalise said. "If we blast the tentufear's heads at the same time, maybe we can destroy it." Esh-Baal shifted direction. "Mister Edwards, ready your weapons!"

Esh-Baal flew to the tops of the arches, ten feet from the demon's heads. She swooped around, blasting flames with her horn. Arms lashed, slashed, and fell. Finally, one of the tarantula heads lunged at Annalise, jaws open to bite.

Mister Edwards roared like a lion and pitched a jagged stone straight into one of its mirrored eyes. The eyes shattered, and the entire tarantula head shattered with it.

The spectators jumped up and cheered. Shards of tarantula-glass skittered across the floor. Annalise screamed, "You did it!"

The tentufear shuddered and froze. The Fate Spinner, who'd been enjoying the show, shrieked at the beast. "DON'T JUST STAND THERE, STUPID! DO SOMETHING!"

Esh-Baal skirted the walls and tops of the trees, away from the demon. "Look," the unicorn said, hovering a safe distance away. A large crack had formed in the stone floor and across the Fate Spinner's mirror.

The Fate Spinner stumbled back, staff tight in her fist, and gaped at her mirror in fear. Maybe the secret to defeating the tentufear, and maybe even winning the labyrinth, was shattering its eyes?

"Miss Meriwether. Look." Mister Edwards pointed at the shattered tarantula head on the ground.

"Mercy."

A child's spirit rose from the shattered glass. He had long copper hair, smiling eyes, and carried a sword. "Thank you for freeing me," the boy said. "Long live the dreamers and the Spinner of Dreams!" The boy's spirit spun into the sky and merged with the faraway stars. He must have been one of the dreamers who'd lost against the Fate Spinner—a soul she'd trapped in her labyrinth.

Maybe the other tentufear heads were trapped souls, too?

"Everyone, aim for its eyes!" Annalise yelled.

The demon shook off its pain and laughed in a grungy growl, pointing its remaining eyes at Annalise. "You're mine."

Annalise raised her darkly marked palm at the beast and answered, "Not if you're mine first."

They countered the demon's attacks—Annalise with her great hand, Esh-Baal with her horn, both with all the golden fire they possessed. They'd dipped low, so Annalise could rip another shadowshine thorn from a tree, when a tarantula bit Esh-Baal's leg.

The unicorn screamed, high and terrible. Annalise leveled her dark mark at one of the tentufear's heads and blasted a bolt of energy so powerful, its head exploded into shards of broken red light.

"Good job," Esh-Baal said, flying higher, weaker than before.

A crack, larger than the last, slashed through the Fate Spinner's mirror. The Fate Spinner screamed in a rage, but all Annalise could see in her eyes was fear.

Their plan was working.

A teenage girl with short black hair stood among the shards of the shattered spider-head in a white-feather dress. The girl bowed low to Annalise. Laughing softly, she soared into the air and chased the golden butterflies until she faded from sight.

Another imprisoned dreamer set free.

The crowd cheered their names.

Annalise counted to four as Esh-Baal readied for another pass. Annalise and Esh-Baal blasted bolts of light at the final tarantula heads and missed. But when they struck its many smaller eyes, each hit made another fracture in the Fate Spinner's mirror, arena, floor, and walls. Esh-Baal dodged tentacles and teeth. When the tentufear sped after Annalise and Esh-Baal, Annalise blasted another of its ugly heads—*crack, smash.*

It shattered into shards of red and fell.

The spectators jumped to their ghost-feet and cheered so loudly, the walls blew dust. The spirit of another dreamer—a young woman with blue eyes, gold hair, and deep dimples—lifted into the crimson-lit sky. She thanked Annalise kindly, waved at the applauding crowd, and vanished.

The Fate Spinner shrieked over the frenzied crowd,

glaring at Annalise. "Eat the traitor—and bring the girl and her monster to me!"

The wraiths booed and threw ghostly rotten tomatoes at the mirror; the glowing tomatoes hit and exploded into dust motes. They screamed her name louder than ever.

"Get ready, dreamers!" Annalise cried. Only the charred head Esh-Baal had speared remained. Esh-Baal tipped nose down and dived toward the staggering, smoking, shrieking mess of a tentufear through a cloud of ash and flame. Mister Edwards clung tighter. And Annalise leaned over, legs gripping Esh-Baal's sides, raised her great hand, and shouted to her unicorn, "Now!"

The power between Annalise and her unicorn surged from Esh-Baal's horn and Annalise's dark mark all at once. A beam of gold light blasted the last tentufear head. Crimson glass sprayed. More cracks grew in the walls, floor, and the Fate Spinner's mirror. And the spirit of an old man with a cane in a ragged suit stood among the debris. He danced a jig and tipped his hat to Annalise. "Bless you, dreamer," he said and disappeared in a glitter of dust.

The crowd went bonkers. Mister Edwards shouted to Annalise over the wind and the audience's cheers, "You are nothing short of incredible." He threw his head back and laughed. "That was amazing!"

"So are you, my friend!" Annalise replied, reveling at the joy in her bones. She realized then what it was like to have friends who laughed with her and not at her—and she was overcome with happiness.

Together, they and Esh-Baal soared.

"You won't escape," the Fate Spinner shouted from behind her fractured mirror. "None of these dreamers in the stands could beat all the monsters I threw at them. And neither will you." The Fate Spinner sneered at Esh-Baal, rising above despite her wounds. "Not even my enchanted sister could escape me."

A prickle of warning inched up Annalise's neck. Esh-Baal pumped her fiery wings and swooped over the stands. The crowd stomped and applauded and cried, "LONG LIVE THE SPINNER OF DREAMS!"

The Fate Spinner rose from her dais, eyes blazing. The tips of her hair glowed red with filament flames as she aimed her staff at her once fearsome demon, convulsing on the dirt before her, headless and dying. "Get up," she demanded through gritted teeth, "AND BRING THE GIRL AND HER MONSTER *TO ME*!"

The poets of hope glittered like winged stars in a trail behind Esh-Baal, Annalise, and Mister Edwards.

Hundreds of white crows caw-caw-caw-cawed above the

bars. A thrill rippled through Annalise; their cries reminded her of home.

Hair splayed in a blackberry fan, Annalise faced the Fate Spinner and roared, "You cannot have me!" Esh-Baal soared past the mirror again. "Dreams are the only true magic that exists. No matter what you do to me, I'LL NEVER GIVE UP MY DREAMS!"

As they swooped past the Fate Spinner, something odd shone through the cracks in the Fate Spinner's mirror: a faint golden light. "Do you see that, Mister Edwards?"

"If you mean the lights of Dreamland, then yes, Miss Meriwether. Yes, I do!"

"I see it, too," Esh-Baal said, and galloped, hooves blazing over the stands. "Let's finish this demon," Esh-Baal shouted. "Get ready—our dreams await!"

The tentufear staggered into a stand. In one last burst of energy, it drew to its full height and rushed them with everything it had. Annalise gathered every ounce of her power into her great hand and felt Esh-Baal funnel the same into her great horn.

Annalise and Esh-Baal locked eyes and grinned.

"Together," Annalise said.

"Together," Esh-Baal agreed.

"Together!" cried Mister Edwards.

One of the tentufear's arms lashed out when they weren't looking and struck Esh-Baal's wing. Esh-Baal screamed.

Her wing went limp. A searing spike of pain struck Annalise's great hand. "Esh-Baal, watch out!"

Tentacles coiled around the unicorn's legs. Esh-Baal teetered and reared. Her passengers screamed. The unicorn's hooves blazed brighter as she fought to get away, but more and more tentacles came. Mister Edwards hollered while biting at the fleshy black whips dragging Esh-Baal down. But the tentufear only wrapped them tighter in its strong arms—so tight, Annalise couldn't breathe.

Esh-Baal strained, arching her neck and rearing. Mister Edwards punched and kicked the tentufear, ripping into its flesh. The string between Annalise and her unicorn dulled. Esh-Baal fired from her horn, and Annalise from her dark mark as the air leached from their lungs, but it wasn't enough.

For the first time on her journey, Annalise let herself think: *What if this is the end? What if I don't make it out of this maze? What will happen to my parents, to my home, to Carriwitchet, to my dream?*

Unwanted tears stung Annalise's eyes. Panic set in and froze her with fear.

No, no, no, no! Stop this. You mustn't give up—you need to fight!

Esh-Baal plunged.

Mister Edwards shouted, "We can do this. We mustn't give up!" Mister Edwards bit the beast again and again, but tentacles wrapped him anyway.

Annalise set her eyes to the poets of hope, fluttering past the bars above. She remembered why she came to the labyrinth and drew upon the very last of her store of strength. Annalise fought and wriggled and finally—she freed her great hand. She blasted herself free from the tentufear, then did the same for Esh-Baal and Mister Edwards.

"You did it!" the fox cheered, pulling himself free from the tentufear's now limp tentacle.

"I knew you could do it," said Esh-Baal, kicking free into the air.

Annalise leveled her great palm at the Fate Spinner's demon. Esh-Baal did the same with her horn. They screamed a warrior's cry and released the power within them. Mister Edwards hooted and hollered as twin streams of golden light converged midair and finally blasted the tentufear away in a spray of darkness and light.

"NO!" the Fate Spinner cried. "No, no, no!"

Everyone else cheered. The poets of hope dropped their golden shimmer of dust, dusting the wraiths in a glamour of light.

Annalise, Mister Edwards, and Esh-Baal watched to see

if another spirit would rise from the fallen monster, when a sudden rumble shook the walls. The wraiths in the stands all gasped at once.

The chains binding them shattered, setting each imprisoned spectator free. The spirits of dreamers floated upward, darting, soaring, laughing, and crying ephemeral tears of joy. Happiness and sincerity, love and appreciation, all radiated from them in shimmering bursts of light. The freed dreamers said to the three at once: "Thank you, dreamers. Long live the Spinner of Dreams—and may the magic of dreams be yours!"

One after the other, the dreamers sped through the bars and into the night. After they'd gone, Esh-Baal flew toward Fate's mirror. The glass was so webbed with cracks, the Fate Spinner's reflection was barely recognizable. Esh-Baal skidded to a halt on the ground a few feet away.

The Fate Spinner leveled her eyes at them, scowling, and shook her head in confusion. "How did you beat them all?" She ran a hand over her plaited hair and growled at Annalise. "How dare you—a nothing girl, a cursed dreamer—stand before me? How dare you *beat* me—the Fate Spinner herself?"

Then quieter, and more to herself, "How did she best me again?"

The dirt floor and walls, webbed with cracks like the

mirror, ruptured with bright golden light from between the breaks. A jolt of energy sparked through Annalise's mark, energy she recognized as truth.

Annalise was sure that the entrance to Dreamland lay beyond the Fate Spinner's mirror.

This is it.

Annalise and Mister Edwards dismounted from Esh-Baal, a distance from the glass.

Unlike the growling black fox, Annalise regarded the Fate Spinner with soft eyes. "If you truly believe people shouldn't dare to dream, and that our heads are filled with nonsense, I feel sorry for you. How sad that you'll never know how wonderful it is to be a dreamer or to have a dreamer for a friend." Annalise smiled at Mister Edwards and then up at Esh-Baal. They returned the look with love.

The Fate Spinner drew away from her side of the glass. Her hair was disheveled; her black makeup smeared. "How funny that you pity me," she said with a coy tilt of her head, "when I, like those Tristle children, know the cold, hard truth. You may have beaten my monsters, but no gates of gold and white will rise through this arena floor and let you into Dreamland." She drew closer to her cracked mirror. "As I said before, there is no Dreamland." Her black eyes twinkled, amused. "Ask me how I know."

Annalise stroked her hair four times, breath quickening,

343

a sour swirl in her gut. Esh-Baal gave Annalise a pleading look, but for the first time, Annalise didn't know what she was trying to say.

"Don't listen to her, Miss Meriwether," Mister Edwards said. "She—"

"She's dead!" the Fate Spinner snapped. Annalise and Mister Edwards gasped. The black and white crows screamed. "That's right. On the day of your birth, I struck my sister down with a curse so powerful, it broke two worlds. That is why," she continued, snarling and baring her teeth, "even though you've defeated me and won my labyrinth, you and your *friends* will never have your dreams." She glared back, chin raised in defiance, and spat, "See for yourself."

Jet-black smoke swirled behind what remained of the Fate Spinner's mirror.

Adrenaline jumped into Annalise's chest like a feral cat and scratched when the smoke cleared, and finally, Annalise saw the truth.

Chapter 33

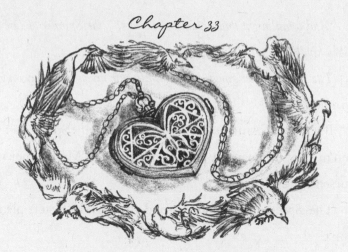

THE SPINNER IN THE MIRROR

A new image emerged on the Fate Spinner's cracked mirror. Annalise recognized the view as the same colorful land she'd been transported to before in the Spinner King's memory: the palace of dreams in Dreamland. Except, this time, Annalise watched the past unfold as a reflection. The same scene from before played like a movie. . . .

"My old dream was so simple," the Fate Spinner said to her sister. *"To be respected and loved by our people. But thanks to your selfishness, I have to conjure a new dream."* Four night wolves drew to the Fate Spinner's side, ears flat and snarling.

A flurry of crows took to the air.

"And what might that dream be, Kismet?" the Spinner of Dreams asked kindly.

The Fate Spinner growled, "I wish to rule my own destiny and rid myself of this curse!"

But now, as Annalise stood before the Fate Spinner's broken mirror, the memory of the day Annalise Meriwether was cursed continued. . . .

The Spinner of Dreams stood in alarm. "Sister, please, don't—"

The Fate Spinner raised her staff and screamed, "It is done!" Black lightning shot from the end of her staff and struck her twin sister in her heart.

The crown slipped from dark head of the Spinner of Dreams; her body transformed into a million black leaves with the blast. Reverie's spirit rose and swirled around the Fate Spinner, who stood by, clutching her staff in horror. "You are a fool, sister," the Spinner of Dreams whispered as her body of charry-black leaves slipped to the Fate Spinner's feet. Reverie's last words echoed far and wide: "No fate can ever kill a dream."

Rumble. Shiver. Crack. BOOM.

The blackened curse that had struck her sister down had burned straight through the earth. A jagged crack, large enough for a castle to fall through, ripped the Mazelands in

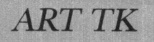

two. Through the gash, another sky, complete with a white moon, glittering stars, and the flickering lights of houses appeared.

In the very far beneath, a newborn baby cried.

A darkness spread out from the Fate Spinner's curse like spilled ink and dripped into the town below. A shroud of black draped Carriwitchet then—a shadow so complete, it eclipsed the town's sun permanently. What remained of the Spinner of Dreams dived through the crack between worlds in a dark and furious cloud, heading for the pure-hearted babe below.

The Fate Spinner had tried to murder her sister. But the spirit of the Spinner of Dreams had survived—only now, it carried a curse.

The Fate Spinner trembled before the chaos she'd wrought, motionless as stone. Shadows hung like dim drapes across her face.

"No!" the Fate Spinner cried through the sky of another world. "I'm sorry, Reverie . . . Mercy, what have I done?" Behind the Fate Spinner, Muse, in his top hat and monocle, dropped to the grass and sobbed.

The vision changed suddenly to the town below the broken sky.

The door of a crooked house shaped like a witch's hat

swam into view. White crows flocked to the roof and cawed. Shadows shaped like wolves plunged to the ground on the horizon and charged into the surrounding woods. The scourge of heart-shaped black leaves holding the spirit of the Spinner of Dreams blew to the Meriwethers' door. Where a few of the leaves fell, shadowshine trees grew.

One heart, larger than the rest, broken down the center and hanging on by a thread, slipped beneath the frame of their front door. Inside, her mom, glowing with pride, held a newborn Annalise. Her dad beamed with so much love, he practically shone. Her grandparents were happier than they'd ever been.

The shattered black heart of the Spinner of Dreams swirled and danced on a dark wind to baby Annalise. Her squinty purple eyes widened with awe, beholding the heart.

Annalise opened her overlarge fist and wrapped the broken heart in her hand. She screamed when it seared into her skin.

Her parents and grandparents, busy chatting to the doctor, hadn't seen the dark heart burn into her palm. And by the time the doctor opened her ironclad fist, the damage was done.

The Fate Spinner's curse, and the spirit of the Spinner of Dreams, had entered Annalise and become a part of her.

And, Annalise thought while watching her magical history unfold, something completely unique had grown.

Something horned, enchanted, and dangerous, born from Reverie's heart, Kismet's curse, and from Annalise. Something powerful, passionate, gentle, and beautiful. A fiery spirit named Esh-Baal.

Muse had told her once: "Even when you can't see me, I am here."

A flutter of truth unfurled inside Annalise then like millions of butterfly wings. Just because Annalise couldn't *see* the spirit of the Spinner of Dreams didn't mean she was gone. Annalise grinned when the truth wove together in her mind:

The heart of the Spinner of Dreams lives within me. And coming here, battling the Fate Spinner and her demons, continuing through the maze, all of it had helped Esh-Baal grow. Now Annalise knew why the Fate Spinner had always been after her. She wanted to finish what she'd started the night of her birth. She wanted to destroy the cursed spirit of the Spinner of Dreams housed within Annalise and Esh-Baal.

But Annalise would never let her.

We are all that remains of the Spinner of Dreams.

The vision from the Fate Spinner's shattered mirror ended, and the full reflection of the Fate Spinner returned. "You see?" the Fate Spinner said, gazing down upon Annalise,

Esh-Baal, and Mister Edwards. "Everything you've done has been for nothing. Either way, I win. There is no Dreamland or Spinner of Dreams, not anymore. When I cursed Reverie and split the world, the curse not only spread to you and your town, but into Dreamland as well. It's been a diseased place ever since." She twirled her staff of eyes. Those that remained unbroken stared wickedly at Annalise. "Petrified trees, black-hearted leaves, dead grass and flowers, mutant beasts and woodland creatures howling at the red moon. Her land is in ruin. What you saw on your way here," she quipped, "was just an illusion to make you feel like you could still win."

Annalise stroked her hair with her great hand, the heat of flames bubbling into her throat. Tears seared her eyes, Fate's words cutting holes into her scarred heart. "No," Annalise replied.

"Yes." The Fate Spinner's lips twitched with joy. "Nothing remains of my sister—but you. You should have taken my deal. You should have entered my mirror when you had the chance. But you failed to do so, and for that, you will suffer." She leaned forward and laughed just behind the cracked glass. "And everyone you love will suffer, too, because of you."

Mister Edwards lunged, teeth bared, at the splintered mirror. "How could you? Knowing there's no Dreamland, no Spinner of Dreams, how could you deceive so many innocent lives? We—we trusted the labyrinth! We trusted that it would lead us to our dreams!" He clenched his tiny fist, shoulders shaking, trying to stave off tears.

The Fate Spinner reached down as if to touch his cheek, hand hovering just before the glass. She sighed with false sincerity. "And I trusted that you would betray Annalise Meriwether, Mister Edwards."

Annalise pulled him close, placed her small hand on his shoulder, and squeezed. "This isn't over yet, my friend." A single golden butterfly perched on the end of his nose. "See? We are not alone."

Above, the white crows circled above the bars and cawed, louder, insistent. The remaining poets of hope, clustered on the dark mirror's frame, flapped their gentle wings and whispered soft as down, *"Dreamland exists for those who believe. . . ."*

"Always listen to the poets," Esh-Baal said. "They are the secret keepers of dreams. And remember, there is no dream without risk, no fear without courage."

Annalise thought she felt the book in her pocket stir as a light breeze drifted through the cracked mirror. Suddenly, the smell of green grass and sunlight and her mom's perfume and dad's cologne wafted through the air. Annalise swore she heard the singing of sunny day birds, laughter and celebration, people calling her name.

The Fate Spinner said the Dreamland gates would never rise again.

But how did she know that to be true?

What if *this*, what was happening now, was the final test?

What if they hadn't yet won the labyrinth?

"This is the end," the Fate Spinner said softer, honey in her voice. "Come through my mirror, Annalise, and I'll let the fox and his husband go."

The thread connecting her and Esh-Baal burned with the color of sunrise. When Annalise tightened her grip on her dagger, the golden light through the cracked glass flared, and the blade hummed in her fist. And in the far corner of the broken mirror, a top hat, fat white tail, two large purple eyes—one encircled in a monocle—peered out from behind the Fate Spinner.

Muse! The cat put a claw to his lips and shook his head. *Shhhh.* He bowed, winked, and hurried off into the background, big paw holding his hat in place. In the distant sky, a blush of lilac and gold spread.

Annalise's great hand zinged.

If Annalise wasn't sure before, she was 144 percent certain now. She couldn't trust fate. But she could trust herself.

She knew what to do.

Annalise stepped up to the Fate Spinner's mirror, aglow

with butterfly's wings, and immediately, the reflection . . . changed. No more did Annalise see the Fate Spinner scowling down at her. Annalise saw herself holding a dagger crafted from a dragon's heart, just as she was in the labyrinth. She saw four black ribbons atop her braid. Shredded, rip-tattered clothes. Bruises and battle wounds. Splatterings of dried golden blood, a blackberry bramble of hair. For the first time, Annalise truly saw herself.

A girl. A friend. A dreamer.

A warrior.

Annalise observed the girl she'd always wanted to be—a girl with the honest, sparkling smile of a friend. She tucked the moment deep in her heart as the image of the Fate Spinner swirled back into view.

"I said, step through my mirror with your monster, girl." The enchantress of all fates glared down with her black eyes, snowdrop skin and hair, colder than arctic winds. "You have no place to go, poor dear." She softened, almost kindly. "I am all you have now. Come home with me to the Palace of Fate where you belong."

Annalise tapped her leg four times with the side of her dagger and looked the Fate Spinner in the eyes. "If it's all the same to you, we want to see the state of Dreamland for ourselves, thanks." Esh-Baal reared behind her. Actually, she might have been laughing. Mister Edwards glowed with pride. "We're not leaving until we do."

For a split second, Annalise saw another in the mirror. A woman in white and gold robes wearing a crown of crows and horns, standing where Esh-Baal's reflection should have been. Annalise inhaled a sharp breath.

The Spinner of Dreams.

And behind the Spinner of Dream rose the most elaborate golden-winged gates and the lilac sun, burning Fate's dark world away. Annalise was certain that behind the Fate Spinner's mirror stood the real gates of Dreamland.

"You're not going anywhere!" The Fate Spinner slammed her staff on the dais. Black crows screamed—caw-caw-caw-caw! Her expression resembled the one Annalise wore when panic barged in uninvited and nestled in for a long winter's stay. "You will never get your dreams—I won't let you!" In a *whoosh* of speed and black wings, the Fate Spinner raised her staff at Annalise, eyes crimped in rage. "Prepare to d—"

Annalise slammed her dagger into the fractured glass and issued a warrior's cry, louder and stronger than she ever had before. "I WISH TO RULE MY OWN DESTINY AND RID MYSELF OF THIS CURSE!"

A shock of black lightning blasted from the Fate Spinner's staff and met the tip of Annalise's dagger. Fireworks of black and gold exploded between them.

The power of fate and dreams surging through her, the

355

thread linking Annalise and her unicorn blazed with electric light. The mirror shattered in a spray of broken black hearts. The poets of hope dived through the frame in a swirl of gold. "It's not over," the Fate Spinner's voice hissed as she vanished in a twist of gilded-black smoke.

The arena walls trembled. The cracks in the walls and floor grew. Golden light brightened through the breaks. The shimmering dust from the poets of hope, which glittered across the dirt floor, slipped through the cracks in streams. The shadowshine trees, born from Annalise's and her unicorn's blood, swelled and rose to the sky, the roots spread and twined down through the cracks. The branches exploded with gold and black berries and bloomed with the biggest, most beautiful gilded flowers and thorns Annalise had ever seen. And still, the sunny light grew.

Mister Edwards watched the arena, bursting with delight. Esh-Baal glanced at Annalise and nodded, deep pride shining in her eyes.

The darkness, the red moon, and the stagnant stench of curses and death packed up and left as the arena crumbled at Annalise Meriwether's feet.

A brilliant burst of light lit the labyrinth and Mazelands in gold. And when the dreamers were almost too weary to go on standing, the entrance to Dreamland appeared.

Chapter 34

GATES OF WINGS AND GOLD

Only seconds earlier, the Fate Spinner had stared Annalise down and tried to destroy her. Now the dark enchantress had vanished, along with her broken mirror. Esh-Baal, Mister Edwards, and Annalise stood in a grand indoor atrium infused with a brilliant gold light. Three walls, constructed with bricks of white and gold, rose to a dome overhead, reflecting an enchanted pale lemon sky. The only dark wall was behind them, made of gray labyrinth stone. The end of the maze.

The gray wall held an iron door that read: *No Winners Allowed.*

Four golden trees with velvety white leaves lined the wall

directly ahead. And, like the grand trees at the labyrinth's entrance, these appeared to be *watching* them. The three glanced at each other in awe, but nobody said a word.

The dagger Annalise had won from a dead king, forged from a cockatrice's heart, was gone. In its place was a silver and gold half gauntlet, like a metal glove, covering her small right hand, wrist, and lower arm. When Annalise flipped her palm skyward, the gauntlet morphed into the dagger, snug in her grip. When she let the hilt go, the dagger changed back into the gauntlet.

Mercy.

Annalise sparkled with delight. Even more so when the trees opened their eyes and spoke.

"Congratulations," the largest, most gnarled tree boomed, extending one leafy arm to the dreamers. "You have arrived at the gates to Dreamland. Gates that have not been opened for over eleven years." It gazed softly at Annalise. "However, as I think you have discovered"—it lowered his knotty eyes onto Mister Edwards and Esh-Baal—"there is magic for those who seek it. Isn't that right, poets?" The poets of hope left the gates and perched on the trees. "And we, the trees, believe if anyone can undo the dark magic that's been done, it is you, Annalise Meriwether."

Dark magic? Undo what's been done? That didn't sound

good. Annalise took a step back and stroked her hair.

One-two-three-four.

Esh-Baal's hooves clip-clopped over the floor in tune with the beat of Annalise's heart. Mister Edwards regarded Annalise with concern.

A squat tree to the left leaned in and whispered, "Oh, young dreamers. It's okay to be nervous. You'd be surprised how many dreamers so close to their dreams suddenly find themselves not quite ready to embrace them."

Annalise was nervous, and she knew her panic and anxiety might always roam the outskirts of her mind. But winning the labyrinth had given her something new as well. An armor, a power, a truth: if she could survive the Fate Spinner's demons despite her anxiety, worry, panic, and fear, maybe she could do anything.

Annalise took a deep breath, then a step forward, and smiled at the regal trees. "Thank you. I've come a long way to rule my own destiny."

The trees bowed to them all. "In that case, come forward. Dreamland is waiting."

The trees uprooted and stepped aside. When they did, the grand gates of Dreamland pushed out of the stone blocks ahead.

The solid arched doors of shining gold stood twenty feet

tall. Elaborately carved wings topped the gates, outstretched as if poised to fly. The scents Annalise had smelled earlier—sunlight on warm summer grass, fresh flowers in bloom, the perfume of a land too long in darkness bursting to life—wafted through the doors. A gilded sign lined the gates just beneath the wings in fancy lettering, banishing any doubts they had: *Welcome, Dauntless Dreamer, to Dreamland.*

A sudden cry escaped Annalise. A wave of emotion crashed through her, weakening her knees. She covered her face with her hands and cried, "We made it." Blackberry hair framed her scraped and dirty hands. "We made it to the gates of Dreamland." Her shoulders shook with every horror and pain she'd experienced on the road to where she was now—the threshold of her dreams.

"You did this, Miss Meriwether," Mister Edwards said softly, voice echoing inside this silent place. He wiped his eyes with the back of his foreleg. "You showed us the way."

Annalise stroked his damp cheek. "Oh, Mister Edwards. I couldn't have done it without you and Esh-Baal."

Esh-Baal's hooves tapped the floor to Annalise's side. Their connection shone brightly between them. Annalise ran her great hand down her black-hearted scales and recalled the reflection of Reverie she'd seen in the mirror of fate. Had she really seen the Spinner of Dreams, or had she only imagined it?

"I saw someone else in the Fate Spinner's mirror before it broke," Annalise whispered shyly to Esh-Baal. The breeze through the doors tumbled Annalise's hair and black-ribboned braid. Her unicorn's great golden eyes shifted toward her. "Someone almost hiding inside your reflection. Did you see her, too?"

Esh-Baal avoided the question. Instead, the dark fire unicorn Annalise had once despised enough to call *monster* lowered her horn, nuzzled into Annalise's touch, and replied, "I was little more than a memory of a dream when I landed in your great hand. A broken heart that wished to be more. I am what I am today because of your strength of will to rise above what others thought of you—what others judged you to be." Esh-Baal continued as the poets of hope soared toward them in a gust, "You, Annalise Lorien Meriwether, along with your very brave friend, Mister Edwards, broke out of a dark world in search of a dream. Thank you, courageous girl, for having the daring to do so, for nurturing my broken heart within yours, and keeping my spirit alive. Without you, I would not exist."

"Oh, Esh-Baal." Annalise sniffed.

Mister Edwards dabbed his eyes alongside them.

Esh-Baal dropped to her knees before Annalise and laid her spiraled black horn at her feet. "Thank you, Annalise. I am forever in your debt."

Mister Edwards knelt at Esh-Baal's wing. "And I am as well," he said, bowing his sleek black head. "For always and forever."

Annalise covered her mouth to hold in her bursting heart. After everything, she was the luckiest girl of all to have found, in all the world, such wonderfully rare friends.

Bubbling over with joy, Annalise hugged Mister Edwards and Esh-Baal. "Thank you both for your help in the labyrinth. For being patient and helping me when I needed it most. For being true kindred friends." Annalise kissed Esh-Baal's cheek. "Thank you for never giving up on me."

At Annalise's words, a golden padlock, shaped just like the silver locket at Annalise's neck, blossomed from the closed gates to Dreamland. Annalise grasped the Spinner Queen's locket and thought about what she'd said: *Deliver it to the gates of Dreamland and they shall open for you.*

Annalise stepped forward and peered closely at the padlock, her friends behind her. The keyhole was the tiniest Annalise had ever seen. Suddenly above the keyhole, words appeared: *You Hold the Key to Your Dreams.*

Still grasping the locket, a soft *click* escaped her fist.

The Spinner Queen's heart-shaped locket, fused shut for many long years, had opened.

Within the locket was a miniature key, engraved in teensy

lettering: *May the magic of dreams be yours.*

The trees tittered, and poets flittered. Annalise removed the key and grinned brightly at Mister Edwards and Esh-Baal before pushing it into the lock. The poets of hope ringed the Dreamland gates, and when Annalise turned the key, every moment she'd lived until now clicked into place.

After Annalise returned the teensy key to the locket and clasped it shut, the gates creaked open an inch, all by themselves, and a brilliant lilac light shone through the crack between the doors. Birdsong, along with the faint caws of crows, the echo of a waterfall, and the cheering and conversation of a small crowd followed.

Mister Edwards extended his arm to Annalise. Goodness, had he ever looked so happy? "Shall we, Miss Meriwether?"

Annalise glanced at Esh-Baal. The beautiful fire unicorn nodded. A trill of excitement rang within her as she took his arm. "Definitely, Mister Edwards."

Then, after all this time, Annalise threw open the doors.

Chapter 35

DREAMLAND

While crossing the threshold, a bitter breeze rushed over Annalise. Her hair blustered back in a gale. Dark clouds roamed the skies, thunder rolled. Lightning crashed. The poets of hope and the sweet lilac warmth she'd glimpsed all vanished. Past the Dreamland gates a massive crack in the earth divided the land in two. The crevasse was black as night. The scents of char from a great fire long since extinguished pressed coldly against her skin. Dreamland lay in ruin. Before Annalise stepped onto the deadened black grass on the other side, she knew the Fate Spinner *had* told her the truth:

When she cursed her twin sister, Dreamland was destroyed.

Yet, because of the magic Annalise held within her, she could still smell the perfume of a meadow in bloom beneath the ruins of Dreamland. She could still hear the distinct roar of waterfalls, the soft songs of birds, and the calls of a happy celebration floating on a warm, sunny breeze. She could still feel the brilliant sunlight cutting through the dark and see a blade of kelly-green grass poking up from the coals of this dead world.

Annalise's black mark prickled with a current of truth.

"I believe in my dreams," Annalise said, hovering in the threshold. "And I believe in Dreamland." The poets of hope rose from the door frame and rushed through the doors. And Annalise crossed boldly to the other side.

Suddenly, lush grass, like green paint spilling out from her battered black boots, rolled out in a flood before her—all the way up a gentle hill, to the horizon's edge. Color and life filled the world. Tepid breezes, sweet and clean, rife with forest and meadow perfumes, tossed Annalise's hair gently around her beaming face. Trees burst into bloom (Annalise swore she heard them sigh *thanks*). Waterfalls draped from distant cliffs. Flowers sprang up and blossomed exponentially. A golden sun rose in a lilac sky, and the dead world fell away.

In the distance, white crows by the hundreds circled the

golden-spired palace of clear crystal quartz belonging to the Spinner of Dreams. The only thing that didn't mend when the dreamers entered Dreamland was the giant crack in the earth. However, a white marble bridge had grown over it so they could pass. Beyond the bridge, a rainbow path of stones dotted the gentle hill, rising to arches of gold, leading to the courtyard bearing Reverie's throne. The same pathway and arches Annalise had seen in the Spinner King's vision.

"Have you ever seen anything more beautiful?" Annalise asked Mister Edwards, walking at her right.

The black fox quickly shook his head. "No, Miss Meriwether. I've never seen anything like this in my life."

A crowd of friendly faces approached from over the hill to their left. They were dressed in formal attire—fancy clothes, top hats, and gowns—enjoying a celebration. They gathered around a long table, decorated with fresh flowers and spread with every kind of drink and food and treat and cake she loved best. The moment they spotted Annalise, the crowd burst into applause and cheered.

"She's here!" the spirit of an old man in a new suit said. Annalise gasped in surprise. He was one of the Fate Spinner's specters Annalise had helped free.

"I knew she'd make it," said another freed dreamer—the teenage girl with short black hair in a white-feather dress.

The boy with copper hair, carrying a sword, cried, "Welcome, Annalise. We've been waiting for you!"

The young woman with long golden hair, deep dimples, and the most beautifully kind blue eyes, smiled demurely, and waved. "Welcome. I'm so proud of you."

The crowd of freed dreamers—some living, some dead, others glittering in the dust of quartz stone—waved her over, calling her name. Annalise walked through the lush grass toward them. Each seat at the table held a name tag on a plate.

The one at the head of the table was set for her.

Welcome, Annalise Lorien Meriwether,
Guest of Honor at The Dreamer's Feast.

This was real. Tears rolled down Annalise's cheeks. Happy tears. She laughed through her fingers when she recognized where she was. This was the place her mom told her about years ago. *"Sometimes the world feels like a dark hallway lined with locked doors. The key is imagining with your entire being that on the other side of one of those doors, there's a table set in a sunny meadow with a seat bearing your name. That there is a crowd gathered in celebration and they've only been waiting for you. And that, when you finally walk through that door, they will cheer and raise their*

cups and welcome you like an old friend. Keep this belief in your heart,
and eventually, likely when you least expect it, you will find the right
door, and it will open for you. . . ."

As she approached the table of dreamers, the Dreamland gates shut gently behind her. Annalise followed the sound—and gasped.

"Is that . . . ?" Mister Edwards gaped with giant copper eyes.

"It is," Annalise answered, excitement, curiosity, and awe mingling in her voice.

Standing before the closed golden doors where Esh-Baal should have been was someone the Fate Spinner insisted was dead. Someone with dark brown skin, shining black hair, kind golden eyes, and a crown to match.

The Spinner of Dreams.

Esh-Baal was the Spinner of Dreams?

Her dress shimmered like a million small wings. Her crown of crows and spiraled black horns sparkled in the sun. The white crows caw-caw-caw-cawed and swooped down to greet her.

Behind them, deep within the labyrinth walls, the Fate Spinner howled a gut-wrenching cry. Her defeat fell like a guillotine, for a moment cutting off all other sound.

Annalise's heart lurched with empathy. She knew that

hopelessness and pain well. *Maybe one day*, Annalise thought, watching a gold butterfly flutter by, *the Fate Spinner might feel something more than pain and misery, too.*

The Spinner of Dreams held out her arms with a quiet, peaceful joy and said something to the crows Annalise couldn't hear. As Annalise stepped through the soft grass to meet her, no doubts about who she was or where she'd come from remained. A golden thread so fine it was almost invisible ran from Reverie's heart to the dark mark on Annalise's great palm.

Annalise didn't know it was possible to feel so happy about so many things.

Suddenly, Mister Edwards let out a small cry as he searched out over the crowd. When he spoke, his words thickened with tears. "I'll leave you to it, then, Miss Meriwether. As you can see, I have someone waiting for me, too."

A handsome silver-gray fox crashed through the mingling dreamers, quartz dust glinting in his fur, grinning and laughing and bursting with excitement. "Reynard!"

Mister Edwards screamed and sprinted to meet him. "Arthur!"

Mister Amoureux. Annalise clasped her hands at her chest, overwhelmed with happiness for her friend. The two foxes crashed together and spun each other around. Tears grew fat and wonderful in her eyes and she laughed and wiped them away.

Everything they'd gone through was worth it to get here.

Annalise searched for her parents but didn't see them. She lifted the locket from her cloak, spun it four times, and moved to give Mister Edwards and Amoureux their privacy. When Annalise turned back to the Spinner of Dreams, the enchantress stood directly behind her.

Chapter 36

THE SPINNER OF DREAMS

A poet Annalise really liked wrote that dreams were born of stardust and heart. That all it took to catch them was a fleeting glimmer of hope, and all it took to break them was a magic we didn't yet possess. Annalise had cast her net and now she possessed something greater than even stardust and heart. Something more solid than hope. Annalise had forged within herself the magic to bring her dreams to life. To stand at the gates of her hard work, heart in her hands, ready for what came next.

The Spinner of Dreams dropped to one knee before Annalise, arms out gracefully at her sides, white crows

circling overhead. A large solid black heart, just like Annalise's, marked her right palm. And it was beautiful. "It is a
great honor to stand before you as my whole self, Miss Meriwether."

Stunned and awkward and unsure what to say, Annalise
curtsied, draping her plum cloak—dirty and ragged, burnt
and torn—like scarred wings at her sides. A shy "Hi" was all
she could manage at first, along with a blush of heat in her
cheeks. Until finally, Annalise straightened, stroked her hair
(four times), and spoke. "I have waited so long to see you, that
this"—she spread her palms to the sky at her sides—"hardly
seems real."

The Spinner of Dreams stood, radiating a peaceful calm.
"Dreams, I think you will find, may seem impossible, but
they are the realest things in any world." She winked. "As
real as a unicorn born from a girl."

"I believe you're right about that." Annalise smiled nervously at her feet. She sighed, more melancholy than before,
and met the lovely gold-fire eyes of the Spinner of Dreams. "I
don't mean to offend, but I'm really going to miss Esh-Baal."

The Spinner of Dreams smiled. "Esh-Baal is a majes-
tic creature, full of magic and fire, but she isn't gone. Rest
assured, your strong and beautiful unicorn still lives within
you." That's when Annalise felt it: a spark, a flame, and the

tip of a unicorn's horn shifting behind the black heart on her palm. "She was a vessel for my body, the way a mother is for a child. The way you are for her." The Spinner of Dreams wiped a golden drop of blood from a cut on Annalise's cheek. "We share blood, the three of us. Esh-Baal will always be your power, an extension of you. And you and I will always be connected by dreams. Dear young dreamer, nothing and no one can ever take her away from you."

Esh-Baal churned within her great hand like before, but it no longer felt painful. Behind them, the party in the meadow clinked glasses and cheered. Annalise stroked the no-longer-broken black heart on her palm. "She really is still with me."

"And always will be. It took your determination to put back together the shattered heart that slipped into your hand the day you were born. It took you learning to love the parts of you that brought you pain, to bring you the power and magic necessary to bring Esh-Baal to life." The Spinner of Dreams took Annalise's great hand in hers. When their skin touched, static surged up Annalise arm. "And it took your belief in your dream to resurrect Dreamland. To bring me home." She clapped her hands once before her. "Now, before we join the celebration, why don't we sit? I believe there is the matter of your dreams to get to."

Annalise rushed her with a hug. "Thank you. For everything. All the times I pinched my marked hand and wished my curse gone. I just. I didn't . . ."

"We all have things we wish we could do differently, even enchantresses." Annalise followed her mournful stare to the Fate Spinner's palace in the heart of the maze. "My sister underestimated the power of a dreamer, and I underestimated her. In the end, what matters is that you try to do better next time, so you don't make the same mistake."

They walked the colored path to the throne. As they approached the arches, a fluffy, crying bundle of exuberance and thrill blew forward, heading straight for them. The Spinner of Dreams clapped wildly and hurried to meet the hatless, despectacled cat Muse. "Ahhhh!" the Spinner of Dreams cried, kneeling to embrace him. "My friend," she laughed, crown wobbling. "I have missed you."

"And I have missed you, Reverie, more than you know." A misty-eyed Muse blinked up at Annalise with all the love, respect, and thanks that a cat could bear. And when he pulled away from the Spinner of Dreams and hugged Annalise, it was with the same ferocity. "Thank you, dauntless dreamer, for following me in your backyard. For giving me another chance, and not giving up. This world—this *Dreamland*—wouldn't be here without you. You brought it back from the dead." He choked up and kissed her great hand. "You broke the darkness the Fate Spinner cast upon you. I, and everyone else here, cannot thank you enough."

Cries of, "Hear, hear!" and "Four cheers for Annalise!" rang through the fresh-flower-scented air.

"Thank you for being there when I needed you, Muse, and for giving me the chance to find my own way." She kissed his cheek and stood. "Speaking of the Fate Spinner, may I ask, what will happen to her? You know, since she . . . ?"

"Tried to kill us, you mean?" The Spinner of Dreams replied, eyebrows raised. "Yes. In my absence, she had ruled the Mazelands, and no one, not even my crow guards, or Mogul the sorcerer, had jurisdiction to stop her. However, there *is* a law protecting dreamers who enter the maze, which the Fate Spinner broke the instant she tried striking you down. Since I have returned, my guards will be hunting her now to take her to Mazelands Prison: a shadow maze that runs directly under the labyrinth. It is the strongest, most desolate magical prison in our world."

"Mercy," Annalise whispered, gazing at her worrying hands. "I feel badly for her. I know what it's like to yearn to be free from a curse, to wish to be loved and accepted for who you are. But maybe her own journey through a dark labyrinth is just what she needs to set her heart right and free herself from her curse."

"I really hope you're right," the Spinner of Dreams

answered softly, and patted the empty space beside her.

Annalise sat alongside the Spinner on her white and gold velvet throne. Muse curled up in a warm patch of lilac-sunned grass at their feet. It was wonderful, but something—or a couple of somewhos—were missing.

"Spinner of Dreams?"

"Please, call me Reverie."

"Reverie," Annalise replied shyly, stroking her tousled braid by fours. "Have you any idea where my mom and dad might be? The Fate Spinner tried to make me believe they were in the labyrinth, but I never got a chance to see if she was telling the truth." Annalise glanced anxiously down the hill toward the Dreamland gates, hoping to see them.

Reverie lowered a wistful gaze to the half gauntlet on Annalise's wrist. The thread tethering them pulsed. "I understand how worried you must be about your parents. And though I can't tell you exactly where they are, I feel very confident," she said with a secret smile, "that they are on their way."

In the distance, strange and colorful creatures, giants, and magical beasts approached Dreamland, cheering Reverie's name.

"My people," Reverie said. "I've missed them so!" She wiped sudden tears from her cheeks and grasped Annalise's shoulders. "My dear girl, you made my dream come true. And the instant you stepped into Dreamland, you did the same for yours. You rid yourself of my sister's curse and earned the right to make your own fate. My only question for you now is—what is the new dream I can grant for you?"

Annalise had done it. She'd broken her own curse, helped Dreamland and Reverie heal. And as she watched Mister Edwards and Mister Amoureux laughing and celebrating together (and eating—mercy, she was mouth-droolingly hungry), Annalise didn't even have to think about what else she wanted (besides at least four cakes and lake full of sweet winterberry tea).

"I would like Carriwitchet restored to the way it was before the Fate Spinner broke the sky. I'd like the sun returned; the crops healthy and strong; the forests no longer petrified, but lush and cool, dappled and green. I wish for the night wolves to stop eating the townsfolk, even though the townspeople are often quite mean. Or maybe, if you can manage it, you could return the night wolves to the Mazelands because maybe they miss their home, too."

Reverie pushed down a grin and nodded thoughtfully, her crown of horns not moving an inch. "Yes, I can see how wolves eating your people would be problematic. I think I can manage that. Anything else?"

"Oh yes," Annalise brightened and talked quickly enough so she wouldn't get nervous asking. "If it's not too much trouble, I'd also like everyone in Carriwitchet, including my parents, to get something they've longed for." Annalise counted birds and butterflies by fours to calm her nervous heart. "I mean, I know the townspeople, well, most of them anyway, didn't come to the labyrinth, and"—she swallowed—"I know some did terrible things. But I feel like they've suffered the Fate Spinner's wrath because of my curse, too. And maybe we've all done a few things we're not proud of on the way toward our dreams." Reverie nodded heavily in agreement. "But since you asked," Annalise continued. "I thought, maybe, we could give them another chance."

The Spinner of Dreams held Annalise's gaze, considering. Her gold eyes looked just like Esh-Baal's. "Well," she said, breaking into a fat grin. "Those are excellent dreams, Annalise. They come straight from your heart, and those are always my favorite to grant. Plus, two of your neighbors did survive the maze." As Annalise wondered who that could be, the Spinner of Dreams snapped her fingers. "Consider it done."

Annalise observed her surroundings, expecting something to happen, but everything remained the same. No glitter fell from the heavens. No electric shock shook the earth. When everyone cheered, Annalise clapped along with them.

"Would you please excuse me, Spinner of—I mean, Reverie?" Annalise asked while gazing longingly at Mister Edwards and Mister Amoureux. They were waving her over from their seats at the dining table while devouring two teetering stacks of deliciously fancy cakes. "I wouldn't want to be rude, but I think that party over there is for me." Her stomach roared as loud as thunder. "And," she replied, trying to hide her embarrassment, "I really, really would like some of those cakes. And, you know, other things. Maybe." She laughed. "And to wait for my parents."

"Of course. Actually, perhaps I'll join you."

The people and beasts of Dreamland joined the party, and Annalise ate at the head of the table of dreamers, at the place set with her name, until she was full. She laughed and traded stories of the labyrinth with the others, her friends at her side. When she'd finished, Muse climbed onto her lap— like he did that day at the shelter—peered up at her with his big plum-colored eyes, and purred. "I'm going to come visit you, Annalise Meriwether," Muse said, pushing his soft cheek against hers.

"You better, Muse." Annalise laughed past the lump in her throat, hugged him tight, and whispered, "I will be waiting for you."

The fur at his cheeks pinked—the same shade as the sunset. Muse dug his monocle out of his fur pocket and flashed it at the sun. The last time she'd seen him do that, he was calling the—

A train whistle blew.

The ground rumbled. The glasses and cutlery clinked. The wildlife and guests paused their cacophony of sound. Train tracks, glowing with the light of stars, pushed up and out of the earth, wound from the base of the hill, and down through the crack between worlds. The dreamers gathered by the table and watched the white crows band together and merge into the Train of Dreams.

"Your coach awaits, Annalise. And I haven't forgotten about fixing your sun and sky. But since the journey is four times as long when the heavens aren't broken, I thought I'd let my train of crows take you home first. For now, I believe there are two very excited people coming through the gates to see you."

Annalise's heart raced. She could barely hold her heart inside her rib cage as she faced the opening Dreamland gates.

There, ragged and tired and bleeding, were her laughing-smiling-screaming-with-excitement parents, bursting through the golden-winged gates toward her.

"Mom! Dad!" Annalise crashed into their arms like a tide that never wanted to be swept away from the shore again.

"Oh, my goodness!" her mom cried, searching every inch of her daughter's face. "You made it!" She laughed and hugged Annalise once more. "You are amazing. Brilliant, brave, the most powerful young woman I've ever known."

Her dad came at her next. "Dad!" Annalise grabbed him and held tight. Red-eyed and swollen, he gripped his EpiPen like a dagger in his battered fist.

"Annalise," he said in his deep, kind voice. "We watched you. The whole way. The Fate Spinner, she . . ." Her awe-struck parents shook their heads at the ground. "She had us watching you fight those monsters." He shook his head, his horror soon blossoming into pride. "But you," he said, shaking his cut-up finger. "You, sweetheart, you showed them all."

Annalise hadn't noticed at first, but her mom carried something in her hand. "You found my bag!" Annalise cradled it like a lost artifact from another age. "I thought it was gone forever. Thank you."

The train gave another whistle. The eyes of the cars blinked inside the dying light. The break between worlds cast a shadow into this world.

Mister Edwards and Mister Amoureux padded shyly up to Annalise.

"Mom, Dad," Annalise said, tapping her finger on her thigh in fours. "Before we catch up, I'd like you to meet my dear friend, Mister Edwards, and his husband, Mister Amoureux, who I haven't had the pleasure of meeting yet either."

Before Annalise could even say *pleased to finally meet you*, Mister Amoureux and Mister Edwards grabbed her up in the happiest hug she'd ever gotten in her life.

"The pleasure is mine, Miss Meriwether," the lovely Mister Amoureux said in a smooth, gentlemanly voice. "You're my hero, you know. Oh!" he exclaimed. "And when we open our candy shop, which we will, one way or another," he said sheepishly, glancing at the Spinner of Dreams uncertainly, "you'll have free sweets every day for the rest of your days, I swear it!"

Mattie and Harry Meriwether shook hands and traded tales with Mister Edwards while Annalise whispered to Mister Amoureux, "You're just as lovely as I knew you'd be. Thank you for your kind words."

The Spinner of Dreams knelt before Mister Amoureux and Mister Edwards. "I haven't forgotten you brave foxes." She rubbed her hands together, and out from between them a golden fire grew, and grew, and grew, and when she clapped a glitter of rainbow dust exploded into the air and disappeared fast as it came. A set of keys fell from the sky and landed at their feet. The foxes looked at each other with big fox eyes. "When you get home, your candy shop will be waiting."

Cheers and laughter and celebrating ensued. And by the time the next train whistle blew, the first stars had poked out of the darkening lilac sky.

The guests had thinned, and the Spinner of Dreams stood by the Train of Dreams, saying goodbye to her guests as they boarded for home. "And, Mister Edwards, I do believe it's time to go."

The foxes, Annalise, and her parents moved to the train's platform. Her parents shook hands with the Spinner of Dreams and exchanged several quiet words—the only one Annalise heard clearly was *surprise*. Mister Amoureux and Mister Edwards said their goodbyes. Annalise waved them onto the train. "I'll be right behind you."

Annalise stood before the Spinner of Dreams for the last time and smiled bravely up at her. "I will never forget this place, or all you've done for me. Thank you again . . . Reverie." Annalise curtsied, removed the Spinner Queen's locket, and handed it to her. "This is yours. Your mother gave it to me when I—when she—before she moved onto the next world." Tears pooled in Reverie's eyes. "It helped me open the gates, but it's your mother's, and you should have it."

The Spinner of Dreams gazed at her mother's locket like

it was something holy, letting her tears fall where they may. Finally, she inclined her head graciously and replied, "Thank you, dear Annalise, for bringing this gift to me." Two white crows plucked it from Annalise's hands and slipped it onto their mistress's neck. "Did you know this locket gives every dreamer it belongs to a different gift?"

"Really?"

"Yes." Reverie traced the mended heart's edges. "Legends say it holds the very first dream ever dreamed. My mother claimed it gifted her with children. It gave my father a dagger to protect us, and when mother let me try it on, it gave me a wonderfully magical book."

A luminous beam grew from Annalise's pocket.

The Book of Remembering! "Goodness," Annalise laughed. "I almost forgot. Muse gave this to me. It helped me remember things in the maze." She handed it to the Spinner of Dreams.

When Reverie took it, the book lost its glow. She promptly handed it back. In Annalise's hands, the book shone bright and fantastic. "It seems this book is no longer mine. Please," she said with a soft smile. "Keep it. It belongs to you. Consider it your connection to Dreamland. And if you ever need help remembering, open this book, and it will remind you."

Annalise held it to her chest. The book glowed brighter. "Remind me of what?" Annalise asked.

"How, against all odds, a girl cursed by fate followed her dreams, challenged an enchantress—and won."

Muse tipped his hat to Annalise and hugged her tight. "I'm going to miss you."

"And I'm going to miss you, too." Annalise returned the book to her pocket and knelt before Muse. "But remember, a wise cat once said that just because you can't see me, doesn't mean I'm not with you." She put her great hand over his great paw. "This goes the same about me, for you."

Reverie bowed low, crown nearly touching the grass. Annalise bowed back the same way, then stepped onto the train car, bag in hand.

"I'll never forget you," Annalise said.

"Nor I, you," the Spinner of Dreams replied.

The doors closed. The whistle blew. And four seconds later, the Train of Dreams dived through the crack between worlds.

The second they plunged through the crevasse in Dreamland, the skies over Carriwitchet changed from dark and broken to sunny, blue, and bright. To Annalise's delight, a pack of night wolves, those that had haunted the Carriwitchet woods for eleven years, galloped upward toward the train windows on an enmagicked road of gold mist leading into the Mazelands. No one except for Annalise noticed them, too busy reveling in their shared dreams. The wolves paused briefly outside Annalise's window, fur black and sleek, gratitude soft in their eyes. She mirrored their thankful nods before they each continued home in peace.

Their group was given a private train car—one reserved for winners, burgeoning with food and drink. "Glad to have you back, Miss Meriwether," the giant white crow said. "Of course, I never had any doubts."

"May I ask you something, Ms. Twixt?"

"Of course, anything you like."

"Do you work for the Spinner of Dreams, too?"

"If I told you that, I'd have to enchant you to secrecy." She winked and continued on.

Once the train and the last of the night wolves had cleared the crack between worlds, the tear in the heavens closed. In front of a perfect yellow sun draping everyone with light, Annalise left Dreamland and her curse behind.

Chapter 37

DREAMS REALLY DO COME TRUE

Once upon a time, there lived a kind but cursed girl, who followed her dreams and believed, even in the face of cruelty, anxiety, panic, and fear, that there was more to life than her curse. And she vowed, for better or for worse, and once and for all, to do whatever it took to change her fate.

And the girl did.

And her life would never be the same.

When the train of crows approached Carriwitchet, Annalise couldn't believe her eyes. Nothing was dead, and everything—everything—was so perfectly alive! The sunlight, soft and golden, shone upon green grass and fields and flowers and trees in bloom. None of the leaves were black. Songbirds sang summer-day tunes. Golden butterflies flew. And if Annalise listened closely, she could just hear the poets' words: *"All hail, Annalise, dreamer of dreams!"*

The houses, no longer black and decrepit but colorful and new, lined clean cobblestone streets. Townsfolk exited their homes, as if in a daze. They stepped squinting into the sun, arms and hands shielding their eyes, then fell to their knees. Weeping tears of joy, they cast their talismans away.

Not a peep could be heard from any passenger on the train. Every dreamer was glued to the scene below. Until finally, the train of crows landed at the edge of the field alongside the cemetery, and those aboard began going home.

Annalise and her mom and dad paid their respects to her grandparents at their graves. Trees swayed in the light winds, and arcs of dappled sunlight shone onto their plots. Annalise knelt at the foot of each grave, Grandma Thessaly and Frida, Grandpa Jovie and Hugo, and did something she never thought she'd do. Annalise untied the four black ribbons atop her mussed braid, then knotted one on each of the fresh purple flowers growing alongside their names.

"I know you were with me inside the labyrinth," Annalise told them. Her chin wobbled and eyes stung with old tears.

"I followed my dreams." Annalise paused to wipe her cheeks. "I hope I made you proud of me."

Four golden butterflies landed on the branch above her. They recited no poetry. But Annalise didn't need them too. Sometimes, the best poetry didn't need to be spoken but kept quietly tucked away in one's heart.

Annalise's parents shook paws with Mister Edwards and Mister Amoureux, who were itching with anticipation to visit their candy store in the center of town, on Olde Faerie Road. Harry and Mattie Meriwether held Annalise's bag and waited for her to say her goodbyes.

"Mister Edwards," Annalise said sincerely. "I never dreamed that on a quest to rid myself of a curse of fate, I'd meet such a kindred friend." Annalise pulled him into a hug. "I am so glad you decided to stay in Carriwitchet, rather than go to Caledonia. Now we can spend a lifetime of dreams, side by side."

Mister Amoureux, standing on the sidelines, sniffed and dabbed his eyes with a hanky. "So beautiful," the silver fox said.

The train of crows fluttered apart behind them, and a flurry of white wings burst into the sky.

Mister Edwards sighed and extended his paw. Annalise wrapped it gently in her great hand—the other, gloved in a half gauntlet of silver and gold. Esh-Baal stirred beneath her mark, maybe saying her goodbyes, too. "And I never dreamed that on a mission as dark and terrible, and dare I say, as wicked as my own, that I'd meet a young woman with a Spinner's heart on her left hand, and one as shiny and beautiful as gold in her chest." Mister Edwards blushed and stared at his toes. "I'm the luckiest fox in the world. Thank you for sticking with me."

"Mister Edwards," Annalise replied. "Dreamers must always stick together. Now, go. Enjoy your dream. I promise, we'll see you soon."

And they did. But first, they had the rest of their dream to attend to.

Annalise and her parents meandered through the field toward home, taking everything in—the light, the birdsong, the clear blue skies, soft summer breezes layered with pine and lilac perfume. The deer and rabbits grazing out in the open, unafraid, no longer hunted by the Fate Spinner's wolves. The tall grass that swayed at their waists in whispers of wind, centuries old. *"Welcome home,"* the lush field said. Then, *"Thank you."*

White crows caw-caw-caw-cawed. They flew right over their heads and landed on the Meriwethers' witch's hat house—black with boysenberry trim. It looked almost the same. Except now it had a fresh layer of paint, stood tall and straight, and required no cage. The garden out front was ripe with leafy green vegetables, black rosebushes, purple hyacinths, fruit trees heavy with winterberries, orange grapes, and de Salzmann plums. Alongside the house was a structure that hadn't been there before.

"Mattie . . ." Annalise's dad raised a hand to his mouth, round with wonder. "Is that—?"

"A boathouse! Yes, Harry, I think so!"

The door was open. Inside were all the wood and tools her father would need to build longboats again.

"Goodness, Harry, Annalise, look," her mom said excitedly. "I think we're getting new neighbors, too."

Her dad raised his eyebrows and clapped. "Oh right, the Spinner of Dreams *did* mention something about new neighbors, along with another surprise. . . ."

As Annalise stepped through their front gate, she squinted at the small house a short distance from theirs, and the people just moving in.

With two children her age.

Annalise gasped.

Nightingale and Bowie! And they didn't even look hurt.

Nightingale, with her silvery eyes, spiraled black hair, and radiant smile, grinned widely and waved at Annalise. Wild thoughts rushed over her brain as if every word she thought was on fire. Bowie was as tall and handsome as she remembered—twin dimples, eye twinkles and all—and he smiled halfway as the two approached her.

Annalise stood stunned in place. The last time she'd seen them, they were flying over the labyrinth walls.

Heart racing, hands sweaty, Annalise must have looked frightful. Covered in wounds in various stages of healing, cloak and leggings ripped, hair singed and knotted—all she could hope was that she wasn't littered with dead spiders.

But when Nightingale breezed up to Annalise, all she said was, "Hi! We just moved in. Isn't that great?" Nightingale extended her hand, and Annalise shook it. A zing pinged through her other, greater hand. A thrum of exhilaration rather than pain. "Ohhhh, I like your gauntlet," Nightingale said, as if people wore such things regularly, and it wasn't the least bit odd.

"Hey." Bowie said next, blushing slightly. "That is a really cool half gauntlet. Did you win that in the maze?"

Annalise laughed. She wanted to ask what happened to them but knew that they'd have plenty of time for that later.

"Yes," Annalise answered. "It's got special powers, actually. Watch this." Annalise had discovered, while on the Train of Dreams, that if she pressed the dragon engraved on the palm, it became, well, an actual golden dragon—a lovely little cockatrice. Their eyes brightened as the winged creature rose from the gauntlet and fluttered around their shoulders sputtering tiny black and gold flames.

Annalise had a very good feeling the Tristles would become great friends to her.

"Wanna come inside with us?" Nightingale asked. "It's only us and our gran, but she just made the most amazing batch of lemon-zing cakes and starry-moon pies ever."

Oh, Annalise thought with a touch of sadness. *They must not have gotten their dream of having their parents alive.*

"Hey," Nightingale said, touching her arm. "Don't be sad. We couldn't bring our parents back, but it's okay. The Spinner of Dreams gave us the next best thing. Wanna come see?"

Annalise did want to see, but she was so tired. She wanted to go inside with her mom and dad, share stories, and rest. "I'd love to. But . . . maybe, can I see tomorrow?" Her mom stood at the door, waving her over.

"Of course," Nightingale said. "We'll be here when you're ready."

"See ya." Bowie pushed his great hair away from his eyes and gave her a short wave before turning and walking away.

A blush in her cheeks, and a skip in her step, Annalise

padded her battered boots through the soft green grass, counting her steps by fours and letting the beauty and wonder and happiness of Dreamland and home sink in.

"Annalise," her mom cried. "Come see the surprise the Spinner of Dreams left you!"

Annalise ran through her door alongside her dad, no bars, no locks, free. Both laughing, they practically tripped up the stairs.

Along the way, Annalise spotted a letter to her mom on the fridge.

> Dear Ms. Meriwether, sorry for the delay in getting back to you regarding your literary submission, DREAMLAND. We at Walker Fawkes Publishing Co. have finally had a chance to review your manuscript, which had somehow fallen between the cracks, and would love to offer you a contract. . . .

That was all Annalise had time to read before her dad pulled her along. When Annalise burst into her bedroom, a hypoallergenic golden Siberian cat with giant gold eyes blinked lovingly up at her from her bed.

"The Spinner of Dreams told us the cat would be a girl,"

Mattie Meriwether said with a wink. "And that she was quite special."

"Oh!" Annalise ran to her. "She certainly looks special." Underneath the thick fur atop her head, Annalise found two very small, very sharp, black horns. She gave her new friend the world's longest ear scratch, and her furry friend purred and purred. "I know just what to call you," Annalise said.

"Oh yeah? What's that?" Her dad seemed more at peace than she remembered ever seeing him. He and her mom looked so happy.

"I think Muse the Second works, don't you?"

"I think Muse the Second is perfect," her mom said.

Everything was just as it should be. She had friends, her parents, the sun and sky, and all her dreams. All was right with the world.

Her dad clapped. "Okay, who's up for lunch and a game of Castles, Angels, and Fiends? What do you say, Meriwethers?"

"Oh yes," Annalise answered, snuggling Muse the Second. "A game of Castles and food sounds perfect."

The tiny cockatrice flew at the cat and blew fire at her nose. To everyone's surprise, the cat blew fire right back.

The Meriwethers honked in giggle-fits.

"Meet you downstairs, Annalise?" her mom asked.

"Okay."

After her parents left, Annalise cleaned up and changed her clothes. While hanging up her battle-ravaged cloak, one of her pockets radiated a faint glow.

The Book of Remembering.

Annalise lifted it free and found the book different from before. The binding was now made of tiny white feathers, and the cover flopped opened all on its own. The golden pages revealed an intriguing story of faeries and kingdoms and magic she couldn't wait to explore. Annalise set it on her nightstand to read before bed.

Before heading downstairs, Annalise glanced out her window. A flash of white caught her eye. On the branch of the old poplar tree with great yellow heart-shaped leaves sat a white cat with big purple eyes, proud as you please on a branch, wearing no hat or monocle. The cat licked his large double paw in the sun.

"Muse the First."

Annalise opened the window. White crows stretched their wings and closed their eyes among the leaves. Muse leaped down and smiled up at her from the grass. "The Fate Spinner was apprehended and taken to the dungeons. I thought you should know."

"Thank you, my friend," she told him.

He bowed. "Until next time, Annalise."

"May the magic of dreams be yours." She watched Muse scurry off.

Muse the Second hopped off the bed, curled around her ankles, and purred. Annalise grinned down at her and silently thanked Reverie. And as Annalise made her way downstairs to her family, a spark of gold fire and the tip of a black horn lit from inside her great hand.

Right away, a wonderful new dream came to Annalise.

A thrill rushing through her, she paused before the kitchen, counting her quick breaths by fours. If there was one thing she'd discovered, it was that all the magic she needed to fight for her dreams lived within her. "Esh-Baal?" Annalise whispered, heartbeat like a thousand wings. "Are you ready for another adventure?"

One-two-three-four.

"I am your fire," Esh-Baal whispered back. "And my fire is yours!"

AUTHOR'S NOTE

The Spinner of Dreams is a work of fiction spun from my imagination, but the way Annalise Meriwether reacts to the events unfolding around her are all drawn from my real-life experiences and the way I process the world.

I've always felt strange. Different. Like an unusual creature on the outside of normalcy looking in. And until I was an adult, I didn't know why.

Like many others, my childhood was steeped in trauma—the worst of it, too personal to speak of here. But it wasn't until my gentle and radiant mother died by suicide that all the light in my world went out. The shock was enormous. I was so traumatized by her death and the other horrors occurring in my life that, by the time I turned eight, I'd developed bleeding ulcers, PTSD (Post-Traumatic Stress Disorder) from trauma incurred by abuse, depression, and panic attacks. Only as an adult would I be formally diagnosed with the above, as well as a bigger part of my puzzle: autism spectrum disorder. I had so much going on around and inside me—things I couldn't talk about, things I didn't understand, things that made me afraid—that I felt like the saddest, wickedest, weirdest, and loneliest girl in the world.

I thought differently from others. I didn't act, react, or process things in the same ways. I felt anxious and haunted. So much so, I sought comfort anywhere I could. I counted things—anything from sidewalk cracks to steps to the strokes of my hair and taps of my fingers, trying to bring order into my disordered world. I had all sorts of triggers for panic I didn't understand. Like Annalise, I only liked the right side of things, including my body, and thought my left side was out to get me. Worried thoughts and images bombarded my brain. The effort and vigilance required to keep them away often felt (and still sometimes feels) like a never-ending battle. I was terrified of being alone.

I lived differently from my friends too. I grew up poor (and still am). Like the Meriwethers, the cord to our TV is duct-taped to the wall so it doesn't fall out. Our dining room table is held together by ratchet straps because we can't afford a new table. We've lost one house to a puff-back (an explosion of woodstove and furnace), another to a devastating fire, and yet another, which we'd built from scratch, to foreclosure after the housing crisis of 2008.

Still, like the Meriwethers, we picked ourselves up and moved on.

There are many similarities between Annalise and myself, the most prevalent being that I grew up wondering *why* I'd been born different. Why others' lives seemed so normal when mine was so hard. I was so convinced fate had it out for me, for years I truly thought I was cursed. What I didn't realize as a child but understand now as an adult is this:

I hadn't only been born a child of fate, I'd also been born a child of dreams.

With Annalise's story, I wanted to show other neurodiverse children (and adults), as well as those who've faced traumatic fates and anyone else who needed to hear it, that no matter what is stacked against you, what terrors you've experienced, how odd and lonely you feel, it is your unique differences that bestow the most powerful strengths upon you—not *despite* your trials and differences, but *because* of them.

Thanks to all I'd survived and lost, something new was forged within me. A golden flutter of hope with a powerful magic of its own—the call of the wonderful dream of being an author. Because no matter what was happening in my life, I always had this big imagination; the ability to easily fall in and out of worlds. As a child, I loathed my strangeness.

As an adult, I celebrate it. Because, dauntless dreamer, my strangeness led me to you.

So, to the one reading now who's spent too many days on the outside looking in; the one who feels like no matter where you go, sadness and ill-fate follows; the one with wild dreams in your heart, fairy tales in your soul, and books in your hands; the one whom others do not understand, I've come to tell you a secret you desperately need to hear:

You are beautiful. You are wanted. You are precious. You are magic.

I see you just as clearly as I see the dream waiting for you along your chosen path. And even if you can't see this dream now, the secret is to believe with your entire being that there is a table in a green meadow, with a place set with your name, waiting through an open door ahead.

You see, I have it on good authority that the Spinner of Dreams has something wonderful in store for you. Now, dreamer, go out and find it.

I believe in you.

Resources

Suicide prevention

National Suicide Prevention Lifeline in U.S:

Website: suicidepreventionlifeline.org

Contact their free crisis hotline: 1-800-273-8255

Contact their crisis text line: text TALK to 741-741

Suicide Prevention and Support in Canada:

Website: crisisservicescanada.ca

Contact their free crisis hotline: 1-833-456-4566

Contact their free crisis text line: text CONNECT to 686868

International Worldwide Suicide Crisis Hotlines:

suicidehotlines.com/international.html

Mental Illness Support

Anxiety and Depression Association of America:
adaa.org

Autism Spectrum Disorder:
autism-society.org
nimh.nih.gov/health/topics/autism-spectrum-disorders-asd/index.shtml

Mental Health America:
Anxiety Disorders:
mentalhealthamerica.net/conditions/anxiety
-disorders
Depression:
mentalhealthamerica.net/conditions/depression
Post-Traumatic Stress Disorder (PTSD):
mentalhealthamerica.net/conditions/post-traumatic-stress-disorder

National Institute of Mental Health (NIMH):
nimh.nih.gov/index.shtml

Panic Attack Hotlines:
National Alliance on Mental Illness (NAMI) free

helpline: 1-800-950-NAMI (6264)

MentalHelp.net: 1-800-64-PANIC (72642)

ACKNOWLEDGMENTS

[Tk]